Iced

Robert Grindy

Livingston Press
The University of West Alabama

ISBN 13: 978-1-60489-192-8, trade paper
ISBN 13: 978-1-60489-193-5, hardcover
ISBN: 1-60489-192-0, trade paper
ISBN: 1-60489-193-9, hardcover
Library of Congress Control Number 2017948801
Printed on acid-free paper
by Publishers Graphics
Printed in the United States of America

Hardcover binding by:
Typesetting and page layout: Sarah Coffey
Proofreading: Erin Watt, Shelby Parrish
Cover design nd Layout: Teresa Boykin, Abbey Ames, Callie R. Murphy
Author photo: Julie Carter

This is a work of fiction:
any resemblance
to persons living or dead is coincidental.

Livingston Press is part of The University of West Alabama,
and thereby has non-profit status.
Donations are tax-deductible:
brothers and sisters, we need 'em.

first edition
6 5 4 3 3 2 1

Iced

Robert Grindy

1.

Streator swam up through dark dreams, breathing hard, confused by his wall. He seemed to be in his own bed, but something was off. That was the wrong wall. He always slept on the other side. Maybe he was dead now. Maybe that's what death was—not frozen forever in a cold lake but waking in your bed facing the wrong wall.

"Hey in there."

He was cold enough to be dead. Most of the covers had come off and he was naked, his boxers tangled around a bandaged leg, propped on a pillow. He tried to lift himself but couldn't. He shut his eyes to stop the shadows on the wall from pulsing with the ache in his head.

"Hey."

Slowly he rolled to his back, blinking away the fog, pulling weakly at the pile of blankets.

"Are you with me?"

A voice murmured through the dark, and he realized it had been coming for some time but muffled as if underwater.

Underwater. He remembered he had almost drowned this night. He had almost been dead. That was the strangest thing that had ever happened to him.

He felt weight beside him. Under the blankets next to him, pressing against his side. A warm hand on his bare shoulder, gently pushing. Attached to the voice. For a heartbeat or two this was a comfort, the familiar gravity of his wife in their bed, until his head cleared enough to recall that he hadn't felt this presence in this bed for many many months.

He managed to prop himself on his elbow and turn toward the middle of the bed. A worried face regarded him closely. Not Roni, as much as he might wish. This other woman. Mora.

His thick head had trouble sorting out what any of this meant. He instinctively tugged at the blankets to cover his naked self

1

against the cold and unknown. He struggled with the blanket over his propped up leg, and the bandages reminded him that nearly drowning was actually only the strangest thing that had happened to him since Monday, when someone tried to kill him.

"Here, I'll get it," Mora said, and she reached over him to arrange the blankets. She seemed to be naked as well. He'd have to add this to the strangest-thing list and sort out the rankings later.

She hovered, considering him closely. He averted his eyes. "How you doing?" she asked. "You ok?"

"Yeah, yeah," he said. "Really feel . . . weird."

"Hurting?"

He thought for a moment. *Hurting* didn't begin to describe how he felt. "Mmm. Everything."

"Want some more meds?"

"No, no, I'll sleep for three days. Who knows what else I'll miss."

"They gave you extra-strength Tylenol, you should be okay, even with the Vicodin. I'll get you one." She slipped out of bed, and in the shadows of the streetlight he saw her cross to the bathroom. How very odd. That was all the reaction he could muster. Odd that she was so very naked. She didn't seem to care that someone she barely knew was watching her lovely in her bones. Back at the hospital there'd been no telling what was under those shapeless scrubs, and earlier in the dark and under all those covers and barely conscious, no telling at all. But now he could see. S*he moved in circles, and those circles moved.* It had been so long since he'd been with any woman but Roni that he had forgotten how every woman curved in different rhythms, smelled in different keys, tasted of different registers . . . *And what prodigious mowing we could make.*

He could see her at the vanity in the bathroom rummaging through the prescription bags from the hospital, flipping on a light so she could read. He shut his eyes against the brightness and lay back down. He heard her pee and flush. She came back with a pill and a glass of water and slipped back into bed. "Take this," she said, helping him sit up, her arm under his head bringing her bare breast so very near his face. Her skin was icy. She was shivering. When he lay back down, she curled up next to him to keep warm, her head against his shoulder, her arm across his chest, her bare legs rubbing against his.

He felt he should speak but was at a loss. He had no idea how this dialogue was supposed to play. "Sorry it's so cold in here."

"No worse than my place."

He was surprised he wasn't embarrassed—he was fairly certain nothing but sleep could've happened over the last few hours, but what did she expect, a man in his condition, with a banged-up head and bandaged leg and a bloodstream full of the finest prescription pain relievers. "So, Vicodin—wow. It always just wipes me out. Not good for, you know, anything."

"No worries. Besides, always time to revise, right? Especially for the fantasy scenes?"

An awkward silence. Here he was supposed to acknowledge that he was eager for take two and that she had been in his fantasies. Had he ever thought about making it with her? He pictured her in his classroom: no, not really. But that would be insulting to admit now. He couldn't remember anything even like flirting with her. Is that what students think when you smile and make small talk? Make jokes about the sex lives of their characters?

He made a half-hearted attempt to play along. "Ah, yes, ensnared by the exotic Indian girl so skilled in the ways of Kama Sutra."

She laughed. "Well, you're closer than most. Half the guys think I'm Arab, the other half think I'm black, the other half think I'm Cherokee."

"That's a lot of halves. So what are you then?"

"Whatever you want me to be, *baby*."

Took him a second to realize she was kidding, maybe even mocking him. Good. They were way too old for this. She wasn't some randy undergrad; she was a full-grown working woman living on her own with a four-year-old kid and an ex-husband somewhere . . . and he was tired of this game already. The short story was done, the denouement unnecessary and tedious. But he didn't want to kick her out—he wanted company.

"So, really, where'd you come from?"

"Born right here. My mom was from Sri Lanka. My dad's Greek. He was in the merchant marine and brought her to Illinois."

But that's not what he really meant. He understood nothing about the whole night. A complete loss. And he felt more loss coming.

"So what's the story with your book?" she asked, out of the blue—or maybe they had been talking about such things and he hadn't been paying attention.

What's the story. She had no idea how complicated the answer was. How could he tell her? And would it be worth it after all, after tea and cake and ices?

"What's it about?"

What's the story. Love and death. What else was there.

"Come on. Tell me."

Tell me a story.

2.

It had been the last Tuesday of the last August of the century when Henry Streator's world became too perverse to live in. Shortly before eleven a.m., he sat in his office chair staring at an article on his computer screen. A former student with a bestselling book. Derrick Doolin. Surely this meant the end of all that was good and right.

Some other day, some other year, he would have dismissed the news with his usual ironic contempt. This day, he had no defenses left. In fact, he might have sat in his office chair the rest of his life watching the cursor blink on that news page if it hadn't been for the knock on his door. He knew that knock. Three quick raps— *why you got this door shut for anyway?* Later, Streator would tell everyone that Tarvis Conner saved his life.

He glanced at the clock. Nearly late. He grabbed his book bag and opened the door.

Tarvis Conner smiled at him. "Hey." He was a small, thin student, maybe 19, with braids hanging from under a Bulls cap on sideways, a huge basketball jersey over a white t-shirt, and baggy shorts he held up by the crotch.

"Hey, Tarvis, sorry," Streator said as he stepped out of the door past him, "I've got to get to class."

"Yeah, I just want you to know I got my thing," Tarvis said, tagging along behind.

"What thing?" They made their way out of the office suite and into the main hallway bustling with students.

"That story thing we was supposed to bring."

Streator could make no headway past three middle-aged women in white nursing-student scrubs sauntering side by side down the crowded hall in front of him, pulling roller bags, chattering loudly, no concern of theirs that he was late for class again and that he really wanted to put distance between himself and Tarvis Conner and Derrick Doolin.

"The story starter? The one due last time?"

"Yeah, I couldn't make it, my car died out on 27th Street."

The biggest of the three women swung her arms in wide arcs as she ambled, so that Streator had to time his move like a mini-golf putt on the windmill hole.

"So bring it to class today."

"Yeah, my car died, and I got to go to the lab to finish typing."

"So okay, sure, sure, go to the lab, I'll see you later . . ."

Streator finally squeezed past the group of women and left Tarvis behind. He picked his way around more slow moving traffic: beefy men in clothes dirty from the auto and welding labs, teen boys in plaid shorts and flip-flops, teen girls with impressive bangs and cleavage orange from the tanning booths. In a knot of young women with hair sculpted in violent-tinged cones and braids, he heard the loudest one complain, "Motherfucker put a motherfucking smiley face on my motherfucking paper and still give me a motherfucking F." He had no worries she was talking about him since he never smiley-faced a paper. His worry at that moment was avoiding the huge backpacks that threatened to knock him off stride when anyone turned sideways.

He dug his file folder out of his bag and stole a glance at his syllabus as he walked. He had overslept, skipped breakfast and a shower, but still would've had time to look at his notes if his colleague Phyllis Nash hadn't stopped at his door and said, "Hey, nice article in the paper today! You must be pretty proud," and hurried on by, ten minutes early for her class. He pulled up the local paper's webpage, and that was the end of any chance for prepping class, let alone focusing on anything else all day. What was it he had assigned? "The Zebra Storyteller?" Was that all? For seventy-five minutes? What would he do with the other seventy?

"You come up with more good ideas between your office door and your classroom door than the rest of us do with a month of planning." That's what Roni had told Streator years ago, when they were both teaching assistants. At the time she exaggerated about Streator's abilities, he knew, because they were sleeping together. Still, he was flattered enough to marry her. Years later she confirmed what he had suspected, that her comment was as much a backhanded criticism of his lack of preparation as it was a compliment.

The days of hallway inspiration of any kind, brilliant or mediocre or desperate, were long gone. The first clock he passed ticked two minutes after the hour; the next clock gave him a minute's reprieve. Even though no two clocks in the building showed the same time, by any measure he was late again, and this was just week two. He blamed Derrick Doolin. He blamed that annoying little Tarvis Conner for slowing him down and the rest of the moseying students for bottlenecking the hall. He blamed the architects of Kickapoo Community College for their early-seventies space-station design of circular pods connected by a web of narrow, curving corridors—intended, he'd heard, to minimize the chances of student rioting or take-overs, as if all of the radical students who had ever attended a downstate Illinois community college couldn't walk side by side down a cattle chute. He was tempted to blame his division secretary for assigning him a classroom clear over in the Industrial Technology pod, or maintenance for not keeping the clocks synchronized, but years earlier his older sister, a second-grade teacher, had given him the Prime Directive for teaching in any school anywhere: never piss off the secretary or the janitors.

Streator knew that even without a Derrick Doolin, a Tarvis Conner, a crowded hall, or wonky clocks, he would still be late. Every day it was all he could do to gather his stuff, pull himself out of his chair, open the door, and begin the long walk to face the faces when the hour hit straight up. Leaving five minutes early was asking way too much.

At the classroom door he made a show of hustling in, glancing at the clock behind him as if surprised, mumbling an excuse about a last-minute phone call from a student. He wondered if he had used that one already for this class. He took a quick sweep of the room to see how many had managed to show. Fourteen or so students, mostly scattered through the back few rows, slouched deeply with their arms crossed or their heads propped up on their hands. A few thumbed cryptically on their cell phones. Most stared at their empty desks, their books and notebooks and pens still stashed in their backpacks on the floor, a double-dog-dare to teach them something today.

His syllabus said he had also scheduled "Big Black Good Man," Richard Wright, and "Plot." He would bet none of them had read any of the Wright story. He himself hadn't read it since grad school. The plot of "Good Black Big Man" or whatever was dim in his memory, something about a sailor, a hotel clerk who's afraid of him, some odd country—Norway? He couldn't remember what he had in mind when he made this damn syllabus. Not enough time to glance through the story, so that meant seventy-five minutes today for one two-page fable. So, he'd give them fifteen minutes for a reading quiz, ramble on about fables in general for a bit, let them tell him why the Zebra story was so stupid, and then he'd explain how this painfully obvious story made the explicit case that the function of a storyteller was to think of the unthinkable so that when it comes to pass—when a Siamese cat pretends he's a lion to trick the zebras in order to eat them—if you've told a story about it, as the Zebra storyteller had, it's already true, and you won't get fooled, so your Zebra storyteller kicks the crap out of the tricky Siamese cat. Then he'd scribble some useless diagrams about rising action and falling action all over the board, watch the middle-school minds in the back smirk while he talked about the importance of "climax," and he'd let them out early. By the time he got back to his office he wouldn't even feel guilty.

His Introduction to Creative Writing class at 12:30 was discussing the Derrick Doolin article when he came in. "Did you see the paper?" asked Trudy, a grandmother with beehive hair in a curious tone of red. She smiled and held up a copy.

"That's so awesome!" one of the young women volunteered.

"Yes. Really awesome. Just goes to show what you can do," Streator said.

He was in a mood to shatter their dreams and illusions but held off. He had already disappointed most of them when he said he had no interest in reading their dozens of notebooks filled with handwritten poetry, rhyming, on boyfriends who light up their lives like rainbows and girlfriends who slice their hearts like razors, or their floppy disks maxed out with their seven-part Chronicles of Jenstan, High Defender of Planet Aqip. The rest of them he would disappoint one way or another soon enough: besides Trudy, a laid–off mill worker who wanted to write stories for her grandkids, there was a bright hospital nurse coming in between shifts (*Megan? Morgan? Mora?*); a 16-year-old homeschooled mouse (*Kristen? Kirsten? Kyrieleison?*) who loved Christian young-adult fantasy; a skinny kid leaning against the side wall (*Jason? Jared? Jake?*) who proved every day that wearing a ball cap backwards reduced IQ fifty points minimum, and was, inexplicably, also enrolled in the Intro to Fiction class; a few other quiet ones in black or camouflage filling space for three easy elective credit hours so they could stay on their parents' car insurance and still get in a shift at Applebee's.

Not surprisingly, Tarvis hadn't made it.

Last time he had them bring in short-story starters, a few sentences launching a character in a place with a conflict. He had intended to work on them last week, but of course, he was behind. So today he had them play a variation of the old standby, Exquisite Corpse: he had them pass their starter to the next student, who was to continue the story until Streator called time, and then it was passed and passed again around the circle, each adding to the story. All he wanted to do was free them from their preconceived notions of their own story, to open up possibilities, to have a little fun stretching their imagination. And to waste time when he wouldn't have to talk.

They attacked the chore grimly. After a few passes, Streator had them read the results.

Grandma Trudy adjusted her bifocals and began: "Simko the Cardinal was all in a dither: who could have eaten all the goobers from the feeder? And knocked it to the ground?! Was it Droopy Drawers the Ground Squirrel? Or perhaps Randy the Root Hog? It was a mystery! Well, she would just have to find out herself . . ."

She struggled with the handwriting of the other students' contributions: "So she pulls out a couple long hairs from her shower drain that are blonde on one end and dark on the other. So she knows right off it must be that bleach-blonde . . . *b-word* . . . from Spanish class she seen flirting with Sean, the only . . . Tru-bart?"

"Trobahn . . ."

"Trobarn warrior with enough knowledge of the secrets of the Flask of Morrow and the Big Wind skills necessary to penetrate the Gate of Graz-iky-something's defenses . . . out in Epcott's barn where the sheriff lifts the trapdoor to find the torture chamber, only it's booby trapped and he's decapitated by these swinging train rails and he falls on top of Priscella. She's still chained up and the blood from his neck stump makes the electric wires that are still attached to her privates—*oh my*—short out and kill her too. And Rory the Ripper escapes to Florida. The end."

The dark-haired nurse bit her hand to keep from laughing out loud. At least one person seemed to understand his misery.

His plan was to have them take a shot at a story draft by a week from Tuesday. Who knows, he told himself, by then things could be looking up—somebody could bury him in a shower drain with a ground squirrel wired to his privates.

By 1:45 Streator was back in his office chair, drained. He opened a bag of Doritos and a Diet Pepsi from the vending machines. Lunch and breakfast. He picked at the chips. He wasn't hungry. His stomach churned, and he could feel a headache building.

This was a Tuesday. His good day with his good classes. Monday-Wednesday-Friday meant three sections of English 101. Freshman comp. Their first essays, personal narratives illustrating a misconception about a group of people, were already piled on his desk waiting for his pen. Not now, not tomorrow. He couldn't imagine when.

Streator opened his lower file drawer for a foot rest and leaned back in his chair, arm across his eyes. His headache was escalating to a roar. The smell of the place wasn't helping. The cooked-corn stink sucked into the building from the ethanol plant next door was particularly vile today. It would be worse outside, so hot and still when he came in, overcast, maybe even an inversion layer keeping the corn smell at ground level.

He bumped his keyboard, and his infinite-plumbing screensaver kicked off. The story on Derrick Doolin came back up. Like a bloody car wreck he couldn't take his eyes off of.

Doolin's pudgy face stared at him from the article's photograph, which looked like it was probably from the book jacket. He wore dark glasses and a grimace. His head was shaved. With his round face and bald head, he looked like Charlie Brown's bad-ass brother. Streator would not have recognized him without the caption.

Doolin had been in his creative writing class a couple of years earlier, fresh from the Gulf War. Streator suggested he write nonfiction, grunt's-eye pieces of his time manning checkpoints in Kuwait, with every approaching car a possible bomb. Doolin said he'd never fired his weapon. Instead he was working on a novel about an elite and of course secret Strike Force Scorpio chasing a terrorist cell all over the Middle East and North Africa. The leader of Strike Force Scorpio, Major Boyle Order, struggled to keep his small, motley crew of tightly-wound lethal weapons alive and on task as they blasted their way from bunker to dune to narrow dirty alley, pausing only to fist-fight with each other, embed lady journalists who wore Victoria's Secret under their field vests, or interrogate smoldering informants slowly peeling off their burkas. Streator saw the first few chapters over the course of a semester. He thought he'd given it a B in a course where grades ranged from A to B-.

But there it was, *The Scorpio Aspect*, in the military thriller imprint of a huge house, number 9 on the trade list and rising.

The article said Doolin had written the book at Columbia College in Chicago, where he still lived. It noted that he had been a Kickapoo student but did not mention Streator's classes. He'd been pretty pissed about the B, Streator recalled. Doolin had a contract for two more books in the series, for some serious cash. It had been optioned to a movie producer.

Streator clicked off the story with disgust, and there was that knock again. Three-bang no-show Tarvis Conner. Streator hesitated. Could he pretend he wasn't in? He shouldn't have left the light on.

His office was so small he could reach the door without getting out of his chair. "Hey, I got my thing," Tarvis announced when Streator reluctantly held the door open.

"Thursday's?"

"Yeah, I couldn't make it, my car died . . ."

"I heard. And today?"

"I had to type it so like I said I needed to use the lab and I don't type too good."

"So you went to type instead of coming to class."

"Yeah, it was due today."

"Last Thursday."

"I wasn't here Thursday."

He took a piece of paper from Tarvis's hand. A full page, single spaced, no paragraphs. "A few sentences? Story *starter*? "

"Yeah, I know, I just got really going and you said we was supposed to talk about it."

"Yes, we talked about them in class today, we did this exercise . . ." Streator gave up and rolled his chair back so that Tarvis could come in. Tarvis took the student chair by the door without being asked. Despite the noisy crowd in the hall, Streator left the door open, to signal *this will be brief.*

"Place a mess," Tarvis said.

It was a mess every other time Tarvis had been there, too. Streator's office was just a little longer than a broom closet, with metal shelves stacked to the ceiling, overflowing with textbooks and old student papers. More piles of books and boxes on the floor left just enough room for two chairs and two sets of feet. He hadn't seen the veneer on his desk top in several years and hadn't missed it.

"The maid quit," Streator said.

Tarvis looked at him and smiled—brilliant teeth, Streator noticed. He didn't seem to know if Streator was kidding.

Streator didn't help him out. He started reading the thing but his head was pounding and he couldn't face the misspellings and comma splices. He handed it back and rubbed his eyes. "Why don't you just tell me what you've got in mind."

"Yeah, okay, see, so it's supposed to be a murder mystery, right . . ."

"No, I just said it needed to introduce conflict, or suspense, or mystery."

"Yeah, so I did a mystery. So for the murder, a rich old guy owns the biggest factory in town, he's like famous rich, runs all over the world, got a big fancy house on the lake . . ."

"Got it. What happens?"

"So it's like winter, okay, and this old guy, everyone knows he's a little weird, know what I'm saying, like he does crazy things . . ."

"He's eccentric."

"Yeah, and one of the weird things this Gunther guy does, he goes ice skating on the lake at night."

"Wait, you can't call him Gunther, you'll have to change the name." The local captain of industry was an old coot named Frederick Gunther, a legend for his charming eccentricities—years ago Streator had tuned out the tedious accounts that everyone in town had about their wacky encounters with the big man.

"Ok, sure, I'll change it. So one morning, New Year's actually, they find him in the lake, he fell through the ice, they find him like his feet with the skates sticking up out of the hole and he's like all froze and these skates sticking up."

Streator chuckled. "That's kind of funny." Not a bad image, he had to admit. Though if someone fell through the ice, chances are he'd go feet first. "So he's dead. Had an accident. Only . . ."

"Only everyone thinks it's an accident, only it ain't."

"Right. So who gets suspicious? Police? Who's your detective?"

"Ok, so I'm thinking, you know, police man figures out the murder or some private eye, that's so stale, everyone does that, like you was saying in class, it don't have to be a cop, it could be like a regular guy or something."

"Yeah, sure, you could do the amateur sleuth. But if you take just a guy off the street, say, a college student or whatever, you've got to work real hard to give him some reason to be suspicious or involved, and then some reason he won't or can't go to the police, or some reason no one believes him, and some reason he's still smarter than the FBI and God and everybody. "

"Right right right, see I figure you come up with someone who's got some inside stuff on who really whacked the rich guy, the kind of shit you only have if you hooked into the street, know what I'm saying."

"Someone like . . ."

"Like you know, a young dude, he knows what's going on,

trying to make something better of himself, get up out of Burke Hole or what have you. "

"So, he's, what? Nineteen?"

"Maybe twenty-one, so he can drink and shit."

"College student? Community college?"

"No, maybe." Tarvis looked a little embarrassed.

"Likes vampire movies, drives an '81 LTD station wagon that never runs?"

"I don't know . . ."

"So basically you're saying you have someone whack Frederick Gunther, one of the richest and most politically hooked-up men in the state, and then you have Tarvis Conner figure it out."

"Well, not *me*, but you know . . ."

"So what's *not-you* know that the police don't?"

"Okay, so he sees a picture in the paper of this guy's legs sticking up out of the ice in this V shape and he's like whoa! cause he recognize right off what he seeing, especially on New Year's, it's a sign, and he scared to go to the police because these dudes they like big-time drugs and gangs and shit, they ain't messing around, I mean they whacked a rich guy . . ."

"Someone whacked a rich guy?" It was Loren Locke, Dean of the Communications Division, sticking his head in the office door.

"Not yet," Streator said. "Why? How rich are you?"

"When you're done here, Professor Streator, step on down, if you would."

"Roger that."

Locke left, smiling. He used to be okay, the only guy Streator had found at the school who knew how to play squash and was reasonable company in a bar afterward. Locke was originally from Albany and had almost finished a PhD from Western Michigan in Shakespearean rhetoric, so the two spent plenty of time beweeping their outcast state, Locke a full twenty years into disgrace with fortune and men's eyes. But then he was appointed Dean, had no time for squash, got fat, and started wearing suspenders and bad ties. And now "step on down when you're done" was never about court time at the Y but something Streator had screwed up. The throbbing in his head ratcheted up another level, now like squash played on the backside of his eyeball.

"Okay, Tarvis," Streator said, taking his paper and tossing it on to a pile on his desk, "it's got potential, I'll give you that, though it's entirely implausible." But what did Streator care if the story was plausible or not, like the kid was ever going to write it. It was the second time Tarvis had signed up for this class. Last spring he only lasted until he actually had to turn something in. If Streator hadn't needed more bodies to have the class make, he would've talked him out of it this semester. Should have anyway. He was a real pain, always interrupting with endless irrelevant tales about growing up in the projects in East St. Louis or somewhere, always coming by the office with excuses for why he hadn't done the assignment but had some rap crap he wanted Streator to read, always going on about some Chinese vampire movie he'd rented, offering to loan it to Streator so he could see how tight it was. Never could get him out the door. It was time to give him the *Get the assignments done and come to class or I'll drop you* speech.

"But if that's what you want to try," he told Tarvis, "what the hell. I've seen worse on the shelves." His standard reply to bad stories. "But already it's way more than a short story you could do by a week from Tuesday."

"See, I thought, you know, I'd at least get it started for class, I'm working on this book and I need some help with the story, I'm wanting to be a writer . . ."

Streator could have laughed. He'd heard it from so many over the years: *I want to be a writer.* Have you ever written anything? *No, but I got a million ideas, and my life, everyone says I should write a book* . . . Have you ever put pen to paper or finger to keyboard? *No, but I got a million ideas. . .* Can you write a basic English sentence without fourteen errors? Have you ever read anything? Have you ever even watched a movie without explosions in it? *No, but I really want to be a writer . . .*

"Fine, knock yourself out, get me something to read by a week from Tuesday. I'll take a look at this thing and check it off. And . . . catch up on any other stuff." There—he had really laid down the law that time. He stood, to signal *we're done.*

"Yeah, I'm on it, Tuesday."

As Streator ushered him out into the narrow hall of the office suite, Tarvis nodded to a tall, thick-necked friend with short-cropped hair and small ears that stuck out. He was waiting in line with several other students for conferences with Prof. Nash. Streator couldn't remember the last time he'd had a line outside his door. Of course he couldn't remember the last time he had scheduled mandatory conferences. "Sam-may," Tarvis laughed, and went through an elaborate set of two-finger chest and lip touches. Sammy slapped away his hand jive, none too happy with Tarvis. But who would be happy with anyone, waiting in line for Prof. Nash to rip you a new one over a paper you spent a good fifteen, maybe twenty minutes writing? Sammy glared over Tarvis to Streator in the doorway and said, "What you doing there?"

Streator started to retort but it turned out Sammy was talking to Tarvis. "That's my creative writing teacher."

"Creative writing?" Sammy sneered. "Shit."

3.

Streator hid in his office the rest of the afternoon. He knew what Locke wanted: a student from the Spring semester was challenging Streator's grade, and the appeal meeting was coming up at the end of the week. Locke wanted to plot strategy. Streator couldn't remember the student's complaint. Something about not getting timely feedback. No defense there.

After he kept his requisite fifty-minute office hour, he tried to hustle past Locke's door without being seen.

"Henry, come on in before you go," Locke said when Streator couldn't avoid eye contact.

"Ah, yes, you beckoned, I almost forgot." No use pretending he was just on his way to the john or the snack machines and would be right back—his book bag was a dead giveaway that he was headed home. Should've left the bag in the office. He wouldn't read the papers stuffed in it or prepare for class tonight anyway; he still carried things home because he still felt guilty leaving empty handed. And then felt worse for ignoring it all in favor of VH1 and the Food Network.

Locke's office was the luxury Dean's model, a double-wide broom closet, so that two or three students could complain at once. Streator took the chair behind the tiny "conference table"— just enough painted steel and brown laminate to keep a physical barrier between Dean and disgruntled student.

"So, exciting news about your student," Locke said with his little ironic smile.

"Which one? They're all so interesting."

"Derrick Doolin. The article today. Your protégé."

Streator stared straight through him.

Locke laughed. "You don't seem pleased, Henry. I can see Alumnus of the Year coming, graduation speaker."

"Spare me."

"I'm serious—in fact, I got a call from Jonathon in marketing today. He was a little cheesed there was so little about Kickapoo in that article and was wondering why there wasn't more credit given to his first writing teacher?"

"Maybe because I thought Doolin was a talentless little pissant?"

"And you told him that?"

"Not in so many words—wait, why didn't Jonathon ask *me*?"

"He left two voicemails. Really, Henry, you've got to start answering messages."

The light on his phone had been blinking for a year. He didn't even notice anymore. "So what does Jonathon want?"

"He wants to push for a follow-up, hopefully get the paper to do an interview with you about Doolin, maybe get you a slot on the Del Welsh show. "

"No."

"No?" Locke was annoyed but tried to hide it with his Cheshire cat smirk.

"No, thanks."

"No, what? No, you won't go on morning radio, or no, you won't even answer a few questions if someone calls?"

"No, I have no intention to get up at six a.m. to chat on the radio with that blowhard Welsh about some student I didn't like who didn't like me, and no, I don't want . . ." Locke was regarding him like he was a spoiled brat refusing to say hi to Grandma on the phone. "Look, tell Jonathon—I really don't even remember this guy and have nothing to say."

Locke got up and shut the door, even though the office suite was empty, except for his secretary engrossed in budget reports that Locke himself should've been doing.

"Is this a sword you really want to fall on?" he said when he sat down again. "You do realize that Jonathon is the president's favorite toady? They just want a little positive p.r., especially in a tax referendum year."

"Jonathon can go on the radio then. He loves that crap."

"And you wouldn't be able to squeeze out a little 'how happy I am for a former student,' for a press release? You know, it wouldn't hurt your position, or mine, if you'd play ball a little more."

Streator clenched his jaw. His headache roared. What did he

mean, "your position"? What position was he in? He didn't even want to ask. "Fine. Whatever. You know I'm a team player." He picked up his bag and started to rise.

Locke laughed and pulled open a file folder. "Indeed you are, so let's chart a game plan for this grade appeal, Tuesday at two."

"I have office hours then."

"I'll write you a note."

Streator was stopped by a train across Gunther Parkway on his way home. A long, grey line of grain cars slowly rattled forward, slowed even more, then stopped. He knew what this meant. Cars and grain trucks were already stacked up behind him. No chance to U-turn and take the long way round. He switched off his engine.

The end of the train disappeared around a curve and into the steam behind Gunther Mills. Then the line of cars banged to a start and inched backwards. The engine approached from the right. But Streator would not be taken in with foolish optimism, especially not today. Before the engine cleared the crossing, the train banged to a halt again. After a pause, it would reverse direction again, several more times at least, as it pushed cars onto the sidings. Seven minutes minimum. His cassette deck had stopped working, and no station in town played decent music. He was stuck singing to himself again.

"Traintraintraaain, train of foo-ood . . ."

A small thunderstorm had apparently just passed. The pavement was wet; the grey and green clouds still rolled over the factory. Steam rose into the clouds and mist in great billows. He hated that he had no windows in his office or classrooms—too expensive to install in the curved walls of the pods—so the weather could shift from tornado to blizzard to perfect sunshine in the same day and he would never know.

The thunderstorm had done little to abate the heat or humidity. Or the smell. He rolled up his windows, turned the car back on, and cranked the air conditioner. The AC rattled and whined but little cool air escaped. He flipped to "Recirc" to keep the smell out, but it was too late. His stomach still churned. The sick-baked smell from Gunther Mills and the other grain processors in town was the defining feature of the place. *The smell of money,* the town burghers were quick to remind everyone. *Completely harmless particulate matter,* factory reps were quick to assert, even as the town hacked and sniffled and pediatricians' offices stacked up with bronchial infections.

He hated corn. And beans. They were adrift in a vast ocean of corn and beans, beans and corn, that threatened to overwhelm every little island town in the county, even flooding into open tracts in the city between the factories and cheap housing developments on the outskirts all the way into undeveloped plots in the center of town—if it was bare, it was planted. Then all of it needed to be cut and trucked and trained and crushed and cooked and trucked and trained again, all of it a pain to Streator in one way or another.

"Peas train sounding louder . . ."

He hated Frederick L. Gunther. Tarvis chose well in knocking him off. Gunther was responsible for the mass of dusty grey buildings beside him, the maze of pipes and domes, the line of cooling towers that looked like miniature Three Mile Islands by the dozen. In went corn and beans, and out came ethanol, lysine, gluconate, starches, syrups, lecithin, fly ash.

By the gates of the factory, picketers moved back to their lines, shaking the rain off their signs. For a year the mill-workers' union had been locked out in a bitter battle, the workers claiming the company was trying to break the union by instituting rotating 12-hour shifts, the company claiming the union's "work to the rules" strategy was an excuse for sabotage. For ten months replacement workers had been bussed in to take the union jobs. For the last three months the picketers could hardly muster the energy to curse the scabs as they drove through the gates. Even worse, the more Gunther and his ilk locked out workers, the more they forced unions to strike, the more they laid off and shut down and moved to Mexico, the higher the head count rose at the community college, and the more stinking papers Streator had to grade. If Gunther and his buddies would just get their heads out of their butts, Streator thought, maybe he could get laid off.

He hated this goddamn train, the graffiti-covered cars still rattling back and forth, each bang a knock on his aching head. He'd heard that years back Frederick Gunther was so pissed off when a long train kept him from getting into his own factory that he had a viaduct built under the tracks by the main gate so he would never have to wait again. As for the rest of the peasants: let them eat Twinkies while they stalled at this and the scores of other crossings all over the city.

"Still a blunder, still a blunder, fool stopped the train . . ."

He hated the pickup he was stuck behind, with the Bush-Quayle bumper sticker, the tattered yellow ribbon, Calvin pissing on Chevy.

He hated his ex-wife for taking the Subaru to her new job in Minnesota and leaving him the Nova, with the broken tape deck and cranky air conditioner that led him to leave his windows down and end up with a wet seat when thunderstorms passed through.

He caught a glimpse of himself in the rearview mirror. He hated his haircut. A week earlier, as he watched from the upstairs bathroom window while Roni pulled away with a U-haul trailer full of half of their furniture and all of her books, he buzzed his bushy hair down to a nub and trimmed his beard to a bad-ass goatee, partly to give himself a hard game-face, mostly so that there would be one thing she didn't know that she didn't know about him anymore. It turns out it's hard to look really bad-ass when your goatee is going prematurely gray. And when you're only five-nine and not particularly muscled. And when you wear relaxed-fit jeans. He now feared he looked as stupid as Derrick Doolin.

The sunlight came long and soft out of the west, breaking through another red-tinged thunderhead. Over the factory towers to the east, the light slanted through the mist and rising steam. Curving over the stacks and pipes and sprawling blocks of industrial gulag, a rainbow. A huge perfect rainbow, each band bright and bursting from Roy to Biv.

By god he hated rainbows.

His hot little house still rattled him a little every time he walked and saw that it was half as empty as it had been just two weeks earlier. In the living room, just their smaller sofa and one armchair and one floor lamp. The dinette set that had been in the kitchen was now lost in the dining room. Big empty spot in the kitchen where the dinette with the microwave used to be. In the fridge he had no beer, but he couldn't blame Roni for taking that.

In fact, she had left several of her Diet Caffeine Free Dr. K sodas, pushed way to the back. He took one to the living room because it was the only thing cold in the house. He turned on the window air conditioner and sprawled on their second-best sofa. He clicked on the TV and absently channel surfed. He kicked off his shoes and socks and thought about fixing something to eat. But that seemed like a lot of effort.

August is a Sunday month, especially for teachers, a time of anxious reconsideration of projects not started, excursions not taken, books not read, empty time wasted, and now September's Monday hurrying near. This August, 1999, magnified the feeling to near desperation for Streator. When the seventies ended, he had just started college and was breathing all its promises; when the eighties turned, with a new wife and new job in a new town, college and grad school behind him, the Berlin Wall falling and a new world forming, Streator felt he was moving across a frontier of possibilities. The end of this decade, though, held no such promises. Just one knock after another.

The first blow that August caught him off guard and could have been avoided. He was nearly dozing in the back of the college's auditorium during another pre-term meeting, endless announcements and strategic plans and employee awards, when his name was called. "Hank Streator," said the President. For a moment it didn't register—nobody called him Hank. A ten-year service award. If he had remembered, he would've taken a personal day and skipped the convocation. Streator slumped in his chair. The President had to call his name again. His colleagues near him joshed and pushed him, and everyone laughed. Such a Streator thing to do. Reluctantly, he came to the stage for a plaque and a backslap. In the group photo, he stood grimly next to the cheerful clerk from the copy center. He thought she had been there forever.

His wife's departure a few days later was a blow he could see coming from far away, and he thought he had braced himself thoroughly. He was wrong. He didn't leave his house until Monday morning, hardly stirring off his couch. He missed his first class of the semester and was late for his second, a new low.

And now, late August, facing down the end of a decade, the end of the century, the end of his thirties just weeks away with his September birthday, what had he to show for the nineties? Ten years shoveling shit out of the Aegean stables of freshman composition. A failed marriage. No book.

Streator slept on the sofa that night and woke Friday morning with something like a hangover. Too much sleep, not enough food. He gave serious thought to calling in sick. As he dragged himself into the shower, feeling as shitty as he could ever remember without alcohol, he knew he'd better do something or he might just curl up and die. On the drive to school, past the rundown strip malls and steaming factories, he decided he had to get out of this town—at least for the weekend, and then somehow permanently. This place was sucking the life out of him.

The long Labor Day weekend stretched ahead of him. He would just go. Somewhere. Take a few days in Chicago. Long road trip to a real college town, Bloomington or Ann Arbor or Madison. Even Indianapolis would be better. Although, really, he couldn't call up his few remaining friends in those places on such short notice, not when he hadn't seen most of them in years. Not when most of them were really Roni's friends. And a weekend alone in a hotel, even in Chicago, had little appeal.

What he really wanted to do was drive to Minnesota, all night, and surprise Roni with a knock on her door in the morning. Some sort of dramatic scene would follow. She would hold the door half-opened in her t-shirt. Maybe she had taken a lover already, and some whiskery colleague or a skinny long-haired grad student would be lounging in his shorts on her sofa. Their best sofa. And then what? They would have at it, have it out, have angry sex (the new lover deleted easily from the scene), have something. He could get no image to coalesce beyond her at the door in her t-shirt.

Attendance was low in his comp classes. He was glad he hadn't bothered reading their essays. He acted like he was doing them a favor by returning their papers ungraded because they needed so much more work. He put them in groups for "peer editing," the blind leading the blind for half an hour while he watched.

Lather, rinse, repeat three times that day. In his rowdy twelve o'clock class, they got into a boisterous argument when someone asked if it was okay to use the word "nigga" in a paper. Streator was the only person in the room, white or black, who argued that "nigga" was just as offensive as "nigger"; all the students were certain that nigga had nothing to do with race anymore and in fact a white person could be a nigga—or for that matter, a nigger.

Since it was the most engaged any of them had been all semester, Streator reintroduced the topic in his one o'clock section. But here it bombed, as did all the rest of his tricks. The dozen or so students straggling in on a Friday afternoon before a holiday couldn't muster the energy to defend their music when he insulted it. A few of the older women were particularly surly. One had apparently seen the light when her daughter brought home a "mixed grandbaby" and now was peeved that he was seen as black when there was just as much white in him; another was old enough to remember using "colored only" water fountains when traveling in the south as a child. No one had any interest in focusing on the question at hand, so he punted and put them in groups.

As they shuffled to their assigned places, a small, nervous-looking kid with a camo hunting cap on frontward asked if he could see Streator in the hall. "Can I just go work on mine in the lab?" the kid asked when they were outside. Michael something. He held his essay draft. The bill of his cap was curved so tight and pulled so low, it was like looking down a tunnel to his eyes.

"Why? What's wrong?"

"Well," he glanced back toward the door, "you know, the topic, I just thought Malveeta and Shirley and some of them might get pissed."

Streator took the draft from his hand and scanned it quickly: *why the Klan wasn't really as bad as everyone said.* He had put the kid in a group with two formidable older women. He really needed to start reading these things first. He tore the essay in two and told him to find a new topic. He couldn't read Michael's face under that cap—mad? embarrassed? scared?—as he went back in for his backpack and quickly left the room.

4.

By the time he was home that afternoon sprawled on the sofa with the air conditioner whining and a blender of margaritas at his side, taking a trip had lost all appeal. He had no energy to move at all. It was so hot. And he was so tired. So sick and tired. The thought of driving for hours with no AC or music made him feel ill.

But something had to change, he knew that. He punched the remote, channels bouncing around and around in the trochaic rhythm he found most hypnotic, until his eyes and thumb ached enough that he turned off the TV and took to staring at the walls. Her goddamn walls.

He had to admit that it had been mostly his idea to rehab the old brick bungalow they found in a neighborhood with sycamores and maples arching over brick streets. He convinced her they were throwing money away on rent; their down payment was less than a good used car. They could fix this place up and make a small profit when they moved, he was sure. They never said *if* they moved, always *when*. He'd been so taken with the arts and crafts built-in bookcases, the wood floors, the low thick beams in the main floor, the oddly shaped dormer rooms upstairs, that he really hadn't considered what a wreck the place was. But the walls— those were definitely Roni's walls.

He came home one summer afternoon to find her ripping down the 70's paneling in the living room and the first floor bedroom they used as an office. He would have rather found her in bed with a whiskery colleague. She was sure whatever was underneath was better than the dark fake wood. She was wrong. Yellow wallpaper straight out of Charlotte Perkins Gilman. They spent a week with a rented steamer in the middle of a summer heat wave trying to get it off. Then they found that the plaster underneath the paper was so bad, so crumbling and bowed and pocked with paneling nail holes, it couldn't be saved. So he and Roni covered the furniture and blocked the doorways with plastic so that it looked like a crime scene, which it was to Streator, and they chunked out the plaster in huge clouds of white dust. And then the lath. Dumpsters full. And then started to wallboard. It couldn't be that hard, she said. They bought home improvement books and consulted friends. It *was* that hard, the cutting and nailing and spackling, the taping and sanding, all far beyond his skills and patience.

Most of one summer they made sacrificial offerings to the walls. By August, they abandoned the downstairs bedroom to raw wallboard and concentrated on finishing the living room enough to paint. She chose an arts and craft green. When it was done, it was more depressing than the dark paneling. Through the paint, under and around their museum prints, they could see—and argue about—the ridges of bad tape jobs, the irregular spackling, the crooked corners. Even worse, the previous owners who put up the paneling threw away the original molding, even the oak baseboards, so that Streator still needed to trim out everything: baseboards, quarter round, maybe crown molding to hide the gaps with the ceiling. That would mean weeks more of miter miss-cuts and staining hundreds of dollar-feet of milled oak, the inevitable daily trip to Menards. By the middle of August, Streator was almost glad he had to give over the walls for Kickapoo's pre-term meetings. Though he was so resentful for wasting all his time off worshiping in the cult of home improvement that he took his anger out on colleagues. And then his students. And, as always, his wife.

That was five years ago. He hadn't touched the walls since. Same raw wallboard in the back room, same untrimmed gaps along the floors and ceilings in the living room, same depressing green. The walls were Exhibit W in her "you never finish anything" prosecution. And they were his star witnesses in establishing that she was a nearly unlivable combination of impulsive naïf and control freak.

The unfinished walls marked the beginning of the end. She saw the future unrolling in front of her in ways that he could not. She said, "I am not dying in this town." She threw herself into her dissertation on Phyllis Wheatley, driving long miles to the closest state university to use the library. She spent two summers holed up in their downstairs bedroom with piles of books and a laptop; he spent those summers not teaching summer school because he was so sick of teaching and not working on the house because he was supposed to be working on his novel and not working on his novel because he was so distracted and depressed from the chronic angers of that house.

He wanted a motorcycle. He wondered if they should get pregnant. She laughed at both ideas. He bought a used Kawasaki.

By the time she had finished her dissertation, they were finished as well. She defended, went on the market, endured MLA interviews and campus interviews before landing a plum tenure-track position at a liberal arts college in Minnesota. He said winters were dark and deep in Minnesota. She said, "Don't worry about it."

During the divorce negotiations they argued about who would get the house. Neither wanted to be stuck with it. Both knew what it would take to get it into some sort of shape to sell. Not just finishing the walls, but sealing the basement, fixing the leaky roof, refinishing floors that Roni had ripped the old carpet off of one winter-break morning, thinking any kind of wood floor had to be better than the gray cat-stained mess on top. Wrong again. Turns out urine stains will soak through a carpet and pad and all but ruin a fir floor underneath.

Streator drew the short straw and won the house. So Roni was free to explore the great north woods while he was manacled to the Temple of Irredeemable Walls.

Well, the hell with that, Streator decided Friday night. He'd just have to prove what he could do without her in the way. Sell this damn house, for one thing. This would be Streator's Plan to Fix His Life, Step: One: Tonight, or maybe tomorrow, he'd go to Menards, he'd get oak trim for the living room, he'd get a compound miter saw, he'd get a five gallon bucket of joint compound since he was sure the old one in the basement was dried up by now, he'd get right on it and spend all weekend busting his butt and come home early from work next week (which he was doing anyway) and have a real good reason for ignoring those papers. He would get the walls beaten into submission in a week or so, get a Realtor in there to see what was a real priority for sale, get the place on the market before the cold weather set in and every buyer could see how drafty it was with so few storm windows and an ancient gravity-flow furnace.

He didn't get up as early as he might have Saturday morning, but he did get to Menards by noon. He decided to just start with spackling and taping; the trim and saw were too much for his VISA. He got out his ladder, tarps, and plastic, moved his computer to the dining room, and dove into the walls in the back room.

But Jesus it looked like hell. He had no touch with a trowel, couldn't get the feathering technique down, couldn't get the tape or corner reinforcements or nail heads to disappear. Truth was, Roni was better with the finish work. Like frosting a cake, she would tell him. He glopped on the joint compound and worked and overworked it until he had practically replastered the entire west wall. Three more to go.

It was stifling hot in that room. Roni had taken off with the window unit he had installed for her when she buried herself in there to finish her dissertation. Like she needed an air conditioner in Minnesota. The window fan hardly budged the humidity. A couple of beers would help. And it might cool down in the evening. If a thunderstorm came through. He could check the Weather Channel.

Locke found Streator at seven o'clock Saturday night half-heartedly sanding the back room walls, a boom box blasting *Darkness on the Edge of Town*. White dust covered Streator like a sprinkled pastry.

"You should wear a mask," Locke said, startling Streator.

"You should knock," Streator said.

"I did," Locke said, coughing and turning off the boom box. "I could hear this from my place." Locke lived two blocks west, on a street of huge old brick houses with pillars and porticos, the former bastion of 1920s doctors and lawyers. He had advised Streator and Roni years ago to buy as soon as they could; if they were going to be stuck in a town like this, he said, they should take advantage of the few amenities the place had to offer, namely lovely old houses they would never be able to afford anywhere else in the country.

"I've come to lure you away for a drink," Locke said.

"I've got beer in the fridge," Streator said. "Or Caffeine Free Diet Dr. K."

"Thanks, no," Locke said, "I like to breathe when I drink."

"Then you're in the wrong town," Streator said, but he dropped his sanding block and went to wash up.

He figured they'd drop into his favorite grungy burger and beer joint a few blocks away, but Locke took them to his own hangout, Reilly's, a tony steakhouse downtown. Wants me on his turf, Streator thought. He had changed his dusty t-shirt but was glad he had kept on his shorts and sneakers grey with spackling.

They sat at the bar. The place was mostly empty. On a weeknight, it would be bustling with middle-management suits from the courthouse and nearby law firms, the only businesses left downtown. Early on a Saturday, only a couple of travelling salesmen stuck overnight. No women. Locke waved familiarly at the bartender and she came right over. She was mid-thirties, long brown hair with highlighted streaks pulled back and up but still all tousled around her face, thick lips with bright lipstick, a big toothy smile for Locke.

"Hey-ey," she said. "Good to see you again. Finally."

"And you, and you," Locke said. They chatted for a few moments.

"I know what you want," she said to Locke.

"Indeed you do," Locke said.

"How about you, Mr. Streator? Still teaching at Kickapoo?"

"Sure, sure." Never failed. Couldn't go anywhere in this town without running into an ex-student. He seldom recognized faces quickly enough to avoid them. And there was always the question of what grade he had given them—might one be inclined to spit in a drink, for instance?

"He'll have the same, of course."

"A beer," Streator said, "something German."

"Come now, Sondra makes the best Old Fashioned in town—I taught her myself."

Sondra blushed and went for the drinks.

"Private tutoring?" Streator asked when she was gone.

"Night student," Locke said. "You know, if you're going to have to live in this town, you have to take advantage of the few perks the job offers."

"So you've said." He watched Sondra fix the drinks. She wore tight black pants and a tight black vest over a white shirt, unbuttoned enough to earn extra tips. In ten years he had never taken advantage of that kind of perk. He'd had his share of flirty students, but even when things were at their worst with Roni, he'd never pressed the advantage with a student. A point of stubborn pride to him. Roni would never have that to hold over him.

He glanced at Locke. How did this work, a guy like Locke and a woman like Sondra? He supposed Locke was handsome enough—*pleasant*, his mom would call him, that little smile and twinkle probably carrying him a long way. He was tall and a little thick now, less hair than ten years ago but at least no comb-over. A willingness to show his money never hurt either: he was the kind of man who wore khakis and a polo on Saturdays. To mow his lawn. "The real question is, did you tutor Carly Simon there before or after she was in your class? Or before or after your divorce?"

"Excellent questions," Locke said as Sondra returned with a Heineken and a cocktail. "Sondra, Professor Streator would like to know . . ."

"Jesus, Loren . . ."

". . . if you are Carly Simon's twin separated at birth?"

She looked them both over like they were teenagers without IDs.

"No? But go on, show him the secret to a perfect Old Fashioned."

She sighed but smiled through her tousled hair. She took one long white-nailed middle finger, showed it to Locke, and then stirred the drink slowly. Then she licked her finger and moved off, singing "You're So Vain" quietly to herself.

"Sure you don't want one?" Locke said with a too-pleased grin.

Streator declined but was beginning to wonder if his pride was misguided.

Locke led them to a quiet booth on the side of the bar, a box of squeaky fake leather surrounded by potted ferns. Harry Connick, Jr. drifted out of the ceiling.

"Is that why you brought me here?" Streator said. "To discuss professional development opportunities?" He took a big slug off his beer.

"No, no. Just wanted to see how you were doing."

"Well, I'm peachy."

"Seriously."

"I'm fine."

The two men drank quietly. Streator wasn't in any mood to give an inch.

"So," Locke ventured, "Veronica left for Minnesota, what, a month now?"

"Two weeks ago. Her school doesn't start until after Labor Day, as God intended. One more thing to be jealous of. As if I needed a longer list."

"You're holding up okay, then? Things all worked out? I know how slow and messy it can be."

"Yep. It's all good. Merrily we roll along. Best thing that could've happened for both of us. Like a big burden released."

Locke sighed and leaned forward. He looked at Streator so long and so seriously that Streator became embarrassed.

"What?" Streator finally said.

Locke seemed about to say something, then thought better of it. He sat back and relaxed. "You're working on your house," he noted absently, scanning for Sondra again.

"Going to sell it this fall."

"And do what?"

"Find someplace with finished walls."

Locke swirled the ice in his drink. Sondra was chatting up a group of loud yuppies in loud ties who had just come in.

"How's that novel coming along?" Locke said without looking at Streator.

"How's that dissertation coming along?"

"It died of natural causes. Your novel?"

Streator shrugged. "Breathing on its own. Actually, I'm going to launch a major rewrite. *Strike Force Kickapoo.*"

Locke looked at him so abruptly with so much concern, Streator was caught off guard. "This Derrick Doolin thing really bugs you, doesn't it."

Despite himself, Streator felt his throat tightening. "It's just. . . the timing, you know, it could've been better."

"But, really, he's just some shitty writer with a shitty book. "

"That's the whole thing. That's it. Here I am . . . and there's this—nearly illiterate . . ."

He didn't want to talk about it. Locke wasn't letting him off the hook.

"I mean, do you remember this guy?" Streator said. "I don't care if he was a vet, he was a real douche, and his writing was a bucket of suck. But now *Derrick Doolin* is sitting in some Chicago loft pounding out chapters til his keyboard smokes. Derrick fucking Doolin is signing books at trade fairs all over the country. Derrick fucking pissant Doolin sure as shit ain't grading freshman essays at a community college in the corn fields til he's gray and blind." There. He had said it out loud. He did not feel better.

At least Locke didn't laugh at him. And he knew better than to offer some condescending advice.

"You want a good novel?" he said. "There's one for you, right there." He nodded toward Sondra.

"Yeah, I bet she could tell stories."

Locke looked genuinely angry for a moment, and Streator felt bad. But Locke quickly reset his expression to "detached." "Her stepfather—a part-time pastor, I think she mentioned—he kicked her out when she was sixteen. She was pregnant, and unfortunately the daddy looked more like Luther Vandross than James Taylor. But she got her GED and then a certificate in cosmetology, and she's still ostensibly working on a degree in Graphic Arts from us. She works nights here and babysits her grandson during the day so her daughter can finish high school."

Streator regarded her again and worked the math. "Grandson?"

"Yes, she's younger than you. Oh, did I mention the lupus? Or the sexual assault?"

Something came to Streator. "Why so much interest in my novel all of a sudden?" They never talked of such things.

Locke hesitated. "It would look good on a curriculum vitae." Now Locke was embarrassed.

Streator stared him down. "Is that a suggestion, or a threat?"

"An observation," Locke said. He waved his hand at Streator dismissively and turned his attention back to Sondra. "I'm going to go rescue someone who really wants to be rescued." She looked his way and smiled. "Sondra Brenly, formerly Schuler. Introduction to Literature. Nine years ago. Got an A."

"Impressive. Wish I could remember students like that."

"She wasn't mine, she was yours. She said your class made her, quote, 'change the way she thought about everything,' unquote. I have no idea what she meant, but I am extremely jealous. And for the record, the answers to your excellent questions? After, and after." And then he smiled at Streator and went to the bar, singing "Nobody Does it Better" quietly to himself.

5.

Streator spent the rest of the night on the couch, staring at his walls. Who was he kidding. He could fresco the place like Giotto and still be stuck with the same wreck. *It's not the house, stupid!* What Major Boyle Order had blasted into the light of day, what Loren Locke was putting his finger on, what nobody bothered to mention? He was a failed writer. Failed at the only thing he had ever been good at his whole life. Nothing of worth to show for his writing, nothing to compensate for the rest of his fuck-ups.

That's why the Derrick Doolin news, out of all the knocks he had taken that August, was the blow that finally brought him to his knees.

In graduate school, a newer, small MFA program in Virginia, Streator was middle of the pack, not a runt to be ridiculed and starved off the department's teat for his own good, but not a star coming out of the program with an agent and a book contract. His thesis was a set of minimalist stories that skimmed the surface of his suburban teenage days, summers in Berkshire camps, his semester abroad in Alicante, written with enough tenderness and humor to pass off "shallow" as "suggestive."

After he finished the program, he helped run a small press, and through quid pro quo with a grad-school friend at another tiny press in Florida, he managed to get his thesis lined up for publication. Streator's press published his friend's precious novel; his friend's press went under before Streator's book came out. Streator ran into him a few years later at the AWP Conference— not a bad guy, a bit embarrassed by what had happened, no longer writing, but working for a literary agency in New York. He told Streator to be sure to send along his novel as soon as it was ready. Streator couldn't remember how long ago that had been, the last AWP Conference he had bothered with. He landed a few old stories in journals run by MFA students. He used to name-drop *Triquarterly,* the one decent literary magazine that had picked up one of his stories just before he was hired at Kickapoo, until he realized none of his colleagues had ever heard of it. And he didn't mention any of it anymore because someone might ask, "So what else have you published?" *Well, there was that story in that lit magazine out of Des Moines five years ago . . .* Or "What have you got out?" Or worse, "What are you working on?" He could hem and haw, he could complain about how he was turned down for a Professional Leave ("We don't call them sabbaticals") because his proposal to work on a novel didn't demonstrate enough "direct benefit to students and/or a specific program," but even the dim ones must've figured it out: he was a writing teacher who didn't write. Even as a self-important undergrad, he had saved his worst derision for that breed.

Sunday afternoon he began Streator's Plan to Fix His Life, Step Two: he drove over to a funky coffee shop near a state university fifty miles away. He bought an espresso and biscotti and settled on an old divan in front of a wobbly table.

He took out his notebook and a pen. He considered his few scribbles, some more than ten years old. What he had been calling "his novel." This was what he had: a fifty-year-old man wasting away as a middle manager for a toy and game company in Massachusetts. Streator's father was a technical writer for Milton Bradley in East Longmeadow. "Where Henry got his writing talent!" his mother always bragged, but Streator always said it was his father's fault that no one could follow the directions for Hungry Hungry Hippo. Although Streator's father was annoyingly content with his job, his wife, and his life, the character in his novel would be lonely, unsettled, widowed—no, recently divorced, his wife had left him—surrounded by the depressing daily cheer of kids' fun, which in reality was a cut-throat, high-stakes, high-pressure game. A setting dripping with irony.

That was his novel. As far as he had ever gotten. Something would have to happen, he knew. But it was just a matter of getting the characters up and running and following along behind to see where they went, what they said, not pressing the matter too much, just *discovering* the story as it unfolded. That was the idea anyway. He was thinking of sending him on vacation to Alicante, where he would meet . . . someone. He decided a laptop would be nice for days like this, and the prices were coming down so much. Roni had a laptop. She took it with her. But no matter, pen speed was best for writing anyway, the physical effort of crafting letters and words and sentences requiring commensurate care in the crafting of ideas—something like that, he had always heard. What was that odd smell he remembered inside Milton Bradley the couple of times he visited as a kid? He could phone his father and ask, but then the questions, the questions . . .

Some sort of reedy new-age folk music tinkled over his head. The "Now Playing" CD by the register said it was Peruvian woodwinds. The handmade flyers on the community bulletin board screamed hipper-than-thou indignation over one current outrage or another, or announced gigs for pretentious bands in sweaty bars. He used to love college towns. The barista had a ponytail. Streator realized he no longer had any patience for ponytails on men. And he hated the word "barista."

He felt like such a poser, he packed up and left without writing anything. He counted the red-tailed hawks on the power lines for fifty hot, flat miles home.

When he pulled into town, he was still hungry, so he stopped by The Tapestrie, a dingy bar near his house where they didn't cook any better than they spelled. He took a sticky table on the side. Edgar, the owner, sat on a stool next to the drive-up window like a crew-cut Jabba the Hut, smoking a cigarette. The waitress/bartender, Streator thought her name was Chantelle, brought him a beer and a horseshoe, a local favorite: an open-faced burger mounded with fries and smothered with cheese sauce. Bacon bits optional. Edgar drew long on his cigarette and complained about the weather. Chantelle settled behind the bar near the only other customer and worked on her cigarette. She and the customer, a young man in white coveralls who smelled like Gunther Mills, concurred with Edgar: miserable heat and humidity. Soon they would launch the " 'posed to be's." " 'Posed to be hotter tomorrow." Or colder tonight. Or tornadoes, or flash floods, or blizzards, or frogs from the sky.

Then 'posed to be back to more of the same. Soon one would say, "Yep. Don't like the weather here? Stick around a few minutes, it'll change." Streator was pretty sure that Edgar sat on that stool every minute of every day and slept sitting on it at night. Why not. The bar was air conditioned, and it was 'posed to be hot as hell tonight.

Chantelle called over to Streator, asked if he wanted another beer, but the first one hadn't settled well at all.

"Diet soda?"

She brought him a flat drink.

"Where you from?" the millworker at the bar turned and asked.

"Massachusetts."

"Figured as much, you got that accent," Chantelle said.

"Like Newwww Yawwwk," said the millworker. "Tell you what, wouldn't catch me living there, too damn big."

"L.A.'s a big town anymore," Chantelle said.

"That where you from?" the millworker asked her.

"No, I ran away there once."

Streator's fries were a goopy, soggy mess, nearly inedible.

"Me and my brother Kirby once rode to San Diego in the back of a U-Haul truck," the millworker said.

"Got hot in there, I bet," Chantelle offered.

"We left the door up. Kirby almost fell out in Oklahoma."

"Sleepwalking?"

"Knife fight."

They commenced to comparing scars and restraining orders. Streator hadn't bothered bringing his notebook into the bar. The smells of Milton Bradley, of the woods and hills of Western Mass and the beaches of Alicante, of restaurants that served soda not pop and banned smoking and all things equine were so far away, it would've been useless to try to retrieve them. As he left the bar with an iron lump in his stomach, he realized why they called it a horseshoe.

Tuesday, only five of his eleven creative writing students were in their chairs when he arrived. Maybe he was weeding some out. Good.

"We weren't for sure we was going to have class today,"

Trudy said.

Give me a break, he thought, he was just two minutes late, not bad for him. "Yeah, yeah. We can talk about . . ." he looked through his pile and found one exercise he had read that matched one student actually there, "Brandon's thing today," he said. "And . . . Megan's."

"*Megan* isn't here," Morgan said.

"We just thought, you know, because of Tarvis and all," Trudy said.

Tarvis was absent, but what else was new. "We'll try to press on as best we can without Tarvis," Streator said with a sharper sarcastic edge than he intended, Morgan's snotty tone putting him on the defensive already.

Trudy stared at him angrily, shaking her head, and the others looked at each other incredulously.

"That's pretty cold," Trudy said as she gathered up her books and stuffed them into her rolling suitcase. "But I, for one, am not going to be late for his funeral."

He found Saturday's paper in the school library. And there, page three, first column, two paragraphs: "Local Teen Dies in Single-Car Crash." Tarvis Anthony Conner. Nineteen. Lost control of his car out off Hackydale Blacktop, somewhere west of town. Early Friday night. Excessive speed. Rolled, thrown from the vehicle. Dead at the scene. Sunday's paper had the obituary. Survived by half of town, nothing else new. Funeral Tuesday at 1:00, Broadway Temple of the Living God.

He was a little ashamed that his gut response to the news when Trudy explained it was, *Well, that's one less portfolio I'll have to read.* And when she left and Morgan followed and he dismissed the others, his thought was, *Well, there's one less hour and fifteen minutes of deathly boredom I'll have to endure.* Cold? She had no idea.

He glanced at his watch. Tarvis's funeral had started half an hour ago. Hadn't even crossed his mind that he could go. Temple of the Living God was one of the churches Roni used to attend, for the music, she said. Tarvis might have been a kid at Homework Haven, where she tutored years ago. She might have known him, or his family. She would've gone to the funeral.

Streator wondered what his own funeral would be like. When a colleague had died of cancer several years earlier, they had filled the college auditorium for a memorial service. What kind of crowd would Streator draw? Who would speak for him? Who would volunteer to sing "The Wind Beneath My Wings?" After Roni left, most of their couple friends stopped coming by. Everybody liked her. She had the unfair advantage of being pretty and charming in an unpretentious Southern way, funny without trying to be, passionate about politics and movies and teaching and books, willing to put up good long arguments defending Chinua Achebe's critique of Conrad's racism without getting anyone angry at her. Streator had taken to disagreeing with everything she said in front of their friends just because her generous spirit was pissing him off. And gee, no one came to see him anymore.

He'd better check out in some sympathetic way, he decided, or the room at his memorial would be empty. He had a recurring morbid fantasy—more so a story he'd worked out in his head—of walking across the Kroger parking lot on one of his late night runs for morning coffee or milk, someone would confront him, and he'd be shot dead on the dirty asphalt next to a spilled Slushee at one a.m. His Kroger wasn't in a particularly dangerous neighborhood; many professionals lived in renovated old houses at that end of town. But you could definitely get mugged there. A guy had been shot in his car in that lot a few years earlier in a drug deal gone bad. Every once in a while he'd see the security guard and stock clerks manhandling some kid trying to slip out with a bottle of whiskey under his coat. In some versions of Streator's story he'd swing a gallon jug of milk and coldcock the mugger, wind up a hero. But in most versions he'd clutch the jug to his chest and the bullet would explode milk all over, in slow motion. "Popular Kickapoo Instructor Slain at Highlawn Plaza." That would pack them in.

The only reason Streator opened his door when the bell rang Tuesday evening was because he was expecting a pizza. But it was Locke. He hadn't been to Streator's house twice in the last two years, and now twice in the last few weeks. "Dean Locke,"

Streator said. "What will the neighbors think."

"How are you feeling?" Locke said with a smile. "Better now, I take it? Keeping the fluids up?" He nodded at the beer in Streator's hand. He came in without being asked.

"Better than what?"

"Your stomach flu. It was flu, right? That's what I told the committee at the meeting you missed today."

Several times through the afternoon Streator had remembered the grade-appeal hearing. But he had given little thought of going. "I'm not as nauseous as I have been. But I can feel it coming back."

Locke sat on his couch. He still wore his dress clothes, without his suit coat. He looked quite uncomfortable. "It's very hot in here," Locke said. He loosened his tie. "Do you have any more of those cold?" He pointed at Streator's beer.

Streator fetched a beer from the kitchen and took the armchair opposite Locke. "Mind the afghan," he said, "that flu is pretty contagious." He tried a smile.

Locke wasn't having it. He took a long draw on his beer. He fidgeted. Streator let him stew.

Finally Locke sighed and said, "Henry, you should have been there."

"I preferred not."

Locke raised his eyebrows. "Is that so, Professor Bartleby. . ."

"Funny thing happened today. Found out a student of mine died. Funeral was this afternoon. Two o'clock."

"One o'clock, and you didn't go. And you just found out today that he died?"

Streator shrugged. "Look, I was in no mood for a bonehead inquisition, believe me. "

"Yes, you look all torn up about Tarvis."

"He was a good kid."

They both studied their rapidly emptying bottles.

"The committee upheld your grade."

"An academic committee chaired by a professor of truck-driver training approved my grading? Hoo-rah."

"Though as soon as the student was out of the room every one of your colleagues chewed my ear off. About you."

He tried to think who else was on the committee. A few names popped to mind. He didn't know they all hated him. "Nice to know they care."

"Dr. Jackie was there, too." Jacquelyn Stoughton, Ed.D., was the Vice President of Student Services, the counselor in chief. "We continued our conversation for about another hour in her office. Seems she had a visit from a few of your 101 students."

"Do tell."

"Seems they and Dr. Jackie are concerned that you're creating 'discomfort in the classroom' for some of your students."

"What the hell? Am I supposed to provide pillowtop desks now?"

"Apparently the students took umbrage at your use of the 'n word'—Friday? Apparently you even wrote said word on the board?"

"You gotta be shitting me. I was making the point that *nigger* and *nigga* were equally offensive. "

"Be that as it may, Dr. Jackie is quite concerned about making any of our customers uncomfortable. "

"Isn't that the whole goddamn point of going to college?" Streator sat forward and jabbed the coffee table. "Isn't that my *job*, to make little narrow-minded turds *uncomfortable?*"

"But apparently not to the point of 'creating a hostile environment.' "

"But *I* was the one . . ."

Locke waved him off. "I know, I understand. We just need to get this said to Dr. Jackie. And Marianne."

"Marianne? Atherton? What the hell does this have to do with HR?"

"She's our official civil rights compliance officer. "

"Oh, you have got to be shitting me!"

"We are all to convene in her office, Thursday at two o'clock. You, me, Dr. Jackie, Marianne, and one or two, maybe three of the students."

Streator grabbed his head. "*Three? Three* fucking students? Who the hell are they?"

Locke wiped his face with the cold sweat of the beer. "Well, I suppose you'll find out soon enough. Malveeta Fray . . ."

"Of course. And her buddy Shirley Harris."

"No, that name didn't come up. One of the Gianoulis clan, and some little Goth-lite came in with Malveeta, Susanne something?"

"Suzy Miffler? She hasn't said two words all semester—Malveeta dragged her in?"

Locke finished his beer and burped in the affirmative.

Streator sank back, shaking his head. "Unbelievable. Should I bring my lawyer? See if Johnnie Cochran is free?"

Locke sighed. His blue dress shirt was dark with sweat. "No, but you might bring in the KKK kid whose paper you tore up."

"How do you know about that?"

"He came by to drop. And complain."

"So there's my defense. I'm just as prejudiced against racists."

"He was really quite amusing. Somewhere he'd picked up a quaint notion that college should be a free marketplace of ideas."

"If he came within shouting distance of an idea like that in class, I'd have given him an A."

"Well, of course he didn't quite put it that way, I'm paraphrasing. His were closer to talk-radio bullet points. But come now—tearing up his paper? In front of him? Isn't that a bit melodramatic?"

"You're right. Cheap theatrics. So give me a bad notice." Streator slumped in his chair, pouting.

The doorbell rang. It was the pizza. Streator went to the door in a fog and paid the delivery driver without looking at anything but the soggy box. "So," the pizza man said as he was leaving, "still teaching at Kickapoo?"

What the fuck else would I be doing in this fucking town! he wanted to scream, but he couldn't get it out.

6.

Streator called in sick the next day. He managed to make Thursday's classes but didn't bother with the afternoon meeting. In his Fiction class, while discussing "A Good Man is Hard to Find," he took up the "Oh, look at the cute little pickanniny!" line in order to lure them into the nigger/nigga discussion, just to be contrary. The pastor's wife got into it with the teenage lesbian Wiccan when they discussed the grandmother's moment of grace with The Misfit. Streator let them go at it. Then it turned out that Towanda had firsthand experience to share about the mindset of ruthless killers, her own aunt having been shot in a home invasion some years ago. Which led to Brittany's close friend nearly killed at a party in a dispute over who was supposed to pay for the keg and weed. Which led to Jason of the Backwards Cap, who broke up the class when he plopped his foot on his desk to show everyone his ankle bracelet, apropos of nothing, maybe just so he wouldn't lose street cred to The Misfit or anyone else. Streator made no effort to rein them in.

In Creative Writing, Morgan took exception when he compared Anne Rice novels to McDonald's food: cheap, tempting, prepackaged, leaves you feeling sick afterward, good chance of killing you if you take in too much. He was a little surprised Morgan was so worked up, because he thought she was the one obsessed with serial killers, not vampires, but that must have been Megan, who had apparently dropped. Morgan's dyed black hair and nose piercing should have been his clue. "But what if you really *like* McDonald's?" she finally asked in exasperation.

"Then you just might make the next Derrick Doolin," he said.

"Awesome!" she said.

Locke caught up with him Friday morning before class. He came into Streator's office and shut the door. He sat down in the extra chair. He didn't bother with his bemused smile.

"You know, I did another brilliant job of covering your ass yesterday," he said. "Blathered on and on about academic freedom and the nature of college education. They had no idea what I was talking about, but I pulled rank, insisted that this was a classroom matter and I was your classroom supervisor. Even talked them out of setting up a special one-on-one session of the mandatory diversity training you've missed for the last few years."

"I owe you my first-born child. Seriously, Loren, what can I do for you?"

"You can do your fucking job, for one thing!"

Streator was taken aback. He'd never seen Locke so genuinely angry, though he quickly composed himself, rose slowly, and perched on the edge of Streator's desk.

"Look, Henry," he shook his head. "I'm going to be direct here, because I like you, because I thought we were friends, and because you're making me drink way too much."

"Direct away."

"I asked about your novel last week," he said slowly, "because your employment depends on it."

"Bullshit," Streator said, shaking his head angrily. "I'm tenured. And even if I weren't, there's nothing in the contract about scholarly work or creative work, god forbid we act like a real college . . ."

"I'm not talking about your employment *here*."

Streator couldn't read this new Locke. He wished he would sit down again. He was pulling a classroom trick, this towering over him to deliver the reprimand. But he was bluffing. Had to be. "You can't fire me. You wouldn't."

"Not me. But I've been having conversations with other people who can. And not just this week."

"I'm tenured. A couple of whiny-ass students . . ."

"What does the contract language say, 'gross negligence, failure to perform duties as outlined in this document'—you do remember what happened to your hero Bartleby, don't you?"

Streator tried to laugh, it was so absurd. "You're telling me that with all the incompetent nincompoops running around this place with jobs for life, they'd fire *me*? ! *I'm* the one who's crossed some imaginary line?"

Locke gave him a palms up *there you have it.*

"The union . . ."

"The union?" Now Locke laughed derisively. "The union will make a perfunctory show of protest, but nobody—hear me well, my friend—*nobody* is going to waste any political capital at this place going to the mat for you, not in a contract year, not for someone who can't make it to class or meetings or return papers, not for someone who openly disdains students, the faculty, the administration, the entire bloody school . . ."

"Everyone hates students and administrators—"

"Everyone *complains* about students and colleagues and the school. Not the same thing."

Streator felt the whole room, his whole life, shrink down to just the space he could fill slumped in this stiff office chair. He couldn't look at Locke. He could barely find Locke out there in that other world. Streator knew he'd been a pain in the ass—that had been his general aim for some time now, after all. Still, he always assumed that someone in this godforsaken place saw the world as he did, someone would understand. When push came to shove, someone would help him shove back. Like Loren Locke. "Nobody?"

Locke sighed and sat down on the chair. The effort to break through to Streator had clearly exhausted him. "You have no idea how often I've defended you. I've played the 'moody creative type' card, the 'he ain't from around here' card, the 'going through a divorce' card . . ."

"How about the 'he's a good teacher' card," Streator said, trying for defiance but barely reaching a whisper.

"Deal me that one and I'll play it."

"Ask your girlfriend Carly Simon, she said so herself, 'Streator changes lives,' or minds, or something, just like the billboards promise."

"One would quibble over your verb tense."

In the quiet that followed, Streator could hear a key in the lock next door, a hushed conversation in the hall. Footsteps. Those crappy thin walls. Even with his own door closed, he knew most of the office suite must have heard this conversation. Locke had tried to save him this by coming to his home.

Streator glanced at the clock. Eleven o'clock. "You seriously expect me to go teach three sections of English 101 now?"

Locke opened the door. "No. Why should today be any different," he said as he left.

Streator muddled through the day's classes. He made nice with the composition classes and even revisited the "nigger/ nigga" topic for something like closure—without actually saying or writing either word. He tried to put on a good show.

And before he left for the weekend, he found Locke in his office and talked for nearly an hour. Streator realized that Locke's previous friendly chats, this week, last semester, even the year before, had been warnings—documentable Remediation Sessions, Probationary Review, as required by contract before termination. When Streator had been roped into the interview committee for Locke's position, HR had insisted they ask the candidates to describe their "leadership style." He couldn't remember Locke's answer, but Streator knew the correct response: "Oblique." But not today. He pulled the paper: the mediocre classroom evaluations Locke had been embarrassed to write and Streator had laughed about, the student evaluations sinking year by year, the docked pay for exceeding personal days and missing graduation, the failure to submit absence reports, the complaints about office hours skipped, the grade appeals lost, the refusal to document outcomes or follow Master Syllabi, the general insubordination he enjoyed wallowing in . . . By the time he left, Locke had convinced him that his job was hanging by the thinnest of threads. There would need to be more meetings, timelines and protocols to follow, meaning that nothing could be settled before the December Board of Trustees meeting, but he wasn't likely to be teaching there in the spring. Unless he transformed himself into a different kind of teacher, and colleague, and human being. Very soon.

Streator saw little chance that could happen, which created a huge, huge problem, undeniably. Yes, he would love to play the tough guy: *Fire me? Bring it on! Do me the favor!* But he wasn't that stupid. He needed a new plan, no joke, and he needed it fast.

Because he had not a lick of savings to fall back on. Because even a pitifully low mortgage in a rustbelt town needs paid. But the prospect of starting over in something new was exhausting. Flopped on his couch in the living room late that night, his bedroom under the eaves too hot and too empty for sleeping, he faced the truth with despair: nobody—not even another podunk community college—wants to hire someone else's too-young-to-be-so-burnt-out problem, not without a killer book at least. And if he washed out here, he washed out at the bottom. Despite all his cocky nihilistic posturing, he was now scared. *Because I got nowhere else to go.* Good lord, he thought, it had come to this: the person he empathized with most in the universe was a pathetic Richard Gere character from the sappiest of all movies.

The morning brought little relief, but he did force himself to sit and focus on the way out instead of the way in. He'd need to find his c.v. and update it right away. But nobody hired for spring semester, not full time. And how could he work up the energy to fake a convincing cover letter, let alone an interview?

Still, this might not be the worst thing to happen, he tried to tell himself. He could recalibrate. Find something that actually got him out of bed in the morning. There was always publishing, editing, for instance. He could look at the job listings online. Something to get him back east, anyway.

But . . . he pictured himself in some office cubicle hacking on other people's tepid prose. Watching someone else get paid for shitty writing while he was paid less for fixing their shitty writing. A couple of friends from grad school were sales reps for textbook companies. One had even come by his office on rounds through his territory. Streator recognized then that there was a job worse than teaching composition: selling composition textbooks. Not as bad as the book scavengers buying the desk copies the sales reps left behind, true, but trying to convince apathetic English professors that your fabulous state-of-the-pedagogy all-in-one reader-rhetoric-handbook was a quantum leap above all the others because of the colored Keys to Success in the margins! The online support! No thanks.

There had to be a way to make money off of the one talent he had. He kept coming back to that little twerp Derrick Doolin: if he could do it, why not Henry Streator?

In the early evening, Streator went for a long ride on his motorcycle, out to the cornfields turning brown and the bean fields turning yellow, his mind anxious and spinning. He wandered back into town and rode around the lake. He parked at a fishing dock and walked out to the end, watching the hazy sun set into the water.

Thick green trees spilled down to the water's edge all around this side of the lake, broken only by sloping yards and private docks of the big estates. Tree frogs pulsed in the still air. Suspicious foamy gunk lapped up on the shore. A couple of small aluminum dinghies trawled by. Nobody swam in the lake any more.

The lake was shallow, fed by the Inoka River and dammed on the southwest side of town. Locke and Streator, raised on the Hudson and Connecticut rivers, derided the barely moving Inoka as a glorified irrigation ditch. The lake it formed was an equally unimpressive body of water, a muddy prairie puddle. From the dam, the string-bean-shaped lake ran five miles northeast up river, wider at two side lagoons where Lorton and Vapor Springs creeks came in. The night of Streator's interview, the committee took him to a restaurant at an old bathhouse on the north shore and Locke told him a story of sailing on the lake with his ten-year-old son: when they tipped over their Sunfish, they couldn't get it to right itself and finally realized the mast was stuck in the muddy bottom, just inches below their feet as they treaded water. Turns out the lake averaged just eight feet deep, twenty-three at its deepest, and was getting shallower every day as silt poured in off the farmland and slowly filled it. With the silt came the pesticides and fertilizers. In the summer the nitrate levels in the lake, the city's chief source of drinking water, would rise so high the city handed out free bottled water to pregnant women and families with infants. Locke told him that the lake was built for Gunther Mills back in the 1920s, to ensure a steady water supply for their grain processing. Occasionally the factory repaid the city's favor with an industrial chemical spill that would bring fish belly up along the shore for miles.

Streator recalled Tarvis's plot outline. A nice irony, killing off

48

Gunther in his own lake, the robber baron consumed by the product of his own greed and ambition. The lake froze intermittently over the winter, so the ice would always be dangerous. And would easily erase clues. Yes, a most excellent murder site. He wished he had thought of it.

For all of his disparaging of his students, Streator had to admit that they were on to something. Like most people, if they read anything at all, it was fantasy, horror, thrillers, military adventures. Everything they wanted to write was derivative, sure, but that never seemed to bother them. That was the whole point, they knew—something that tasted just like the last burger and fries they liked. That's why they resisted Streator's efforts to steer them from the cliché. Tried and true was what they wanted to read, so why shouldn't it be what they should write? And was it such a crime to want to make a little money on what you wrote? Nobody in his MFA program ever mentioned the English professor who got filthy rich with a little novel about a tightly-wound Vietnam vet named as an inside joke after a French symbolist, the spelling changed to "Rambo."

What he could use was a good story, Streator concluded. Nothing subtle. Something you could find in the spinning wire rack at Kroger. *Strike Force Kickapoo* indeed. But he'd be damned if he had one.

7.

He rode home more anxious and depressed than when he had left. Maybe he was a writer, but was he a storyteller? Hell, even Tarvis Conner had a story. Well, maybe not a story, but an image.

And there had been something appealing about that image: those feet sticking up out of the ice. The rich quirky industrialist ice skating on the lake. The setting a rustbelt factory town presided over by the murder victim.

A murder mystery. Maybe the most elemental of stories: everyone will keep reading to find out whodunit.

His mind kept circling back to Tarvis's idea. A murder mystery in this nowhere town? Why not? Not the New York-LA-Chicago boilerplates, but still a town big enough to have crime, ghettos poor and rich, quiet cul-de-sacs and busy boulevards.

And a victim? Someone who walked with kings. Someone taken down by a prole from this dreary town.

Why not? Why not?

Because it wasn't his story. It was Tarvis Conner's story.

But Tarvis Conner was dead.

And besides, it wasn't even a whole story he'd told him, just the barest bones of a situation. Would hardly count as stealing. And Tarvis Conner was dead. Who would ever know?

He found Travis's thing stuffed in a folder in his briefcase. It went all over the place incoherently. Some background about the dead rich dude, the character obviously modeled after Gunther. Something about his home security system dying from a Y2K glitch on New Year's. A long stretch about the police finding him in the lake, legs up in a V. A confusing point about the legs as some kind of sign that only a select few would recognize.

Why not. It was a good hook. The story didn't have to be great, or even realistic. Just catchy.

Why not.

A bad book could bring in some serious cash.

50

He could do this.

He dug out a yellow legal pad and started scribbling random thoughts. A murder, yes, the industrialist on the lake, looks like an accident. But who could solve it? The police, a private eye—what private eye ever really did anything but hunt down deadbeat dads? And there was the problem that Streator didn't know anything about detective work. Readers liked "police procedurals." What he knew about police procedures came from watching *Inspector Morse* and *Prime Suspect*. All that "Deputy Chief Inspector have the Detective Sergeant get the CSI report off to the DA ASAP while we canvass the witnesses and bag the perp" stuff. . . boring. Sure he could learn: it was called research. But he was more than a little lazy. And time was short.

But what if Tarvis had the right idea there, too? Someone outside all the police procedural techno crap, someone who had a compelling reason or need to figure it out? The amateur, sure, there was a tradition there, too. An old lady with knitting needles? A kid from the hood? No, no, but someone who had a particular kind of inside knowledge, someone who had connections all over town. An English professor at the local community college, he joked with himself. But as soon as he thought it, the idea was no longer absurd: he did know people all over town, from the pizza joints to the picket lines to the toney bars. College professor— *community* college professor—as detective? It was just goofy enough that it might work.

Streator stayed up most of the night filling and scratching and tearing on his yellow pad, his mind swirling with possibilities. He could do this. Ten years here, he could write this town. Immediately images flooded his mind: blue tanker cars full of corn syrup, the steaming factories, the rail yard under the viaduct that looked like Gatsby's valley of ashes, the bungalows and farm houses and tiny postwar ranch houses, the junk-filled woods, the shallow fetid lake, the booger-freezing cold, the shuttered downtown, the strip malls with dollar stores and title loans and payday loans and rent to own, the screeching cicadas and winking fireflies. He could write this place.

He woke on his couch Sunday morning and ate corn flakes while flipping through the scribbles on his yellow pad, most of it incomprehensible. He set up his computer on the dining room table and started banging out notes and ideas, plot lines and possibilities. His protagonist could be—well, someone like himself, he decided, but a more interesting version of himself: edgier, funnier, sharper, faster. But not an English professor—just too close. Psychology professor? Sociology? They were always getting tangled up in their students' lives, always playing the counselor, the soft shoulder, having them write all that touchy-feely self-exploratory crap. But could he pour himself into someone who thought the social sciences were really sciences? Not a chance. Hard science, then? Bio? Chem? Math? The supreme rationalists? They would make good detectives in that "elementary my dear Watson" kind of way. No, Streator didn't know enough of real science to even fake it half-assed. And people like that, like Roni's parents, biology professors in the Triangle, were innately boring. Might as well choose a librarian. Philosophy? Art? History? History. That was it. More or less the humanities, and his hero would teach required courses that put him in touch with everyone in school. And Streator knew enough history to fake up a few class scenes, to have his hero drop a few "you know, despite their inimitable noveau riche backgrounds, robber barons of the Gilded Age regarded their wealth as their birthright" references here and there. The sage on the stage lecturer it would be, the long hair sweeping back, the rumpled tweedy look Streator himself could never pull off, the rationalist with the appreciation for a solid narrative. But no more than late 30s and damned good looking. He'd call him . . . he looked at his poster from the British Museum . . . Rosetta. Russ Rosetta.

And a student, a damsel in distress: she could be older—the advantage of the community college setting—returning, maybe divorced, but hot of course in an early 30s way, a kid or two? He'd have to think about that, but maybe. Probably, if it were to be at all realistic; they all had kids. Rich dude dies and she's upset, Rosetta can tell, he's that kind of guy, that kind of teacher. She confides that she's worried. She can't be directly involved, but—a brother. She's worried her brother is mixed up in it. Can't get the police involved because of blah blah blah. He slowly starts to help her, they slowly start to get involved, the two of them unravel the truth . . .

And what is the truth? The possibilities pour out of him: union conflicts, a mob hit—no, too obvious in a town that has declared itself a "war zone," but a good red herring early on. But some secret of a rich guy that would link him back to a plain joe like her brother: drugs, prostitution, pornography, all his noir favorites.

Quickly Streator discovered that even the computer was not what he needed—he wanted to see everything all at once, a way to connect one possibility to another, something more visual. He wished he had a large bulletin board or whiteboard. He paced his house restlessly. He saw his newly spackled but unpainted walls in the back room. Huge blank slates.

He cleaned out the back room, taking all the tools and tarps to the basement, sweeping and dusting all of the spackling mess. He pulled his old desk into the center of the bare room and set up his computer with an orange extension cord to the wall. He was surrounded by off-white blank walls. He took a fat carpenter's pencil and started writing on his walls.

He had never outlined any fiction before—verboten in MFA land—but he had never tried anything this sprawling. He scrawled out lists of characters, events, scenes in big letters. He drew lines and story arcs and timelines, retreating back to his computer, leaping up to the walls . . .

The worst crime in a town like this was always gang-related, Streator knew. For several years the inner city had been awash in shootings, especially in neighborhoods like Burke Hole. So that was an obvious place to start, to link a murder to an ordinary part-time student—but then the brother would have to be black, and so would his sister. If he eventually hooked up the sister with Rosetta, he'd have to write an interracial romance. That certainly would be a hot button to push. He'd think on it. But once you added the element of race, then the real seedy side of this town just ripped wide open: the openly understood code of "country schools" in the real estate ads that meant "no black kids," the police harassment, the neighborhood color lines . . .

And the victim? Clearly a Frederick Gunther type. He'd have to move his character somewhat away from Gunther just to avoid the libel possibilities, which was too bad, because even from the little that Streator had heard of Gunther, the old man was a larger than life character. He was said to cater his business lunches from the Korn Krib, a converted grain bin outside of town that served a mean horseshoe. In his later years he managed to keep himself in headlines with outrageous statements about how to fix America—burn Dr. Spock's books, boycott the Hollywood homo-jewboy cartel trashing our values, attach birth-control patches to welfare checks, outlaw labor unions, legalize bordellos. He had heard that in his days as his Big Daddy's second-in-command factory boss, the younger Gunther was all but a plantation owner, especially during the war when his workers were mostly women, many young black women from the south; rumor had it that Junior Gunther helped so many young workers "get in the family way" that Big Daddy Gunther had to start his own home for wayward girls to shut everyone up, and that's how Gunther Hall, still going today, was formed and that's why half the families in this town were named Lloyd, the name Big Daddy chose to designate the fruit of Gunther's loom.

The hell with libel. He'd change enough to get by. It was all going in. Let the lawyers sort it out later. The more he wrote and scribbled, the more excited Streator became. The great irony would be this: his ticket out of this shithole town would be this shithole town. He dug up every scandal he could think of from his ten years there: his colleagues with gin in their water bottles; the Director of Student Life embezzling money from student club accounts; too many sordid affairs to choose from. And the locals: the priest who ran the Catholic hospital and gave a kid AIDS; the spa owner who set up his wife for a cocaine bust and married his masseuse a few months later; the councilman's wife who dragged a dead horse around the town square with her husband's pickup at two in the morning. Everyone was complicit, most importantly the fat-cat factory owners who lorded over this dying town, who spewed noxious waste into the air and rivers, who sent workers on twelve hour rotating shifts and broke their unions with replacement workers, who let men die from falls and steam and explosions, who brokered inside deals to corner the international market on soy lecithin . . . He'd have them all on a plate. Or at least a version of himself who much more resembled John Cusack would have them on a plate.

All day Sunday and into the night he spun out a Byzantine plot over his walls and into his computer. Monday he sleep-walked through his comp classes and rushed back home to his walls.

He decided that his local ghetto gang was hooked into the drug trade out of South America, doing the dirty work for Colombian drug lords who think his factory boss—Warren Geddes, Streator named him—was screwing them out of payoff as he moved into South America with his soybean plants. A Colombian boss named Velasquez convinces a Geddes underling to funnel in cocaine with the soybeans, using help from local gangs in a B-list city where the feds wouldn't be looking and the local cops are easily bought off. But it all goes bad when Geddes finds out and makes trouble; no two-bit greasy Colombian drug dealer owns Warren B. Geddes, not on your god damn life! So Geddes has to be taken out. Velasquez turns to the local muscle. The gangbangers infiltrate Geddes' compound on the lake early in the morning of New Year's 2000 when everyone has partied themselves into a new millennial stupor and the Y2K bug has screwed up the security system. They take him out "skating" on the thin ice, shove him through head first, leave his legs up in a V for Velasquez. But the sister's little brother was there. Now the Velasquez gang thinks he's going to squeal. Little brother goes missing, sister is worried, she confides in her favorite professor who always takes such a personal interest in why a top student's performance suddenly goes south, and they don't go to the police because . . . well, he'd work that out later.

By Tuesday he started writing. Slowly at first. Still much on his walls.

But as he figured out piece after piece of his puzzle, it came faster. He found himself connecting every player in town to every other, all of it rooted out one inch at a time by the intrepid community college history professor, cautiously asking just the right questions of country-club life guards, lawn service guys, YMCA yoga instructors, bank tellers, pastors' wives, volunteer firemen, pharmacy techs, lingerie sales clerks, shift bosses, bar tenders, UPS drivers, the whole field of erratics carried into his classroom who made it impossible for him to buy a burger or rubber in this town without hearing, "Still teaching at Kickapoo?" The truth ran deep into the housing projects and back out into the McMansions on the lake—even the trophy wives still needed Gen Ed, he had discovered over the years. And those wives and soccer moms from his classes, maybe even some of those young waitresses at Applebee's, well, of course Rosetta could charm them into opening up, in more ways than one—he'd have to figure out what kind of player Rosetta could be while still pursuing the sister and not losing sympathy with the audience, but that could be part of the tension, maybe a lesson he'd have to learn about love and commitment and all that horseshit.

The writing poured out of him quickly and naturally. It was good, he could tell. Well, it was good enough, at least.

He was right. In a few weeks he had a lengthy outline and a couple of sample chapters. He found a listing online for his friend Brent Medina from grad school, the agent in New York whose little press had folded before it published Streator's thesis. He called him up and said, "You still owe me a book."

Medina had just left his old agency and was starting out on his own. He needed talent. He was intrigued by Streator's pitch and had him e-mail him his outline and samples. He called back four days later, a Monday, and said, "Finish this. Now. And don't show it to anyone else."

But as he finally headed for bed on Monday night, a new thought came to him, and he was seized with panic and doubt: what if Tarvis had showed someone else his story? The day he gave it to Streator, it appeared to be hot off the press, and Streator had the only copy, he was sure. But what if Tarvis had told someone else about his idea? Would that matter? What if someone knew he was stealing a dead student's story? He was too far in to change direction—there was no time, and he had no other direction.

Now he really couldn't sleep.

8.

He became more anxious as Tuesday morning crawled along toward his 12:30 creative writing class. He was early, which seemed to put the students on guard as they trickled in. He tried to sound relaxed, chastened even, but his knee was twitching as he steered the conversation around to Tarvis, what a senseless shame it was to lose him, what a wake-up call it was to make the most of your short time on this earth. Grandma Trudy eyed him suspiciously. Why was he bringing this up now? Streator wondered if anyone had seen the new things Tarvis was working on, how much promise he showed, such a shame, like his novel idea . . . No one took the bait.

Later that day, Streator lurked down the hall from Prof. Nash's classroom door and caught up with Tarvis's friend Sammy coming out between classes, loudly messing with a couple of other boys from his posse. "Hey, you're Tarvis Conner's friend, right?" Streator said casually as he passed by. "Real sorry about Tarvis. Real shame."

Sammy muttered noncommittally, a little surly even; he looked away to his boys, who didn't seem to know how to act when a strange professor wanted to make small talk. Streator gave them the same bit he used in class about Tarvis and his writing, wondering again if Sammy or any of the others had had a chance to read his stuff.

Sammy wasn't having it. "What it matter to you what shit he wrote." The tattoos on his neck seemed to pulse with his veins. "Dude's dead, just leave him that way." He glared so hard Streator made a quick uncomfortable getaway. He felt fairly certain that Sammy knew nothing about Tarvis's writing, but the sirens sounding told him Sammy didn't want anyone poking into Tarvis's affairs, for whatever reason.

Streator remembered that Tarvis always used the small computer lab in the library. When the lab emptied out in the late afternoon, before the night students came in, Streator pulled up the Word files on all the computers; students without disks often saved their work to the C drive, often inadvertently. But nothing was left over from Tarvis.

By Wednesday afternoon, Streator had even talked the school's IT guy into hacking into Travis's student email account with a weak story about a group project, a dead student, the rest of the group stranded without his work . . . Nothing there. Tarvis apparently didn't use the Kickapoo account for anything but very rare notes to professors when he was blowing off class.

Streator was more and more convinced that there was no paper trail for Tarvis's thing and that probably no one at school knew anything about it. That just left his family.

The obituary said he was survived by his mother, Angela Conner. The address in his school records took Streator to the Burke Hole neighborhood just south of downtown. Locke had told him that the neighborhood had been something of a ghetto for Italian miners in the 1920s, immigrants who came to work the Burke #3 coal mine at the end of the street. Now it was a ghetto of a different color and had the highest crime rate in the city.

Tarvis's street did have some run-down and boarded-up houses and vacant lots, but many others were clean and tidy, with flower beds out front and vegetable gardens out back. Shade trees lined the right-of-way between the sidewalk and the street. Not a lot different from his own neighborhood at first glance, Streator thought. Though the sidewalks needed more repair.

The Conner house was a high square two-story with a small stoop and faded white aluminum siding. A tired woman in a flowered smock and white pants, a nurse's aide uniform Streator guessed, opened the door reluctantly after he had knocked several times. She stayed behind the screen door.

"Hi, Mrs. Conner?"

"Nuh-uh. Who you looking for?"

"Sorry, I'm looking for Angela Conner? Mother of Tarvis Conner, he was a student of mine."

"Tarvis?"

"Yeah, I was looking for his mother. "

"Angela don't live here."

"Ah. Well. Thing is, I was his English professor . . ."

She opened the screen door and stood in the doorway. She was short and wide. He could see a boy of about nine peeking from behind her, eating a Popsicle, in long shorts and no shirt, big basketball shoes untied on his feet. "So you still at Kickapoo?" she said.

"Yeah, sure."

"You don't remember me, do you?"

Geez Louise, her too? "Sorry, I get so many students." Her face didn't register at all, not a blip—a gap in her front teeth, a scowl furrowed permanently into her forehead, dark circles under her eyes. Her hair was clipped short. "I don't remember your name."

"Alberta Jameson."

Nothing. "Sorry, must've been a while?"

"That's all right. It was probably ten years now. English class. We wrote all those papers, like to kill me."

"English 101?"

"Don't think so. I dropped that one. You give me a good grade, I remember." She still scowled.

He wracked his brain. "Developmental English?" His first year there, the only time they talked him into it, all those needy students you had to nurture and cajole and introduce to Mr. Subject and Mrs. Verb.

"Maybe, I guess."

"So, you finished then?"

"Naw, I got a few more classes—I started working, you know, just never got back, always meant to."

"Well, maybe some day. So I guess I've got the wrong house? I'm trying to find Tarvis Conner's mom?"

"You in the right place, but she don't live here. She's up at Keller." Keller Correctional Center, a women's prison 40 miles northeast. Kickapoo ran classes there. Streator was supposed to help with the program review. He hadn't managed to find the time. "Tarvis lived with us. I'm his aunt."

"Oh, well. Listen, I'm really sorry about Tarvis, he was a good kid, I liked him a lot."

"He was taking classes with you?"

"Yeah, creative writing . . . he didn't mention it?"

"I didn't know what classes he took. I work nights at Graceland, I never hardly seen him."

Bingo. "Yeah, creative writing, he was quite a writer, lots of imagination . . . he never told you about all the good stuff he was working on?"

"Just those damn raps he always bugging us with."

Bingo bango. "Well, anyway, what I really came by for, Tarvis and I used to trade videos, he wanted to write movies, so I lent him some DVDs, and he wanted me to watch these, so I thought I'd bring them back." He showed her a couple of old horror movies from his collection.

She looked at them and scowled even deeper. "Why don't you just keep them. We don't have no DVD. No one here watch this nasty stuff but Tarvis. His tape player broke. He used to go out to Uncle Archie's."

"Oh, okay, sure, I'll keep them. I was wondering, though, I hate to ask, the last DVDs I lent him, the thing is, they were kind of rare ones, at least hard to come by and sort of expensive. I was wondering if maybe you still had them? He put them in his backpack, that was the day before . . . his accident."

She let him in. The living room was dark but clean, with family pictures on the walls, mostly kids' school portraits. A small TV in the corner played the *PTL Club* loudly. He could smell some kind of meat cooking in the kitchen. "Dontrice," she said to the boy lurking next to her, "show Mr. Streator Tarvis stuff, I got to get supper finished before it burns, your daddy home any minute and I got to get to work."

Dontrice clumped upstairs without a word, still sucking his Popsicle. Streator followed.

Apparently Dontrice and Tarvis and someone else had shared a room. Two bunk beds and a single took up most of the space; the rest was cluttered with clothes, bright bedspreads on the floor, plastic toys. The walls were covered with posters of rappers and basketball players taken from magazines. A shelf on the wall was stacked with tall trophies, the kind Roni used to hand out at the Homework Haven. "Tarvis stuff there." Dontrice pointed to a small desk piled with papers and music magazines and then plopped on his bed and kicked off his shoes.

Streator poked at the papers but saw nothing of interest. A few rented DVDs and videos were hidden in the pile. No computer, as he had said. On the floor next to the desk was his backpack, though, and inside was the mess of a notebook he apparently used for all of his classes. Streator flipped through, saw a few random jottings from creative writing in-class exercises, several pages of what looked like raps, stray notes from a political science class, but nothing about his Gunther story. But in the bottom of the backpack was a floppy disk. Streator glanced at Dontrice, who was on his back playing with his feet in the air. Streator slipped the disk into his pocket and picked up the rented videos. "Thanks, bud," he said to Dontrice and went back downstairs.

"Find them?" Alberta asked when Streator poked his head in the kitchen where she was setting a table.

"No, afraid not. Just these rentals."

"He probably left yours at Uncle Archie. He used to go out there and watch, he got one of them DVD players. You could ask him."

"Oh, sure, not really a big deal, maybe next time you talk to him . . ."

"We don't talk," she said brusquely. "He's in the book. Archie Lloyd down on Millhouse."

"Sure, yeah, I'll give him a ring," feeling more awkward now that he had breached some family squabble. He looked at the rental tapes in his hand. "You want me to take these back for you?"

She scowled at the videos. "I appreciate it."

"Really sorry about Tarvis," Streator said as he made his way to go.

She looked a bit teary. "It ain't right. He like your class?"

"Sure, I think so."

"Not surprised. You was a good teacher. You give me a lot of confidence. You know, you the first person ever told me I was smart."

Geez, he'd really said that? And she remembered? If every casual utterance was for posterity, he really was going to have to watch his mouth. "Well," he said, embarrassed, trying to change the subject, "Tarvis was a good kid."

"Amen." Alberta shook her head thoughtfully. "And all for hot wings. It ain't right with God."

"Wings?"

"He delivered for Wing Zone. What else he way out there in the country for?"

Streator stopped at Family Video on his way home. He thought about just dropping the videos in the box, but he was feeling somewhat guilty and unusually generous. The least he could do for Tarvis and his family was pay his late fees.

The clerk at the counter was one of his current 101 students—Streator even remembered her name, Amanda, without looking at her tag. He asked her to look up the late fees.

"Just these three?" Amanda asked as she scanned them in and punched her computer. "Or like the whole account? Because just these three are... $18? But the whole balance due is like ... $64?"

"Sixty-four? Holy crap, what the hell's on there?"

"There's like . . . five more still out. *Shaolin vs. Evil Dead*; *Yongary, Monster of the Deep*; *Hot Brown Sugar Dreams #7*; *Ivory Does Ebony* . . ." Amanda started smirking as she read the titles.

"Ok, geez, these aren't even mine, I'm just doing this as a favor . . . you know Tarvis Conner?"

No use explaining. Her smile said she wasn't buying it. He fished out his credit card and cleared the whole account. No matter how many millions he made off Tarvis's story, Streator thought, they were officially even.

Tarvis's floppy disk had the files for the short pieces he had written for creative writing, a few old 101 essays, and little else.

Streator was in the clear. He threw himself into his book with the kind of abandon he'd never experienced. Even when he was in graduate school, he had cruised at half speed. Now he understood what it meant to work at writing.

He drifted through his classes on autopilot. He came late and left early, scribbled the bare minimum on any assignments he managed to return. He carried around his disk , so that even in class, as students wrote essays and took exams and worked in groups, he could pull up his work at the teacher's station. He skipped out on most office hours and went home to write. Nights, weekends, late afternoons, even an hour squeezed in before breakfast, a time of day he'd rarely been coherent let alone productive.

His fortieth birthday came and went with little fanfare. The division secretary bought a cake for the suite. He cut the first piece at 10:45 and disappeared into his office. His parents and sister called, sent gift cards for chain restaurants, sure he wasn't cooking anything. He was somewhat surprised at how little the day bothered him. Now that he had a plan, he wasn't afraid of his forties.

Then Roni sent a card, two days late. It was sweet and thoughtful, damn her. She hoped his birthday cake didn't catch the house on fire—not a reference to his forty candles, but to the tablecloth she torched trying to make crème brulee for his thirtieth birthday. This one hurt. Another one of those unexpected blows.

The small and tidy handwriting on his birthday card made him ache, it was so familiar, so much more evocative of how he thought of her than even a photograph or perhaps even her voice. With that tight pretty script came back notes left on pillows and refrigerator doors, inscriptions in books and on pictures, long letters when he was travelling without her, grocery lists on scraps of envelopes. He could still see the note she left in his grad-school mailbox asking him to help her move. He couldn't fathom that he hadn't seen that writing in months, hadn't talked to her in weeks, and that was just a quick phone call, every other contact through email, which carried nothing of who she was. He realized she was still the lens through which he judged his own life. The monologue in his head was still, really, a dialogue with her. She was still the one reader for everything he wrote.

He didn't touch his keyboard for two days.

When he returned to the writing, he attacked the story with a vengeance. Meals became stacks of white bread and peanut butter, jelly optional—he'd heard that John Gardner worked that way. Sleeping, showering, shopping, laundry all became optional. As did his classes. Sick days and personal days quickly evaporated. He didn't care.

Students complained to Locke, who badgered Streator. "Just following orders," Streator told him.

"Punching your ticket out of here," Locke told him.

Students took their cue from him and strolled in late, skipped more than was common this early, missed homework, let the discussion questions he lobbed in drop uncaught. Many stopped coming altogether, usually with no word, though Mora from his creative writing class came by his office to have her drop slip signed.

"Sorry, I really like the class," Mora said at the door, "but they keep changing my shifts at the hospital and I've already missed so much."

He took her drop slip and signed it quickly. He was supposed to try to talk her out of it, figure out some way to get her caught up. "Maybe another semester," he said. "You're good at this." This time he wasn't lying: she actually had a facility for language and a sense of what made a story.

"Thanks." She smiled. He would miss that smile. She was about thirty, dark-haired and pretty, the only one who laughed at his jokes. "Yeah, maybe next year when my boy is in school. . ."

She lingered awkwardly but Streator's mind was already back on his book, and in a moment she was gone, the door shut, maybe he had said goodbye or good luck, he couldn't be sure.

Streator hardly noticed when the heat gave way to an autumn chill except that he had to turn his lights on earlier. He ignored the leaves killing his little patch of lawn.

Jonathon from Marketing and Public Information snared him in the hallway with a super idea: how about inviting Derrick Doolin to campus for a reading, a talk with students, a big to-do!

"Super-duper, knock yourself out," Streator said, proud that his reply didn't come out, *Go fuck yourself.*

9.

By late October Locke managed to convince Streator that if he didn't make a little better attempt to teach his classes, they'd fire him the next week. Streator complied, mostly; he had almost fried himself anyway, so a few hours a week showered and shaved and talking to real people was therapeutic enough to justify time away from his computer.

He caught a break when an entire day of school was cancelled for a mandatory Staff Development Day. Sexual harassment, diversity training, a lot of Who Moved Your Cheese stuff. At least that was what Streator heard later from distraught colleagues; he himself spent the day hunkered down in his office writing his novel, venturing out every seventy-five minutes to sign his name on the sheets outside the session doors so that he wouldn't be charged a personal day.

He did attend one session, however: "Gang Activity in Our Town," presented by a young detective from the local police department. Here Streator took copious notes and picked up many colorful details of gang dress, signs, organization, lingo, funny stories of dumb drug couriers that the cops nabbed easily at the Greyhound bus station and the truck stop on the interstate. Later, Streator poured bits and pieces of this straight into his novel and intended to call the baby-faced detective to pick his brain some more, but in the rush of writing, it was just easier to make shit up.

At four o'clock, Locke dragged him into a department meeting because they were discussing the Kickapoo courses taught in area prisons. Streator was ostensibly a member of the program review task force, but he had only attended one meeting in the spring and had ignored the file of papers to evaluate. He slouched grumpily into the classroom where the rest of his colleagues plus a few adjuncts he didn't recognize were being briefed by Phyllis Nash, the chair of the task force. Prof. Nash was a small woman in her fifties but commanded attention with her laser intensity and commanded respect by out-working and out-caring everyone in the department, despite having done this for twenty-six years. Streator immediately felt guilty for coming in late. Prof. Nash described the limitations of teaching composition in the prisons: no student access to computers for word processing or Internet research, few resources other than a textbook, restricted "homework" time. Instructors were given Kickapoo master syllabi to follow, but it was unclear how closely they were able to adhere to the outlines. Classroom observations were difficult because of security issues. The instructors were not hired by Kickapoo but by the Department of Corrections, as much for their experiences in dealing with the inmate population as for their subject-matter expertise, she seemed to insinuate.

When she asked for questions, an impatient Streator couldn't hold back: "So you're saying they handwrite 'essays' on the spot after ten minutes of reading some *Newsweek* op-ed piece together, they fix their spelling errors, it's graded by some social worker with a B.A. in Study Skills, and we're supposed to sign off on these as college English courses, because . . . we feel sorry for them?"

His colleagues groaned and sighed; one of the unfamiliar adjuncts on the side, a stern woman in her thirties with short dark hair, looked like she was going to come out of her chair. Prof. Nash held up her palm, took off her reading glasses, pushed her graying bangs to one side, and locked on to Streator. The room quieted. Over the years, she had always been more cordial to Streator than he had a right to expect, but she suffered no fools.

When she was done—his logos dismantled, his ethos discredited, his pathos dismissed—all Streator could do was toss off a "whatever" shrug and slink back to his office before the meeting ended. Two minutes with the blinking cursor in his novel and he had no memory of the meeting.

Apparently some guys won a World Series and then some others won elections, planes crashed, the earth quaked, everyone fretted about the Y2K bug bringing an end to civilization. Streator pushed on relentlessly. His noisy furnace rattled against the deepening cold, but he didn't hear it. He was numb from lack of sleep but that only seemed to keep his mind swirling with ideas. He chugged Jolt and pressed on. Orange drift fences reappeared on the bare fields along Gunther Parkway; Streator made a mental note to rewrite a scene to include them. His back ached, his shoulders ached, he thought he might have carpal tunnel syndrome, but he swallowed ibuprofen by the handful and pressed on. He startled himself in the mirror one morning—some haggard stranger stared back at him. His ragged hair was growing back more gray than it had been before Roni left.

In mid November, Streator called Medina and told him it was done.

Medina laughed. "What do you mean, 'done'?"

"I've got a draft. A full draft. Ready for you to read."

There was a pause on the other end of the phone. "Wait, what? You're kidding, a full draft?"

"Yeah. I've been working."

"I guess so, I was expecting, like, what, spring or something. You sure it doesn't need to ferment a little longer?"

Streator explained to him a bit of his job situation, how there was no time to lose, how hard he'd been going. Medina was sympathetic, eager to get to work. He had Streator e-mail him the manuscript and suggested meeting in New York as soon as possible. Streator recognized some small familiar note of urgency, if not desperation: he thought he was picking up that Medina's solo venture into agenting wasn't going as well as he had hoped, that he, too, could use something profitable in the pipeline very quickly.

Streator flew to New York over Thanksgiving break and hunkered down in Medina's Brooklyn apartment for the long weekend. Streator had forgotten how tiny an expensive apartment could be—the second floor of Streator's bungalow was roomier and his mortgage less than half of the rent for this flat, and it was doubling as the office for Medina Literary Agency. Temporarily, Medina assured him.

In grad school, Streator had been friendly with Brent Medina though never much liked him. Medina wasn't the top talent in fiction but was the top schmoozer. He had five or six years on

Streator and had worked in public relations before returning to school. He lectured to the rest of them unabashedly about the need for networking. He was barely in town a month when he started his own reading series at a local bar and always included an open-mike session, and always read from his own work. When he wasn't appointed editor of the department literary magazine, he started his own journal and traded favors with other editors around the country. He hardly left the elbow of visiting writers. Rumor had it that he slept his way through every AWP conference he attended, and he attended them all. Tall, thin, dark, and smooth—it was a possibility, Streator allowed. Streator only went to a few of Medina's bar readings, but he remembered that every young poet Medina brought in had that all-black troubled-sexy look and lingered over the word *fuck* in every poem. Streator was surprised when he heard of Medina's divorce, mostly because he hadn't known that he was married.

Medina seemed to have found his calling as an agent, although, as Streator suspected, it was a rough go starting on his own. Several writers he was counting on to make the leap with him from the old agency had bailed out. Unpublished writers were quick to find him in the guides, so he had a mountainous slush pile of unsolicited manuscripts but little of promise and could only afford part-time help to manage it.

Medina laughed out loud as he read the manuscript. He loved what he called "the snark factor," the mocking comic tone oozing out of the narration. In fact, Midwestern grotesque was the new Southern grotesque, he said; salacious absurdity with rubes from flyover states had never been more marketable. "Buddy, you and I are going to make some money," he told Streator when he finished. Not some seven-figure auction, not Oprah's Book Club, he said, but he'd get a deal: multibook. A series. They'd certainly sell the movie rights though it would probably never get made; a PBS mystery would be the prize, but a better bet, if it got hot enough, was basic cable.

"A series?" Streator hadn't thought of that. "I hate to say it," Streator said, his exhaustion leading to unusual candor, "but I feel like I've shot my wad right here. I can't imagine anything more to say about this place or those people."

"Yeah, that's one of the problems," Medina said, holding the manuscript, "you've dumped in everything but the kitchen sink and it's all over the place. Hold a little back for the next one!"

Streator was unsure. "You want my history professor to keep on solving mysteries? You really think this little grubby city has enough interesting crime to keep this guy going?"

"Jesus, don't you read *anything*?" Medina said. "Miss Marple dug bodies out of the same little English garden for fifty years!"

They hacked on the manuscript for two days. Medina may not have been much of a writer but he was a ruthless editor, and for every cut or revision he had a story about the personal taste of this editor or that editor at this house and that house . . . Streator was too tired and too desperate to resist. "I am at your mercy," he said. "I wanna be a paperback writer." Medina came up with the title: they'd call it *Iced.* He liked how it played off both the murder scenario and the crack cocaine at the center of the conspiracy. He could see a cover with the two legs sticking up in a V.

At the end of the weekend, Medina printed off and kept the revised manuscript with him. "I didn't mention this before because I didn't want to get your hopes too high," he said as they were leaving, "but now that I've seen it, I know just who to show it to. And I've already mentioned it to her. And she's already interested." He paused for dramatic effect. "Ellen Kendall," he said slowly, with a knowing smile. The name was supposed to mean something to Streator but didn't.

"An editor?"

"Ellen Kendall? Kendall Books? Good God, Streator, you're going to have to get up to speed if you really want to do this," Medina said contemptuously. "Ellen Kendall has her own imprint . . ." and he rattled off the convoluted family tree of a megapublisher.

"Is she good? Hell, what do I care—will she take it?"

Medina named three writers on Kendall's list, all of whom he was supposed to be impressed by, but only one Streator had heard of. "She has a small list but likes crime and mystery and literary too. It's a good fit. And I think I can get her to read it toot sweet," Medina said with a frat-boy smile. "I'll just move it to the top of the pile on her bedside table."

Now Streator remembered why he had never really liked

Medina. He'd been friends with Roni before Streator knew her.

Streator flew back numb from New York and tried to regroup and refocus. December came in with a couple of quick storms, thin freezing rain slick enough to keep his Nova sliding all over Gunther Parkway but unfortunately not heavy enough to close school. What he could really use was about a half-dozen snow days.

He spent the last couple of weeks trying to salvage his semester. The handful of students left in his classes came infrequently. Some of the noisy ones in Malveeta's circle had made a stink before Thanksgiving and were allowed to transfer to another section. Streator let Dean Locke clean up that mess; that's why he was paid the big bucks. Streator was glad to be rid of Malveeta's noise particularly. She was fifty-three, had worked at the hospital umteem years while raising eleventy kids, and was not to be swayed from any direction but hers: "Shouldn't we have those papers back by now?" "A 'B'? I can't get a B in this class, I'm going into the nursing program!" "The Bible is the inerrant word of God, it's the only research I need." And the worst: "My daughter teaches English, she looked at this and thought it was good." "My daughter teaches English and she says one should never start a sentence with 'and.' " "My daughter teaches English . . ."

"You don't say?"

". . . and she never lets her students use contractions."

"Well, it is certainly clear, then, that in terms of a clue, she don't got one," Streator told her. That took care of Malveeta and two of her friends. The rest of the students knew they had Streator over a barrel. It was an unspoken agreement: they wouldn't complain anymore, but they weren't going to do any real work. Or worry about any real grades.

Streator was exhausted beyond caring. Even with the manuscript finished he still couldn't sleep. He could hardly eat. Someone out there in some unimaginable New York office held his life in her hands. He felt like a figure skater sitting on the crying bench waiting for his score to come up—*Ooo, the judge from Kendall Books gives him just a 5.2 for style* . . . Every day he pulled up the *Iced* file and reread it, tinkered here and there, tried to convince himself it wasn't a piece of crap. Resisted the urge to call Brent Medina.

It turned out that Locke had overestimated how quickly the wheels of bureaucracy could turn at Kickapoo. The Board of Trustees went into executive session at their December meeting to discuss personnel matters but didn't come out of it with Streator's termination notice. Locke said, "Don't hold your breath for January. They meet before school starts again. The VP told me to start thinking about which adjunct could be bumped into a one-semester full-time, if need be."

Friday afternoon at the end of finals week, Streator sat at his desk staring at the piles of papers he was supposed to grade by Monday eleven a.m. He wondered if he should bother. If the Board fired him in January, he would feel really stupid for reading these. When the phone rang, he assumed it was a student calling about a grade even though he told them explicitly not to call. He could let his voice mail pick up. Medina had told him not to expect to hear anything until after the new year.

"Streator," he answered with a sigh.

"Ellen Kendall wants to know where you've been hiding," Brent Medina said.

Streator looked around at his closet of an office. It had been a very good hiding place indeed.

Medina said that Kendall wanted him to come to New York the first week in January to discuss some additional editing and other matters, such as his commitment to publicity events. She would have a contract for him to sign. Two books, for starters. More would be likely. He could expect a healthy advance on royalties. Medina named a figure that would take Streator almost three years to earn at Kickapoo.

After he hung up, Streator did what he'd been dying to do for the last ten years: he filled in course grades on his roster based almost entirely on how much he liked each student. Then he typed up a very brief but somewhat smartass letter of resignation and left it in Dean Locke's box.

10.

Twelve thousand years ago, a mile-high sheet of crushing ice crept down from the northeast to within a few miles of Streator's home, leveling everything in its path, before it stopped, paused for a hundred years, and left.

For thousands of years after, hunting people roamed through the grass and swamps but apparently found no reason to build a permanent settlement here—they came, they ate, they left.

In 1802, two French trappers built a trading post where Lorton Creek met the Inoka River. When the Kickapoos, their best customers, were driven west several years later, the traders also left.

In 1820, Alexander Behr and his wife built a cabin on the north side of the Inoka near the site of the present courthouse. They stayed a few years until his wife became scared of Indians, and then they left.

In the mid 19th century, thousands of overland immigrants hurried through the area, pausing only to pay a ferryman to help them cross the Inoka River, before bustling on to the heads of the California and Oregon trails.

After steel plows and field tiles tamed the prairie and wetlands, two railroads converged and a town was born, which eventually grew into a city. In the 1970s, downtown merchants blocked the development of a new mall, so the developers built one anyway, in an unincorporated village just outside the city limits. Within ten years almost all of the downtown businesses had left.

During the next twenty years of Reaganomics, globalization, and labor troubles, nearly 10,000 city residents left.

In the ten years that Streator had lived there, these people from his small circle of friends and neighbors and colleagues all left: the Andersons, Jack and Louis, Meredith, Paula, Steve, Adele and her kids, the McElroys, the Augustinos, Gary and Jamey, Luke and Justine, the Cowden-Strasbourgs, the Clarks, Trish and Ted.

And then Roni left.

It was a town to leave. And now it was finally Streator's turn. He felt strangely anxious about the prospect.

He spent Christmas with his family in Springfield and had planned to stay out east until his meeting with Kendall after New Years, but by the 26th he changed his flight and headed home. He hadn't realized how much Roni had run interference with his family until he tried to go it alone.

Everyone out East kept asking him what he was going to do now. He really didn't know. There was no reason to stay there, in that town, in that house. But he had no idea where to head. Someplace he could write. He wasn't sure where that could be. Of course, he'd be obligated to pump out several more Professor Rosetta Mysteries, and he seemed to have committed the good professor to this town. If Streator left, would he have the access to the material, the daily exposure to the local color, to keep the series going? He remembered that Jack London had spent one winter in the Yukon but milked it the rest of his life. That could be his new goal: to be as popular a hack as Jack London.

He was glad he had returned early. He could get his office cleared out while the school was closed so he wouldn't have to face any staff, just make a quick and clean break. By the 29th, he managed to cart his books home, clear important files off his computer, and throw some papers into boxes. He had several more hours of sorting and hauling to really get the place empty, but he just didn't have the energy.

By New Year's Eve, he was so sick of the end of the millennium crap—endless "Best Of" lists, Y2K jabber, the debate over 2000 v. 2001 as the actual beginning of a new century—he thought he would just stay home. But then Locke invited him to Reilly's downtown, to celebrate the book and the new year, to show he had no hard feelings. Though he was put out that Streator hadn't let him read a draft and wouldn't tell him what it was about. All Streator would let on was that Locke would recognize the town. "Blowing the lid off this dump!" Streator said, a couple of beers into bold.

Locke looked at him funny.

"What?" Streator asked.

"Nothing," Locke said with his smile. "I just never thought, you know, you'd have much to say about this place."

"What?" Streator said, shouting over the synthesizers of the 80's cover band, "I lived here ten freaking years!"

"Henry," he said with his most condescending smile. "You never *lived* here. You passed through for ten years. You were never more than a tourist."

So not the party he had hoped for—Locke was patronizing and annoying, the music loud and annoying, the champagne cheap and annoying. The women his age annoyingly scarce. Locke's Sondra was the most attractive woman there, perhaps one of the youngest, and definitely one of the few singles. When he was tipsy enough, Streator made a half-hearted play for a small lawyer with a short skirt and tightly bound hair, somewhere north of thirty and south of fifty. She appeared to be unattached. She also seemed uninterested. He may have had a fat contract waiting for him, but still he rated no chili peppers.

On New Year's day, Streator woke cold, tired, and slightly hung over. He wandered out of bed late and dragged a comforter downstairs. He had slept remarkably well considering that he still wasn't used to his bed. He'd been sleeping on the couch since Roni kicked him out of their room last spring. After she left, he told himself it would be great to have a real bed back. But then he told himself the room was too hot. And then he told himself it was just easier to crash on the couch during his late-night writing frenzy. And then it was too cold and drafty up there. But when he came back after Christmas, he climbed the stairs and curled up tight under a huge pile of blankets. Everything was so different, an empty room didn't seem so depressing.

The weather had been brutal most of the week, temperatures at night dipping near zero, snow flurries off and on for a week. His furnace wasn't up to the challenge. Later he would drive to the newsstand and get a *New York Times*. But for now, he sat wrapped up on his couch and drank his coffee.

A new year. Hell, a new century. He already felt different. An odd feeling, something he was struggling to identify and accept. Almost like he was happy. Almost like he was proud of himself. It was going to be a good new year. That's what he knew.

He reconsidered his walls. Not as bad as he once thought. He'd have to get a few gallons of Kilz Stain Cover Primer to cover the writing in the back room, but otherwise he was leaning to dumping the place as-is, even if he took a loss. The sooner he could get into a place with an adequate furnace and something like insulation, the better.

He turned on his computer and drank a cup of coffee while his Windows slowly rolled on and his modem squawked and beeped at him, taking forever to load, as usual with his dial-up and only 128GB. A new computer was definitely on the list for 2000, and looking into DSL. Eventually his Yahoo homepage came up, with New Years' headlines from around the world: parties, fireworks, concerts, same as every year, just bigger, more insistent on being momentous. No word of any millennial raptures, alien abductions, end of days collapses. Even the Y2K computer bug was a bust: Streator's IBM worked just fine, and there were only a few reports of scattered problems.

His only e-mail account was still through Kickapoo. He hoped they hadn't shut him off yet. The off-site, web-based access was linked through the school's homepage. As the page loaded, he saw an announcement that Marketing must've launched during the break: "Best Selling Author Derrick Doolin Coming to Kickapoo!!!" Jonathon in Marketing never met an exclamation mark he didn't like. Late January, the school would be graced by Doolin's celebrity presence. Streator was grateful he would miss it.

But Streator 2.0, newly upgraded by Brent Medina, realized he should cheerfully attend and network. In New York, Medina had asked him if he knew any writers who could give good blurb. Streator laughed and said no, and then jokingly, "Except Derrick Doolin."

"Derrick Doolin? Perfect." Medina insisted that Streator contact Doolin, even after Streator explained that the former student wasn't likely to have anything good to say to his former teacher.

"Who gives a shit?" Medina said. "You can't think that way. It's business."

"Leave the gun. Take the cannoli."

"Exactly. He'll get it."

He had bought a copy of *The Scorpio Aspect* in the Newark airport. Lurid yellow cover with Derrick Doolin's name in huge block letters. Streator had tried to read the book on the plane but couldn't get past the first couple of chapters, in which the bloody fights were recounted with as much pornographic detail as the sex scenes, the guns and knives more lovingly described than the women's naked bodies. He hadn't written Doolin yet. He should get that little chore done. He should look up Doolin's contact info and write a chatty congratulatory e-mail, looking forward to seeing him in a few weeks. Then maybe later, mention his own forthcoming book and work around to asking about a blurb.

It would be a good productive way to start the year. He decided he would reread the article in the local paper about Doolin first. He pulled up the local paper's homepage to get to their archives. He watched a big black headline slowly form line by line down his screen. And then he nearly fell out of his chair.

"AGRIBUSINESS GIANT FREDERICK GUNTHER DIES IN LAKE ACCIDENT." In the early hours today, New Year's Day. Found on the lake, near his home. With ice skates on his feet.

Streator's fingers trembled on the keyboard. He felt bile rising in his throat. He could hardly read. The details were still sketchy. Someone in Gunther's household had noticed him missing some time after midnight New Year's morning. They frantically searched the roads and called the police. As it became light, someone noticed something odd out on the lake. It appeared to be two legs sticking up through the ice a hundred yards from shore. A small picture showed the fire department search and rescue team sliding out on the ice in a rubber dinghy to retrieve the body in the early dawn light. One small shadow in the distance looked to Streator like the V shape of Gunther's legs.

Streator went into the bathroom to vomit but nothing would come up. He slumped on the cold tile floor next to the toilet. He could hide there forever and no one would ever find him.

He washed his face and went back to the computer. The rest

of the article had nothing but background on Gunther. The wire services had picked up the story but were mostly repeating the local coverage. Same picture.

Streator paced his house from TV to computer to couch and tried to think clearly. This couldn't have been an accident or a coincidence. It was too close. Close? It was exact: who, when, where, how. Col. Gunther, in the ice, with the V, on New Year's Eve. And not just any New Year's: the Big One. Just what Tarvis had written. Just what Streator had stolen. In a book now sitting on his publisher's desk.

That little shit Tarvis Conner—he knew something. He'd heard something. He wasn't nearly smart enough to guess at this. *"Someone who's hooked into the street, someone who knows what's going down."* He was always a pain in the ass when he was alive, but even more so now that he was dead.

He tried to work his way through it, to calm himself. He had the panicky, gut-churning feeling of the guilty, but why? What exactly had he done? Stolen a story idea, but that was no crime, just unethical. He had no way of knowing that this was going to happen, so he wasn't complicit. He should go to the police, show them Tarvis's thing, let them sort it out. He wouldn't have to tell the police about spending the last few months working up Travis's real murder scenario into a book.

But that would be pretty hard to keep from his publisher. He wracked his brain to try to remember copyright law, previous suits over plagiarism: how much could he steal before it was trouble? More importantly, how much could his publisher know he had stolen before they balked? And then there was the fact that his scenario came to life after he had written it, but before it was published, while the police were still investigating what Streator's source had known about it . . . wouldn't that scare any publisher?

His instinct was to ride it out, not bring it up, hope Kendall and Medina wouldn't see the story of some bigshot from a flyover state, and if they did, wouldn't make the connection. Avoid the whole thing and hope it got better on its own.

He knew that was the wrong instinct. That was the instinct he had relied on most of his life in most contentious situations. The instinct that was partly responsible for the mess his life was in.

By noon he had talked himself into doing something. If nothing else, he had to know how big his worrying should be. He defaulted to worse-case scenarios; perhaps there was a scenario he wasn't considering.

He e-mailed Medina. So that he could control his tone. *Happy new year—funny article in the news today, don't know if you saw it . . .* a link to the news story. *This doesn't make a problem, does it?* That should give him a buffer of a day or so; Medina wouldn't be checking his work e-mail on New Year's Day.

An hour later he was watching the local TV station for more details when the phone rang. "Medina, Brent" on the caller ID. Damn it, Streator thought, don't these type-A's ever take a day off? He considered letting it go to voice mail. He picked up.

"This Gunther, this is the one you were telling me about," Medina asked, "the one you modeled Geddes on, right? The one you were worried about libeling, right?"

"Yeah, I don't know, to tell you the truth, this has me kind of spooked."

"It's pretty wild, all right."

"Do you think . . . is this like a huge problem?"

The pause at the other end was excruciating. "Well. Probably not. I mean, lots of stories are taken from real-life crimes. Publicity, even controversy, it's always good."

"That's what I was thinking. Every week *Law and Order* takes some real crime and makes a story out of it—'ripped from today's headlines!' "

"Of course, those are never written *before* it happened exactly as they described it, exactly *when* they described it, and *before* anyone has seen it. That might give some pause."

"What—literally? Delays?"

"I'm sure they'll want to run it through legal, see what they think. I mean, as long as the lawyers are convinced there's no way you could've known anything about this in advance," he laughed, "I mean, they can't publish a book by a murderer, am I right? But other than that . . . it should be okay."

It should be okay wasn't the assurance he wanted. "So . . . in terms of a new timeline?"

"Well, it always grinds slowly, but if legal has to get into it first, that means months."

"Months? Before what?"

"Before anything's signed or money changes hand."

As he feared. He couldn't tell him that he was stupid enough to quit his job already, that he had been planning on bringing a fat advance check back from NYC.

"So . . . Friday's meeting?"

"I'll call Ellen and confirm, but yeah, I'm sure she'll still want to see you Friday, get this settled one way or another."

"One way or another? There's a chance they could pull the plug?"

"There's always a chance, of course, right up til the paper's signed, even afterward sometimes, and this is a . . . wild situation, I've never heard of this. It's hard to tell how she or her company will react, I mean the whole publishing world is so volatile right now."

Streator hung up and whacked his head with a couch pillow. The lawyers would be scared shitless of this whole thing, especially if they found out about Tarvis—*when* they found out about Tarvis—and the whole thing would go down the toilet. If it got out that any of them had some advance knowledge of this death or were withholding evidence, they'd all be royally screwed, Streator worst of all. He had to go to the police. Show them Tarvis's assignment. Cover his own ass.

11.

The noon newscast on the local TV station had interviewed Detective Roger Cruiks about the Gunther death. Ten years earlier, Officer Roger Cruiks was a member of Streator's very first English 101 course at Kickapoo Community College. Cruiks had been one of the brighter bulbs in that class or any later class, though Streator had no luck at all curing him of cop-talk in his writing—"the individual proceeded to resist actions taken to subdue him" sort of thing, ingrained from several years on the force and several more in the military before that. Streator had been surprised to learn that you didn't need a college degree in hand to be a police officer.

Cruiks had been a compliant, good-natured student, didn't mind the kidding Streator gave him about his name and his politics, even invited him for a ride-along. Streator wished he hadn't declined; the experience and the contacts would have come in very handy lately. But if this whole fessing up was going to go smoothly, meaning a little discretion about his involvement with Tarvis, he was going to need someone sympathetic on the police force to talk to.

Streator drove around the lake and parked along the road next to Vapor Springs Cove. He wandered up toward the entrance to the Gunther estate. His breath came steamy and the dirt shoulder under his feet was crunchy with stale snow. Quite a few other gawkers had come out in the cold, too, and lined the roadside in twos and threes under their parkas and wool caps, pointing out at the lake, smoking cigarettes. Several flower arrangements had already been left at the gate at the end of Gunther's driveway. Several more were left on the lakeshore.

He sidled up to a knot of teenagers laughing over something on the flip screen of a tiny camcorder. Streator peered over a shoulder. One of the kids related that he'd been out delivering papers early New Year's morning, saw the bustle of activity out on the lake, ran home for the family camcorder, and captured the search and rescue team struggling to yank Gunther out of the ice. In one shot, he had zoomed in tight enough to see Gunther's legs up in a perfect V, the skates clearly visible. It was the shot Streator had envisioned for his book cover. He felt queasy again.

But there was nothing to see now. The rescue dinghy sat on a trailer. A white TV van with a broadcasting dish idled nearby. Several police cars were parked near a boat dock outside of the Gunther compound. No yellow tape, no CSI team in white coveralls. Just a couple of cold cops in uniform standing around drinking coffee, waiting, listening to the chatter on their radios, every once in a while taking a hand out of their jacket pocket to touch the radio receiver on their shoulder, turning their heads to nonchalantly mumble something incomprehensible. Like tobacco chewers taking turns hitting a spittoon beside them. A few other men and women in parkas and trench coats over cheap suits stood with them—reporters, probably.

Streator edged nearer, trying to listen but keeping to the public roadway, looking out at the lake. A man in a suit and wool overcoat came through the gate and chatted with the officers and reporters. As he was leaving, he noticed Streator and stepped over.

"Hey, Mr. Streator!" He reached out to shake with a gloved hand. "How's it going?"

Roger Cruiks, as he had hoped. Cruiks was a big man with an eager face, older than Streator, not as gray but more bald.

"Hey, Roger," Streator said, "How you doing, good to see you." He had run into him here and there over the years and Cruiks was always friendly, genuinely glad to see him, which always surprised Streator. "Keeping busy, I see."

"Oh yeah. You still teaching at Kickapoo?"

"Sure, sure. You taking classes?"

"No," he laughed, "not since they went and promoted me to detective. Just never seemed to find the time."

"Well, *Detective* Cruiks is on the case, I see."

"Oh yeah. Big time. What brings you down here with the vultures and rubberneckers?"

He should tell him. Just tell him. But he wanted to ease into it. He needed to feel out the whole situation first before giving anything away. "I was just out for my constitutional, like to come this way around the lake, you know, New Year's resolution to get back my girlish figure . . ." he patted his soft belly. Cruiks laughed. "I'm so out of it," Streator said, "I didn't even hear the news til just now. I saw the crowd and wondered what the heck—these guys were filling me in. So the big guy bought it, huh?"

"Yep," said Cruiks, laughing a bit, shaking his head.

"So does he usually go skating at midnight or what?"

Cruiks smiled and looked back at his fellow officers. He shook his head again and lowered his voice confidentially. "Slipped away from his nanny. The family's pretty pissed off. Think they'll sue her ass."

"His nanny?"

"Nurse, guard, whatever. Not the first time he's run off, apparently, which is why someone was supposed to be watching him. I guess he says, 'Ok, I'm going home now,' and out the door he goes."

"Alzheimer's?"

"Old goat like that, maybe syphilis. Quite a cocktail of pills he had lined up on his dresser, let me tell you. You didn't hear that from me. Course, who hasn't heard."

"So he made a break for it, huh, for one last hurrah."

"New Year's eve, seems like the nanny had a little too much to drink. They had the doors all alarmed, but I guess the Y2K got it. There's another lawsuit for you!"

"Yeah, the Gunthers could get rich off this." Tarvis had mentioned the alarm crashing from the Y2K bug. Someone was counting on it. That sick feeling crawled up Streator's throat.

"Next thing you know he's out here reliving his glory days."

"Of what?"

"Speed skating—the Olympics, back in ought-nine or whatever."

"Never heard that."

"I thought everyone knew that," Cruiks said. His radio handset squawked and he spoke rapid cop code into it. "Hey, gotta run, have a good one, stay warm . . ."

He knew he should stop him, he knew he should just get it all off his chest—but he couldn't. He couldn't convince himself that he had to.

Streator stayed and stared across the ice for a few minutes. He'd written his winter scenes in late summer and early autumn. But standing there now, he wouldn't change much in those scenes. He'd done a damn good job.

But it didn't matter. All that work, the first real work he had ever done as a writer, the first thing he had ever thrown himself into . . . all down the crapper. Just like that. And he was afraid that Kendall and Medina would out him as plagiarist in the publishing world as well. It was an even smaller club than academia, Medina kept proving to him.

By the time he got home, a bigger problem was coming to the forefront of his teeming mind: he was unemployed in Greenland. As soon as it came out that he had been planning to make his fortune off of a dead student's idea, not even Timbuktu Tech would hire him to teach part-time remedial comp for $300 a credit hour.

Locke answered his door Sunday evening holding an oversized cardigan close against the cold. "Henry," he said, surprised, "what *will* the neighbors think."

Streator hadn't bothered with his coat for the two-block walk, just his sweatshirt. He hadn't noticed the cold. Locke ushered him in quickly to his oak-paneled foyer. "What's the matter?" he asked finally when Streator did nothing but stamp the snow off his wet Chuck Taylors and stare at the floor.

"I could use some help," Streator said. He couldn't remember ever asking that before. It was the hardest two-block walk of his life.

Locke took him inside. Sondra waved at him from the kitchen. Locke took Streator into his living room and shut the French doors. He sat in a deep armchair by the fire and managed to squeeze out something of the story.

"So, hold on," Locke said, "your book had Gunther—"

"Geddes . . ."

"—feet up in the lake, ice skating, New Year's day, 2000?"

"In a big V."

"In a big V." Locke shook his head in astonishment. "Henry, how the hell did you come up with that?"

"Lucky guess." The look on Locke's face said he didn't buy it. "Well, let's just say . . . I borrowed the idea, from someone, and now I'm thinking this someone, he might have known something."

"Jesus. Henry, you have *got* to go to the police."

"Yeah, yeah, sure, I will. But—like I said, I think they're going to kill my book, at least the deal is going to get delayed, a lot, and now I'm screwed, I mean royally screwed. Every which way, but mostly finance wise."

Locke sat back on his leather couch and sighed. "You want to come back," he said.

Streator stared at the painting over the fireplace, a Frederick Church print of a Hudson River view. "Yeah." He gathered himself to face Locke. "I know. I really screwed up. And I know you've got adjuncts slotted in for next week—but I could use a little help here."

Locke looked genuinely sorry. This surprised Streator. "You know, I would, Henry, I really would, in a minute. I don't give a damn about what the VP says, it's my call, and I would do it." Not just sorry but sad.

"But."

"But there are other issues."

"Issues." Jesus, he hadn't even slept with a student.

"You remember Malveeta Fray?"

One of the few he did remember. He definitely hadn't slept with her. One of the older women in his English 101 class leading the charge against him over the nigger/nigga discussion. She had dropped his class about Thanksgiving. "I thought that was all smoothed over."

"So did I. She transferred to Phyllis Nash's section, and surprise surprise, she did even worse there. When her grades came in, she threw a fit. Not about Phyllis. About your class. She took it to the VP. With a lawyer."

"For a grade appeal? What's the big deal, it wasn't even my class."

"But your class was the root cause, the lawyer argued. If she hadn't needed to transfer sections so late, she wouldn't have done so poorly."

"She didn't have to transfer. I was fine having her." And probably would've given her an easy grade, he thought.

"But she was still—distressed and uncomfortable, I think she said. Seems you can't un-poison that well."

"Good lord." Streator slumped in his chair. "So the fact that I was gone already made it easy for you all, I take it."

"Not really," Locke said. "They still threatened to sue."

"For a freaking grade change?"

"She didn't want the grade changed. Well, she wanted a W. What she really wanted was a refund. Our money-back guarantee."

Years earlier, Kickapoo had instituted a warranty of sorts: if a student who successfully completed a Kickapoo course didn't have mastery of the listed course competencies, Kickapoo would pay for a course repeat, or something, Streator was fuzzy on the details. It was an obvious marketing gimmick coming from the tech side of the building to help sell Kickapoo students to auto shops and electronic service centers. The transfer divisions had ignored it, and Streator had never heard of the policy ever being enforced.

"I didn't think students even knew about that."

"Well, the lawyer sure did, and she argued that the grade from Phyllis Nash was evidence that your course had not allowed Malveeta opportunity to master the outcomes or some such bullshit . . ."

"Come on, it doesn't even fit the stupid policy."

"Doesn't really matter. You know how they are. The customers are always right."

"So the VP gave her money back."

"No, no, my friend. This went all the way up to the Board. The President was not at all happy. Especially when half of the rest of your class called him the next day and wanted the same deal."

"Christ." Streator held his head in his hands. "Malveeta called them."

"It would seem so."

How could one student hate him so much? What had he ever

really done to her, except try to get her to look outside of her narrow little window on the world?

Locke didn't bother explaining the rest. There was no way in hell this Board would sign off on his rehire.

"You didn't tell me any of this," Streator said.

Locke huffed. "Well, you did quit rather dramatically before the grades even came out, so no, nobody was inclined to keep you in the loop. Actually, though, I'm surprised you didn't hear. Everyone's talking about it."

Streator shut his eyes. His brain was redlining but the clutch to his mouth would not engage.

Somewhere Locke said, "I was going to bring it up last night. I thought it would be good for a laugh."

The two blocks home were longer than the two blocks there. In his cold living room, he didn't bother turning the lights on. He sunk deep into his armchair, paralyzed with despair. He had no job and no prospect of a job. He had no book and little prospect of a book. He had no savings. He was pretty sure he couldn't cash out his state retirement. On the bright side, his credit cards were maxed out from his recent plane fares, he had a non-refundable ticket for a flight to New York, and he had a house he could never sell for a profit. He was going to be bankrupt in every possible way in a town that smelled of burnt baked beans.

And he still needed to call the police and tell them what he knew about a possible murder.

86

12.

Sunday morning, his cell phone rang while he picked at a mushy bowl of cereal. Medina. This time he let it go to voice mail.

After a long while staring at the phone, Streator listened to the message. Medina had been in touch with Ellen Kendall—in fact, he took a great personal risk and contacted her on her ski vacation in Vermont, and she was not very pleased by the day's turn of events vis-a-vis *Iced*, not even by the prospect of increased publicity, apparently more skittish or perhaps just more conservative than Medina had estimated, not one who relished controversy in her professional dealings, so she would need considerable reassurance that nothing was amiss that might come back to bite her professional ass, which meant that at Friday's meeting, which she had agreed to keep, Streator would need to smooth and schmooze bigtime, let her see what a groovy and upstanding young man he was, explain the funny coincidence of how he happened to hit upon a scenario that played out so closely in real life, and by the way, how exactly had he come up with this story, call back to run through this whole thing one more time.

How could he possibly explain this? He didn't know himself how it had happened. He went for a long drive, just to clear his head, just to feel like he was doing something, just to get away from phones and computers and televisions telling him what he didn't want to hear, asking him what he couldn't answer.

He found himself driving around the lake again, near Gunther's house. But the shoreline was now empty, no police or on-lookers, nothing to see but inscrutable ice.

On his way home, Streator detoured through Burke Hole, down Tarvis's street and through the surrounding neighborhoods. He wasn't looking for anything in particular, just trying to get a handle on this kid—what could he have known? With the shade trees bare and the flowers gone, the sidewalks covered with dirty unshoveled snow, the whole area seemed much more shabby and depressing than it had in September.

The newspapers said this neighborhood was the center of gang activity. And on the concrete pillars of the overpass for the railroad that cut diagonally through Burke Hole, Streator saw graffiti in red spray paint that looked like gang signs: unusual dots and swirls, odd letters. And on one grey stanchion it was spelled out: Vice Lords.

Very bad boys, the Vice Lords, a bigtime national gang, the officer had explained on Staff Development Day. If Tarvis was mixed up with them, anything was possible. Streator couldn't help but wonder about that kid Sammy, one scary looking dude.

Back at his home, he sat with the phone in his hand. Whom to call first: Detective Cruiks, or Agent Medina?

Calling either one seemed like throwing in the towel. He couldn't get himself to punch the buttons. But he had nothing left to do, nothing left to play.

Except that he did have one other asset, Locke had reminded him: he knew something about a very high profile death. Maybe a murder. He wasn't involved, but he was in a unique position. He didn't know much, but he knew more than anyone this side of the Hudson. And he was a writer. That's what writers did—find an angle on something that no one had thought of. Or knew about. He was a writer—he had re-convinced himself of that in the last few months. Goddamn it, there had to be a way to make money on this.

If not fiction, then nonfiction. Something about this whole sordid thing. If there was something sordid. Something investigative. Locke had mentioned that, too, when he was trying to talk him through some way to salvage his book. Streator was so distraught sitting there by that lovely little fire in Locke's well-appointed home that he had dismissed the idea without really hearing it. Not his forte. He didn't like talking to people enough to be a good journalist.

But that was too damn bad, he told himself curled up on his own cold couch. The time of Streator by the Scrivener and his "I prefer not" was long gone. His only life-ring now was to somehow exploit his insider position with some kind of inside-the-crime piece. He could pitch that to Kendall on Friday, if she could keep the lawyers at bay. He could tell the story of the story, somehow downplay that he had been planning to rip off a student's idea. Or hell, if he had to fess up, that wouldn't be the worst thing, would it? Some sort of bad boy coming clean? Redeeming himself? Or, or—maybe they wouldn't pull the plug on the novel, if he could show how far removed he was from what had really happened— if he knew what really happened. At any rate, whatever he did, he'd need something else, something more than just some kid's one-page thing. If he could get a hold of something juicy . . . surely Kendall or Medina or somebody would bite. There had to be a way to make money off this. He'd have to come up with something fast, in the next couple of days.

The key was Tarvis Conner. Somehow he would have to draw a line from this kid to one of the richest men in the state. He had no idea how to do that.

The last time he had seen Tarvis, out in the hallway, he and Sammy went through some elaborate two-fingered gestures. Gang signs? He dug out his notes from the Staff Development Day workshop on gang activity but could make little of his messy scribbles, a complaint of his students. His notes referred to the police department's Gang Book, which had pictures of signs and tattoos. The detective at the session had told them that the Vice Lords were a huge outfit, born in Chicago, now part of a loose network of prison and street gangs known as The People, bloody rivals to The Folks, a group that included the Gangsta Disciples, the Vice Lords' archenemy. Both organizations had been active locally, leading to the violence the town had become known for; antagonizing graffiti of the rival gang's symbol upside-down was enough to spawn bloody retribution. The Vice Lords were still Chicago based, still active in prisons, now hooked up throughout the Midwest and South, very dangerous and heavily armed. The detective said they were targeting smaller cities like this to fuel and then corner the drug trade, specifically crack cocaine, driving out or swallowing up the small-time local dealers. The Wal-Mart of the crack biz.

He found the card for the officer who had given the talk, Detective Eric Ramage of the Street Crimes/Tactical Unit—who knew this town was big enough for its own Street Crimes/Tactical Unit?—and called his office, but Ramage was not in on a Sunday after New Year's Day. Streator left a long rambling message about hoping to get some help with a student who may have become involved with gangs. He kicked himself once again for being such a lazy-ass researcher; if he had contacted Ramage months ago, he would have an easier time getting to him in a pinch. Now he'd have to rely on the Internet instead of the local Gang Book. He did find Vice Lords hand signals on the web but no match for what Tarvis had flashed at Sammy. Still, those were definitely V's, and Sammy didn't want anyone else to see. V for Vice Lords? Tarvis had he said that the legs in the ice would be a signal that others would recognize: a V.

He could find no arrest records for Tarvis online, but the databases were hard to access and juvenile records were likely sealed.

Kickapoo had not yet shut down Streator's account, so he was able to access school records. Tarvis had graduated two years earlier from Truman High in town. A gangbanger graduating would be unusual; in fact, it wasn't exactly a given for any one at Truman, as Streator had heard that their dropout rate was about 18 percent overall, over 50 percent for African-American males.

He wondered about Sammy but didn't have a last name, so he pulled up Prof. Nash's class roster. Nobody named Samuel on the list. He thought about calling her at home. He hadn't talked to her since she had dressed him down at the department meeting. Again, he couldn't get himself to punch the numbers.

He called Cecilia Burton instead. She taught night classes in reading at Kickapoo, and he thought he remembered that she had worked as a counselor at Truman, maybe just retired. She was home and very surprised to hear from Henry Streator; he probably hadn't said three words to her in three years of department meetings. He came up with a long-winded story about a student he was worried about, someone he had hooked up with through Big Brothers years ago and had practically adopted to keep out of trouble, but this kid had been acting erratically, especially today when they were supposed to get together for a New Year's outing. Streator told her he was convinced that the kid had fallen in with the wrong crowd but wasn't being straight with him.

"I know I'm probably violating all kinds of FERPA laws here," he said to Cecilia, "but my little buddy has this new tattoo he won't talk about and he started hanging with this big guy, Sammy, I don't know his last name, and Tarvis Conner, that kid who died, all their friends. Have you heard anything about those guys, especially if they're hooked up with gangs? Maybe Vice Lords?"

Cecilia said she knew Tarvis Conner, or at least knew of him, when he was in school, but the Sammy that Streator described to her didn't sound familiar. "I don't remember ever hearing anything about Tarvis and gangs or drug trouble, anything like that. Vice Lords don't stick around school very long," she said. "Some of his folks go to my church, but I think the last time I saw him was in the school musical, must've been spring of his senior year."

"A musical?"

"*Little Shop of Horrors*. He was the voice of the plant. Everyone thought he was a hoot and a half. *'Feed me, Seymour!'*"

A dead end there. He didn't sound like Vice Lords material, but he had been out of high school for two years. Lots could happen.

Like your mother could go to prison.

He tried the online archives of the local paper. Normally they charged $1.50 per story retrieved and you had to put in an order and wait a week or so, but Kickapoo students and faculty could access the files through the school's library page. He found nothing on Angela or Tarvis. Then he remembered his own archive.

He dug through the boxes he had lugged home from his office. Buried in one were files of graded essays he was supposed to read for the task force reviewing the Kickapoo program at Keller Correctional. And sure enough, in a file for a developmental English class, there was a handwritten essay from Angie Conner.

It was a Personal Narrative, describing "An Event That Changed Your Life." A bad photocopy of four paragraphs on white binder paper, big looping handwriting in light ink. Angela wrote about the first time she tried crack. How the icy hot devil had grabbed her and never let go. Somewhere in the middle she squeezed in that her crack addiction led her to turn tricks before she moved over to meth and got arrested for dealing and now was in for five years, which didn't seem fair because her cousin she used to use with, she got treatment not jail thanks to some guardian angels who could come help her any time now, thanks! Though the cousin got HIV anyway so maybe the guardian angels could've been a little more on the ball. No sense of narrative structure at all. A few decent details, particularly about smoking crack. A cliché-filled conclusion about getting right with God and more dreams of guardian angels. Never mind the subject-verb errors and fragments. All in all a mess. A C at best, even for developmental. The grade marked was A.

There was nothing in her essay about Vice Lords or Tarvis except a mention of how much she missed her son, but still Streator felt like he was circling closer. If she was dealing in Burke Hole, then she had to be hooked into the Vice Lords. And if she was hooked into them, odds were that Tarvis was too. She would be a good one to talk to, if he could, if he had any idea of how to get something out of her. He could drive up to Keller and visit her, but what could a total stranger ask an incarcerated mother about the criminal activities of her dead son? "*Hey, nice to meet you, how's the food, and by the way, did Tarvis help you out in the family business? And how would he know about the impending murder of a rich guy?*" He definitely wasn't desperate enough to try that, not yet anyway.

Streator decided not to call back Medina until he had something new he could relate. All he had been doing so far was chasing shadows. He'd have to find a way to calm down and focus—but enough bits and pieces were coming in to the light to make him push on. Maybe he could work up the nerve to go to Keller some day this week. In the meantime, he'd just have to find a new avenue.

When Streator had moved up from South Carolina, he was surprised—and dismayed—at how much of the South he still heard from the locals. True, they didn't usually milk "pie" into three syllables—in fact, their slow drawl was more reductionist, mushing "insurance" down to "INshurnce" and "poem" down to "pome." Still, the rhythms, the lilt, the down-home expressions seemed to echo what he'd heard in South Carolina, which his colleague in history confirmed: the predominant local speech was labeled by linguists as Upland South, brought along as this part of Illinois settled from the bottom up with families moving north out of Kentucky, Tennessee, the Carolinas in several waves, as early as the 1830s, as late as World War II.

But even more Southern than the accents was the habit and subject of the locals' public discourse: interminable, inconsequential, and unbounded. Even in the frozen food aisle at Kroger when he was meditating on cut broccoli versus florets, some old guy riding a scooter cart would slide up and let him know they sure wanted enough for that corn, didn't they, he grew it for fifty years and now he couldn't get himself to buy it, course he wasn't supposed to eat it, got the diverticulitis, and the checker in the Fast Lane would complain about her aching feet, not as bad as when she was a flagger on a road crew and her varicose veins swolled up something fierce, and the bagger pitches in on how his mom got one of them foot jacuzzis, you ever try them, you should, I tell you what, at the end of a day like today . . . And like the Southerners he knew, the locals often as not saved their best and longest story or most important point about the state of the universe until you had the doorknob in your hand, or they had the knob in theirs and you were holding a pizza box getting colder by the minute. Usually he found this intolerable. Today he counted on it.

"So, how's it going?" the delivery guy from Wing Zone said as Streator paid for a big bucket of wings for lunch.

"Fine, good." *Wait for it . . .*

"Still teaching at Kickapoo?"

And there it was, right on time. "Yeah, sure"—thank god a name tag—"Lenny. Happy new year. Sorry I didn't recognize you. What was your last name?"

"Ormand. I didn't hardly recognize you at first either, you used to have a lot more hair, then I got to thinking, hey that guy looks just like my English prof!"

"Right, right. English 102, about three years ago?"

"Last year."

"Ah, right, sorry, the years fly by, the students, the names . . ."

"I bet," he said without the slightest hint of irony. Lenny didn't seem at all put out.

"You taking classes still?"

"Not this semester. Taking some time off, you know, get me some money together. My wife left."

"Sorry to hear that."

"Yeah, she still blamed me for Kiki, like it was my fault I had Guard training that weekend."

Obviously some story he must've told Streator and expected him to remember. He had no idea.

"I mean, shit, just 'cause I was the one wanting the pool makes me the bad guy? And she's off the hook for not watching her? How does that work?"

What in the hell was he talking about? Best just to steer away, hard. "I don't know, wow . . . Seems like a bunch of Kickapoo students deliver for you guys, though? You know Tarvis Conner?"

"Oh yeah."

"He was in my class. Real damn shame."

"Yeah, he was a good kid. Everyone liked him. Well, except maybe our asswipe manager. He was always getting on Tarvis for taking too long on his deliveries, he's like, 'Where you been, boy, I coulda delivered six orders to the North Pole by the time you make one run to South Lake.' He always thought Tarvis must be out cruising town with his music blasting. But that wasn't it—half the time he was lost, I swear to god he couldn't read a map at all, and besides he drove like an old lady."

"Tarvis? Seriously?"

"Yeah, he had that big old Wally Wagon, he was so short he could barely see over the hood, he looked like some old grampa peering over the wheel. He give me and Kyle a ride a couple times, he was like 'Everybody buckle up!' and he's doing like 25 in a 45, forgot to look when he changes lanes and almost sideswipes this dude, then jerks back and he almost goes into the other lane and hit some other dude . . . we was laughing our ass off—we're like, hold on there, grampa!"

"Well, he must've cut loose and got that thing cranked up out on Hackydale that night."

"Maybe. I could see him wrecking going like 20, though. He was the shittiest driver. But he must've be doing something crazy, 'cause that old beater was a tank, I tell you what, them old LTD's what they use in the destruction derby, you can't hardly kill them without an RPG and even then I don't know."

"So, any legal fallout for you guys?"

"For what?"

"Oh, you know, guy gets in an accident delivering, maybe he's trying to rush too much, manager's on his case about being so slow?"

"When he crashed?"

"Yeah."

"He wasn't delivering for us. He wasn't working that night."

"He wasn't? Someone told me—"

"Yeah, I'm for sure. I was in that night. Besides we don't deliver that far out in the country. 'Limited Delivery Area.' We don't go west past Sickle Street Road."

13.

It took Streator nearly an hour to find the spot where Tarvis had wrecked off of Hackydale Blacktop. It wasn't far from town, but even with a MapQuest printout and the description from the newspaper article, he had trouble with the county roads. Many weren't well marked, or had confusing designations like "3750N." All were laid out in a grid following section and township lines, true, but often a road started one direction, took a right angle turn at a corn field, then maybe another right angle in a different direction a mile later. A road that started as rough pavement might come to a T-intersection and become gravel, and then end altogether at a grain silo. With the winter sun so weak in the late afternoon's gray clouds, it was easy to get turned around.

What the hell was Tarvis doing in the middle of godforsaken nowhere late at night? Kid like that—or a guy like Streator—way out in the cornfields, might as well have been on the moon. Sure wasn't delivering wings—somebody had lied to his Aunt Alberta. Why would they do that? Especially for something so easy to check, Streator thought. They must have been pretty desperate to keep her from knowing what he was really up to.

Streator finally decided that when the newspaper article said "off Hackydale Blacktop," they meant on one of the numerous farm lanes off Hackydale, probably one without a name. Streator drove slowly east and west for several miles on Hackydale, exploring all of the paved side roads, named and unnamed, certain he was in the right neighborhood but not confident of which corner was Tarvis's. He passed white farm houses and their outbuildings huddled behind windbreaks of thick trees, back off the road on gravel lanes. Their mailboxes showed six digit addresses and solid Midwestern names: Showalter, Munson, Hanks, Bruckner, some of them familiar from Kickapoo—in fact, he'd had a Bruckner in creative writing last fall, Megan? He thought he remembered that she had dropped early.

As he headed back east toward town, figuring he must've

gone too far west, he finally found what he was looking for. A road marked 2200N made a hard right-angle turn south just a quarter mile off Hackydale, the road narrowing after the sharp right and now marked 1015 W. No warning sign. At the turn, a dirt track on the left ran north. If you went straight, you were into the fallow fields. And straight ahead was a little flower memorial, a small wooden cross with faded plastic flowers. Streator had seen these memorials all over the country roads, and even on power poles in town, with notes and flowers and teddy bears nailed to them, where reckless teenagers had managed to kill themselves.

Streator pulled his car off to the left at the intersection, where the dirt track heading north ran over a culvert, the only break in the deep ditches on all sides. He got out to look around. The wind blew curls of snow across the stubble and hard dark earth.

On Streator's interview trip to Kickapoo, the prairie landscape where he landed left him discombobulated. After all his years in the hills and woods of Massachusetts, Pennsylvania, Virginia, and South Carolina, he felt out of joint and out of place in this part of the Midwest. He found the flatness and lack of trees outside of the towns to be beyond boring: it was aesthetically unacceptable, annoying even, and he found it nearly impossible for him to get his bearings, to find any point of orientation.

In his first January there, with the corn and beans down to stubble and black dirt, the landscape shocked him. The bleak openness was frightening. On a Saturday before school started, he'd headed out to the college to prepare for the semester without paying attention to the weather reports. It was cold and very windy in town and had snowed the night before, but the main streets were plowed. When he left the shelter of the trees and buildings and river valley for the open prairie, however, he suddenly found himself in a howling white out, the snow blowing across the road in a solid horizontal scream. He crept forward slowly, panicked that some over-confident "shoulda been here last year, you want to talk about blowing snow" grain-truck driver from Gunther's was barreling down on him from either direction. He escaped back into the safety of town and rarely left it the rest of that winter or any winter. When he did have to set out for a distant city in the winter, he felt like Scott in the Antarctic desperately mushing from one relief shelter to the next. Ten years later, he was still unnerved.

Streator hugged his parka to himself and pulled his stocking cap over his ears. The frozen gravel crunched under his boots as he walked around. The ditch on the far side was certainly deep enough to flip a car, the corner easy to miss. The writing on the flower memorial had faded already, but something on the little cross looked like it could have said "Love you Tarvis." Not far away, face down in the field, he found a yellow highway sign with a big right-angle arrow that must've been marking the corner. The wood post was snapped off clean.

But what did that tell him? Nothing. Streator slowly scanned the bleak country. Tarvis Conner in his '83 LTD wagon way out here—it made no sense. Since he was driving east and south, he was headed back toward town. But where had he been? In the late summer, when Tarvis wrecked, it would've been less forbidding but perhaps more isolated with the corn up ten feet high, blocking sightlines in all directions. West down 2200 N the nearest house was a half mile away, across Hackydale. He could see no grain elevators marking even the smallest of railroad hamlets in any direction. A couple of sheet metal corn cribs in the distance, a ramshackle pole barn down the dirt track where he had parked his car. From the map he saw no sensible way to use these roads as a shortcut to anywhere—not to the interstate, a state highway, another town. Hackydale connected with other country lanes but nothing that went anywhere in particular, just access roads out into an empty corner of the county.

The wind shifted a bit, more from the north than the west, and Streator thought he caught a whiff of something odd—a chemical smell, sort of ammonia-like, maybe a little sweeter but not at all pleasant. He was used to the processing smells in town and the farming smells around town, but this was something different. Streator knew the farmers put ammonia on their fields, but nobody would be doing any work outside on a day like this. Seemed to be coming from the north, from the direction of the pole barn, maybe a hundred yards down the dirt track. No power lines ran to it. The one window was covered with black plastic. He thought he saw the faintest line of smoke or exhaust coming from a ventilation pipe. Streator walked out into the field to get a different angle. On one side was parked, or maybe abandoned, what looked like an old brown jeep, but taller and more square, like an old Landcruiser or something. Probably a farmer in there working on his combine or whatever, running one of those big kerosene heaters to keep warm. Probably what he smelled. Though when he caught that slight scent on the breeze again, it didn't smell like burning fuel, unless they were burning piss in paint thinner.

Streator had limited exposure to drugs. At parties, he would take a hit when the joint was passed his way, even inhale. That was about it. His more affluent roommates in college occasionally indulged in coke, less often in Quaaludes or magic mushrooms, but Streator was never tempted. He did watch a lot of *COPS*, however. He thought he remembered something there about the peculiar smell from the manufacture of the rural drug of choice, methamphetamines.

Back at home that night, Streator found the Internet buzzing with meth stories. The problem was worst in rural areas, where cooks set up makeshift labs in isolated farmhouses, shacks, trailers. Farms supplied plenty of the key ingredient: anhydrous ammonia, a common fertilizer stored by the hundreds of gallons in huge, unguarded tanks, easily tapped by crank cooks sneaking around at night. Pseudoephedrine, another common ingredient, was easily obtained from drugstores and supermarkets in large quantities. County sheriff deputies were overwhelmed; it was impossible to patrol the hundreds of square miles of isolated rural areas. Their best chances came when some place blew up or caught fire. And Streator had remembered correctly that cooking meth was a smelly process. Seasoned law enforcement said they used their noses to find the labs, the smell described as close to urine, ammonia, ether, acetone, or rotten eggs, depending on what method was being used. In some states, lawmakers were distributing scratch-and-sniff cards to help teachers and others identify the smell. The most common description Streator saw was "cat pee."

Recent reports showed that city dealers—street gangs, even?—were moving in hard. The stuff was astonishingly addictive and fairly cheap. That would be a market that someone like the Vice Lords couldn't afford to ignore, Streator thought. They wouldn't want to manufacture the smelly stuff in town. Might they use runners to bring it in from the country? Someone who loved driving around in his big old beater, someone whose mother was an addict and a dealer? What else would Tarvis Conner be doing out there in the boonies?

Streator was reasonably certain he was getting a handle on Tarvis, but that still left him a long way from Frederick Gunther's feet up in the lake. The news at ten offered nothing new. He reread the wire service articles on Gunther, which outlined his career in brief and the Gunther family saga: German immigrants who became 19th century millwrights who became 20th century grain-processing barons. The company website had even less of interest.

He spent a couple more hours that night surfing the web but nothing was revelatory. Still he kept skimming, trying different keywords, different search engines—AltaVista, Lycos, Dogpile, WebCrawler. He kept the television on and flipped through cable news channels as his slow connection downloaded stories. Nothing helpful.

Finally he crawled off to bed but couldn't sleep.

A few times during his childhood, Streator's father would have him come to Milton Bradley for a top-secret research session, where kids would test drive new games and toys in development. Once when he was about nine, they had him play with a new building blocks toy, designed to rival Legos. The twist was that these blocks and pieces were oddly shaped, somewhat suggestive of recognizable pieces of cars or building or rockets or whatever. But there were no directions or even pictures of what to build—no space ships, robots, dragsters, anything. The idea was that the kids' imagination would be completely unbounded as they discovered creations of their own design. Streator remembered staring at the pile of parts, half-heartedly sticking together pieces here and there, turning it around and over, stealing a peek at what the other kids were doing with theirs, until after a half hour or so he had a thoroughly dissatisfying lump of protruding parts, not this or that. He felt the same frustration now as he tossed and turned in his bed. He recalled that the toy never made it into production.

100

14.

Monday morning he found nothing new on TV or the Internet. By late morning he headed downtown to the public library, a limestone Carnegie building that was far too small for the town but had managed to escape the wrecking ball because of the sentimental attachment of a small group of preservationists. The local history room of the library was staffed by elderly volunteers in odd hours here and there—nothing on Mondays. The main collection had a few local histories; most were obviously Chamber of Commerce booster books and nearly thirty years old, but still they were much more revealing than anything in the newspaper.

Streator discovered that the Gunthers were relatively nouveau riche for the area industrialists, not one of the three or four original families in town to make it big in grain processing when the railways came in the mid 19th century. In fact, the city was well established as a major processing center when the Gunthers finally came into money. They had owned a small water-driven mill on Vapor Springs Creek, but it soon became obsolete when big modern mills—Lentz's and Warnick's—opened across the river. After World War I, Albert Gunther did his best to keep up with Lentz and Warnick and the others, building a more modern but very modest mill up on the flat above Vapor Springs Creek. A fuzzy photo showed a family of stern Gunthers lined up by height near the new mill, the family home in the background. Frederick, the oldest of five but not yet a teenager, was almost as tall as his father even then.

Without rail access on that side of the river, however, Gunther's little mill was never real competition for the growing factories in town. Gunther's served mostly a handful of local farmers still carting corn in wagons.

What the Gunthers did have was land—pretty useless land, up and down the draw where Vapor Springs Creek came into the Inoka River, lapping up onto the prairie plains on both sides.

Most of the land was too steep and wooded for farming, but the Gunthers apparently hung on to as much as they could and eked out a living running their mill, selling timber, and farming the few viable acres.

In 1923, when the large operators realized that expansion of their mill production was limited by the amount of water available, Lentz and Warnick cajoled and bribed the city into damming the river, creating the lake. And that, gushed the local history authors, was the remarkable foresight that enabled the city to expand to its present stature as a center of agribusiness in the region. The permanent supply of adequate water allowed the mills to expand rapidly, and other industries followed: small factories and foundries for auto parts, kites, potato chips, water valves. And, lo, great prosperity came unto the city of the plains.

The small-time but apparently quite shrewd and even ruthless Albert Gunther rode this growth to remarkable heights. First he played hardball with the city when they came calling for land up Vapor Springs Creek, the area to become one of the three major basins of the new reservoir. What he negotiated was not just a good price for his useless land, but something more important: a bridge across the narrowest part of the new reservoir, a bridge from the town and its railways across to his modest mill. Gunther Mills expanded on the south side of the reservoir and became competitive with the big boys on the north side. Following came twenty years of consolidations, unfair market practices, hostile takeovers, bad luck and good luck in depression-era investments, sweetheart deals with the government during World War II, and gambles on the possibilities of soybeans. By the end of the war Albert Gunther had bought out Lentz, moved his base to the mills on the north side, demolished his old southside plant, and became the largest, richest grain processor in the city, soon in the region. Of course, the book was written before globalization swept its broom across a rusting Midwest and most of the heavy industries in town had closed or moved overseas, but agribusiness, especially Gunther Mills, kept the city afloat, riding waves of biotechnology booms like lysine and ethanol toward the century's close.

From what Streator could glean from the circumspect local history and the few microfiche articles he had time to skim,

Frederick Gunther was something of the Prince Hal of the Gunther clan. Albert's eldest child and only son, Frederick came of age just as the Gunthers came into their enormous wealth in the 1940s. He jitterbugged his way through a local private college until even Daddy Gunther's growing political connections couldn't keep him from the draft in 1943. But the old man got him attached as an aide to various diplomats, and his time in Europe as the war was winding down and then after read like a Grand Tour— London, Paris, Rome, Zurich, Athens. An avid skater in his youth, he learned the sport of speed skating in Switzerland, and he was indeed a member of the US Olympic team in 1948 in St. Moritz. Though nominally an employee of Gunther Mills after the war, he didn't seem to have many obligations other than gallivanting around the world, a hayseed playboy of sorts.

In 1961, however, the old man died and Prince Freddie morphed into King Frederick, surviving a power struggle on his board of directors and even a play for control from one of his sisters to emerge as chairman of the board of Gunther Mills, a throne he didn't relinquish until just several years ago when he became king emeritus because of failing health. Apparently his playboy days weren't all for naught as he had parlayed his international connections shrewdly and took Gunther Mills world wide.

Faithful wife Marta, acquired in Brazil after Frederick's ascension to the Gunther Mill's throne, emerged as the philanthropic angel of the Gunthers, her foundation endowing Gunther scholarships, the Gunther Pod for the Performing Arts at Kickapoo Community College, Gunther Park, Gunther Cancer Care Wing at the local Catholic hospital. And of course there was Gunther Hall, a sprawling brick manor with spacious lawns overlooking the lake. Originated by Freddie's mother in 1946 as a home for "wayward" girls and then an orphanage, under Marta's steerage it added substance abuse rehabilitation, domestic violence shelter, and residential mental health services for teenagers to its mission. Streator had heard (and used in his novel) that every time a Gunther had need of certain social services—first some place for pregnant mill workers Freddie had taken advantage of, then for their offspring, then Marta's alcoholism and their daughters' sleeping pill addictions and abusive marriages, then their granddaughter's bulimia—they added a new wing to Gunther Hall.

Streator had put little stock in any of the rumors beyond their prurient value. But a small detail caught his eye as he was skimming an article about Frederick L. The L, he had missed earlier, stood for Lloyd. Locals always joked that the huge clan of Lloyds in town was the result of Freddie's dalliances with the young, nearly helpless female mill workers who came streaming up from the south during and after the war. The story went that Freddie's mother, a stout no-nonsense German farmer, took pity and set them up in Gunther Hall and even went so far as to give them the Lloyd name, some said to remind or shame Freddie. It all seemed so far fetched that Streator had no qualms about including it in his novel—without the middle name connection, he wished he had thought of that—but now he wasn't so certain. Surely the middle name was just a coincidence, the sort of thing to fuel rumors?

He remembered something else: he retrieved Tarvis's obituary, and sure enough, he was survived by a handful of Lloyds, including an uncle, Archie Lloyd, he of the working DVD player. Tarvis was a Lloyd. He needed to find out more about Gunthers and Lloyds. He was starting to feel a little desperate, and nervy.

Except for the barbed-wired-topped fence, Keller Correctional Institution for Women looked more like a hospital campus than a prison, maybe a sixties-era community college with drab, low-slung buildings. Come to think of it, Keller's campus was more attractive than Kickapoo's once you were inside the fence, Streator thought. More green space.

The line for processing visitors was surprisingly long and slow for a Monday, full of cranky grandmas corralling impatient toddlers. And only after Streator had filled out his DOC 1048 Prospective Visitor's Form, shown two forms of identification to staff, and made it to the front of the line did he discover that his trip was a complete waste of time.

In his haste and wiredness, Streator had not explored the clunky and poorly designed Department of Corrections website thoroughly enough, missing the tab leading to a PDF with detailed instructions for visitors, including the information that all visitors must be on the offenders' Approved Visitation List. In advance.

"So, we can't just ask Angela if she'll see me? Put me on the list?" Streator asked the stone-faced staffer manning the check point.

"No sir," she said. "Not unless you're legal."

"Legal, how?"

"Lawyer or something."

For a moment Streator was tempted to lie and claim to be a lawyer, but the weight of all the official authority of forms, bars, barbed wire, gun belts, and grim guards squelched that impulse quickly. Most of it, anyway.

"Huh. See, my friend is a lawyer, I'm a free-lance writer, and he gave me Angela Conner's name, I'm trying to interview her for an article I'm doing on women incarcerated on drug charges, you know, it's my thesis that we'd all be better served if they were hospitalized, you know what I'm saying . . ."

"Yes, sir."

"So I just assumed because he made the referral, and he's legal, it would be okay?"

"Your friend should have told you to write the inmate and get on her list," she said. "And wait a second—you said Angela Conner?" She gave him a funny look, even peered around like she was looking for someone. "You mean Angie Conner, the inmate, right?"

"Yeah, that's her."

She scanned a computer screen. "She been released to Transitional—four weeks ago?" the officer said. She looked at Streator suspiciously.

"Really," Streator said. "I'll be darned. So . . . you say she's released to—what?"

"Transitional."

"And . . . that's . . . ?"

"Like a half-way house or something."

"Ah, good for her. But—I thought she had like time left on her sentence?"

The officer sniffed contemptuously. "Sentence. Like that

matters. Only thing matters is what kind of lawyer you got."

"So she's out—I don't suppose you could tell me where?"

"No, sir. You could try Parole." Her skeptical look said *Good luck with that* and *even if I knew, no way in hell I'm telling you, coming in here with that lame-ass story.* "We got lots of other drug addicts you could interview if you get on their list, but otherwise—" she motioned to the line behind him.

Streator berated himself all the way back home. He didn't have time for such stupid mistakes. The drive to Keller and back on a bad two-lane highway took longer than he thought it would, nearly an hour each way, and with the shuffle through the prison bureaucracy, he had had wasted almost three hours on a dead-end. He was burning daylight and feeling a bit panicky.

If not the mom herself, then, maybe her sister, Alberta Jameson.

When he had visited her in September, she didn't seem to know much about Tarvis's life and was hesitant to talk about her sister, but talking to her now surely would be better than nothing. She seemed to think she owed Streator something. Maybe he could cash in.

An unusual number of cars were parked near Alberta's house in Burke Hole. Streator could hear several loud voices talking at once inside when he knocked on the door. Some man peeked out the curtains of the front window. He could hear someone else fussing inside, and then a small, slender woman cracked open the door.

"Hello," Streator said. "Is Alberta home?"

The woman scowled at him, which didn't seem to suit her friendly face. Her hair was braided short and tight, and she wore a white t-shirt and some kind of uniform pants. Something about her looked familiar—another damn student.

"She ain't talking to no one," she said and shut the door.

Streator had no idea what that was all about but had no time to worry it out. On the drive back to his house, a thought came to him: if the students in the prison classes were anything like his, he'd bet that Angela's writing teachers had heard much more than what appeared in the essays.

When he pulled up the Kickapoo records at home, he hit a snag: the prison sections weren't listed on the regular school records that Streator had access to. Nothing in the essay file from the program review had an instructor's name; it was supposed to be a blind outcomes assessment. And he didn't know any of the instructors at Keller, anyway—they were hired by the Department of Corrections, not Kickapoo.

He was fast running out of Tarvis contacts. The kid Sammy still might be a good lead, if he could figure out what the hell his name was. His encounters with him in the hall bordered on threatening, and he was tight with Tarvis. He certainly looked dangerous. It was puzzling how his name wasn't coming up. But Streator did know one other name.

He could hear Uncle Archie's dogs barking before he even opened his car door. Two or three, and big, Streator decided, as he sat in his car at the end of the long gravel drive, trying to determine whether the dogs were out in the dark or inside the house. Inside, he finally figured.

He'd found Archie Lloyd's address in the phone book but wasn't familiar with that part of town on the south side of the lake. Down South Bay Drive he was into post-war housing neighborhoods, looping cul-de-sacs of small white two-bedroom ranches. At the outer edge of this neighborhood, in a wooded area that seemed to have steep draws cutting through it, he found Millhouse Estates Road, and then the gravel lane to Uncle Archie's house set back from an open field next to a thick woods. In the early evening dark, Streator felt like he was far out of town, but knew that he must have just twisted and turned into one of the underdeveloped pockets tucked away here and there in the outer rim of the city.

As the dogs barked inside, the front porch light came on. It was an old squat farmhouse, its big front porch enclosed with storm windows so that he couldn't see the front windows or door—very uninviting. Streator ventured to the front concrete steps. He never knew with these enclosed porches whether one was expected to knock on the outer screen door, which would be hard to hear from inside, or treat the porch as the public space it used to be and come on in to knock on the front door proper. But the barking dogs convinced him that he had been heard, and that he should keep walls between him and their teeth. He rattled the storm door.

Inside the porch the front door opened and a large man in tan Carhartt coveralls stepped halfway out, turned sideways, one arm and leg still inside, holding back what must've been the dogs. "What you need? I ain't buying."

"Are you Archie Lloyd?" Streator asked, nearly shouting through the closed storm door.

"What you need?"

"I'm a . . . friend of Tarvis Conner. I'm looking for some stuff, Alberta said he might have left it with you?"

Uncle Archie shook his head, stepped back for a moment and then came back out to the porch, shutting the front door behind him, ambling slowly to the storm door. "Say what, Tarvis what? God damn dogs, can't even hear myself think, now what you need?" Archie leaned on the jamb to steady himself and opened the storm door. He was tall and barrel-chested, with a ragged beard and short hair receding half way back across his head. Maybe in his sixties, Streator guessed, so probably a great uncle.

"Hey, how you doing, I'm Henry Streator, one of Tarvis's professors at Kickapoo . . ." Uncertain how long Uncle Archie would lean there listening in the cold and dark, Streator rushed through his very-sorry-about-Tarvis bit and his bit about the DVDs he was wondering if Tarvis had left there, how he wouldn't bother except they were hard to find, a couple even belonged to the school really, he decided to throw in to make it more urgent.

"Alberta sent you here?" Archie asked suspiciously. "She didn't say nothing to me."

"It was a while ago, she said Tarvis used to watch his DVDs out here sometimes, so I thought . . ."

"Well, I don't know nothing bout any goddamn movies but there's a whole pile in there, go root around if you want, let me get the goddamn dogs . . ."

Archie kicked back the dogs and yelled at them—two black and brown mutts, Rottweiler mixed with junk yard, as hard and thick as Archie himself, maybe as old—but did nothing to corral them as Streator followed him inside. The dogs barked and jumped on Streator and snarled at each other and circled and sniffed. "Good boys, down you go, good god you're a load . . ."

The living room was baking hot and smelled like dogs and cigarettes. A huge big-screen TV, a boxy rear-projector, jutted out from one wall, taking a big chunk out of the small living room, blaring a football game in surround sound. Facing it was a long sectional couch in black leather. No wonder Tarvis came here to watch movies, Streator thought. The rest of the place wasn't nearly so up-to-date, however; the thick brown carpet and the green walls said that the room hadn't been redecorated since the sixties, maybe earlier. Uncle Archie plopped on one end of the couch and pulled a lever to flip up foot rests. The armrest had a console with cup holders; one held a Michelob, the other an ashtray with an idling cigarette that he picked up. "There's what I got," he waved at a pile of videotapes and DVDs on a sideboard near the TV. "I don't know what all Tarvis brought over, he'd stay up all goddamnn night with them vampire movies and shit."

Streator untangled himself from the dogs and pretended to pick through the pile of videos, realizing he had no real plan here, no idea what he should try to get from Uncle Archie. In the pile were buddy cop movies, blow 'em ups, a couple of horror shows, and a lot of porn. Not much chance of any Kurosawa or Bergman lurking in here, Streator decided, even if he had been dumb enough to loan Tarvis anything from his own collection.

"So you're Tarvis teacher? What you teach out there?"

"English. Writing mostly."

"English, god damn, I best watch my mouth, that was my worst class, you teach like that diagram a sentence shit?"

"No, not really."

"Bunch of ladies in my church go out there, they complain to high heaven about them classes. You know Georgia Davis? Shirley Rice?"

Shirley Rice was one of Malveeta Fray's English 101 buddies—best to change the subject. "Tarvis had me for creative writing."

"Creative writing! Shit. What you do in there?"

"Stories, poems, that sort of stuff."

He shook his head contemptuously. "Jesus. Tarvis write that shit?"

"Yeah, he was pretty good, too. He never told you about what he was writing?"

"Hell no, I never knew what class he took. I thought all he ever did was drive that old car around and come here to watch them bullshit movies and go bang that country gal . . ."

"He had a girlfriend?"

"A girlfriend?" Uncle Archie asked incredulously, giving him a what-kind-of-dumbshit-are-you look. "Little fat country gal? Met her at Kickapoo, so it's y'all's fault the boy's dead."

Streator shook his head, not understanding. "Alberta never mentioned any girl."

"She didn't know. She didn't *approve* of that sort of thing. She's a god-fearing woman, don't you know," he said sarcastically. "Look what good that do her now. She better hope she got God on her side."

So it was a secret from his aunt, and even his Wing Zone buddy didn't seem to know. Tarvis was keeping it all hush-hush. Why would that be?

"I kept telling Tarvis, I say what you doing chasing that pasty tail way out in the country, god damn you telling me there ain't no gal in this whole damn city . . ."

Way out in the country. Someone from Kickapoo. That mailbox on Hackydale Blacktop. "Wait—was this girl's name . . . Bruckner? Megan Bruckner?"

"Maybe, yeah, that sounds about right."

On his way out, Streator saw that on a shelf next to the door was a handgun. That must have been what he had been holding inside the doorway when he first answered the door.

Two scary dogs and a big old gun. That was one spooked Lloyd.

15.

So someone told Tarvis's aunt he was out there on Hackydale Blacktop delivering wings . . . because he or someone else didn't want her to know he was out there seeing some girl? Because that wasn't the only reason he was out there? Both?

Streator headed back out to Hackydale. He couldn't recall anything in class to make him think Tarvis and Megan were a couple, but he'd be the first to admit that he was paying so little attention last semester, they could've been making out in the corner and he wouldn't have noticed. Tarvis was chatty with everyone. Streator couldn't remember if Megan had come back to class at all after Tarvis died.

He had grabbed yesterday's bucket of cold hot wings and ate while he drove. He realized he had forgotten to eat all day, and now he felt queasy from too much coffee and Diet Pepsi. The wings weren't helping his stomach, but they were all he had. The corner was harder to find at night, the country roads in the winter black nearly indistinguishable. Steering with one hand while licking the wing sauce off his other didn't help his driving. But he did find the corner.

He stopped for a moment, turned off his lights, and rolled down his window. Out at the old barn down the north-running lane, a weak light shone above a side door. The cold wind from the northwest brought that chemical-cat pee smell again.

And just a half-mile down the west-running road, back across Hackydale, a mailbox at the end of a gravel lane said, "Bruckner."

The small Bruckner farmhouse was nearly hidden behind a thick windbreak of overgrown firs. Megan looked shocked and bewildered, as well she should, to see her ex-English professor on her porch, reddish wing sauce staining his pants and jacket and fingertips. He knew whatever reason he gave for coming out here on a bitter cold night would be lame and suspicious, but he didn't want to just call, he wanted to see.

"Megan, hey, how you doing, I'm really sorry to bother you. . ."

"Oh my god—Mr. Streator? What in the world?"

"Sorry I didn't call, I know it's . . . do you have a minute? Could I talk with you a minute? It's kind of important."

She showed him into the living room, all decked out in country cute: plaid furniture, shelves full of hand-painted knickknacks, a red apple theme running throughout. But dirty, cluttered, with overflowing ashtrays, beer cans, pizza boxes, odd smells. He took a seat on the edge of an enormous Barcalounger with the leather ripped on both arms. He leaned forward on his knees earnestly. She sat with her feet tucked up under her on a blue plaid loveseat. She wore a baggy sweatshirt and gym shorts that revealed odd rashes on her legs. She seemed to notice him looking and pulled an orange and tan afghan around her legs. She looked chubbier than in class, and her hair was different. The blonde was growing out so that half of her head was dark.

"So, listen, I wouldn't have come all the way out here, and I tried to call, but I'm just . . . so worried . . . about a student—someone you know, I think." She seemed to be buying it but then she was distracted by headlights coming across her front yard. Streator heard a rattling car pull around back.

"Your folks?"

"My brother," she said. "Stepbrother. My folks are in Florida."

"Lucky them," he tried to laugh nervously, thinking the more flustered he sounded the more convincing he'd be. "But anyway, like I said, this student, I'm really worried, I tried to get counseling to look in on him, but you know how they are."

"Yeah, I know."

"The thing is, he was a friend of Tarvis's, so I think . . . I'm really sorry about Tarvis, you guys were going out?"

"Yeah." She sighed. Her eyes glistened. "He came out to see me that night he wrecked. It was a surprise—he was supposed to be working."

"Yeah, Lenny Ormand mentioned everyone liked him at Wing Zone."

"He was supposed to be working at Subway that night."

"Subway?"

"The one out at the truck stop."

112

"He had two jobs?"

"Yeah. That's where we met. He worked a lot. We didn't have hardly no time."

"Such a shame. Why was he even on that lane? It's not the main road back to town."

Megan hesitated and squirmed. "The turn on to Hackydale is easy to miss at night, and Tarvis was always getting lost out here. But most everyone goes that way anyway if you know what you're doing. Cuts off a couple miles."

The back door opened. He could hear someone banging cupboards in the kitchen. "Whose car's that?" an angry voice demanded. "I seen that car . . ." Someone came to the door from the kitchen—a scarecrow, a cadaver, some male creature between the ages of twenty and sixty—one of the mangiest humans Streator had ever seen. He was gaunt, yellow, and sores and scabs pocked his face. He stopped short when he saw Streator, startled and then angry in amazing succession. "Who the hell is this?" Ten teeth in his whole mouth? Not many more, Streator figured. And he reeked of sweat and ammonia and solvents.

"This is my English professor, Duane—he's . . . got some school stuff . . ."

"What the fuck he coming all the way out here for?" Duane said, confused and angry now, but wandering back into the kitchen, "That your little shitbag Jap shit car out there? Fucking English professor," Streator heard him mumbling to himself, "I know what the fuck he wants, you can't fucking tell me, first that little fucking nigger coming out here . . ." Streator heard cabinets banging. "Where's my fucking Cheetos, Megan, and did you drink all my goddamn beer again . . ." Streator heard a chair scratch across the floor and a can open. Then just belching and low murmurs and the crinkle of a Cheetos bag.

Megan looked horrified and terrified. She pulled the afghan around herself higher.

"I shouldn't tell you," Streator began again, a little spooked himself, "but I've got to ask—you know a guy named Sammy that Tarvis used to hang around with?"

"No, no one named Sammy."

"Big guy, real thick, short hair, lots of tattoos?"

"No." She looked like she was sincerely trying to remember. "We didn't hang around with a lot of his friends, though. His friend T-Bone looks kind of like that I guess, but we didn't hang around with him or nothing."

"T-Bone?"

"Yeah, that's all they called him, I don't know, he was Tarvis's friend from high school but I went to Hackydale-Wonoka, not Truman."

"How about family? Maybe a cousin or something?"

"No, the only family of his I ever met was one time we went to his uncle's house to watch some movies."

Streator nodded thoughtfully. "Well, anyway, I hate to ask and I can't tell you why . . . but I can't help this Sammy unless I know: was Tarvis . . . did he ever buy or sell drugs? Like crack, or meth?" Duane's mumbling and crunching in the kitchen dropped several notches.

"No, no, no. He wouldn't, not ever, I'm sure."

"You're sure?"

"Very for sure. He . . . he just wouldn't. He hated that stuff." She looked even more scared.

"Do you know," he learned forward even more earnestly, "was he ever in a gang? Like the Vice Lords?"

"No, no, not that he ever said, not when I knew him. He said he hated all that stuff in his neighborhood, he said he . . ." She glanced very slightly at the kitchen. It was definitely quieter in there. "No, no gangs. No drugs. Not Tarvis."

Streator sat back for a second. He didn't believe her. He could see how scared she was.

"Well, one reason I asked, I'm pretty sure . . . well, I'd see Tarvis and Sammy, you know, flashing like gang signs I'm pretty sure." This really did seem to bother her. She shook her head. "And the things he wrote, not the things we read in class but just the things I read, a lot of it had drug and gang stuff in it," he lied.

"Huh," she said, "there was nothing like that in the stuff he showed me."

Whoops. "Well, just a couple of things, just for class . . . so he showed you the things he wrote?"

"Yeah, sometimes. He talked about it a lot anyway. He was

114

excited about some book he was writing about a rich guy dying in the ice with his feet up or something like that, I don't know, he had it all worked out like it looked like an accident only there were hit men or drug dealers or something."

Houston, we have a problem. "Wow. Did he ever write it up?"

"I don't know. Maybe. I've got all his notebooks. His mom said I could have them. He filled a bunch of them. I haven't looked at them though. They make me so sad." She looked like she might start crying.

"Wow. Boy, I'd love to see those notebooks sometime." She didn't respond. He'd have to press that another time. He really needed to see those notebooks. "So where do you think he got an idea like that, rich guy getting killed by drug dealers?"

She shrugged.

"Well, that just makes me wonder, you know, what I was asking about before."

The back door slammed and Megan jumped. She glanced at the kitchen and suddenly went off in a rush, "But he was no gangbanger, I swear to god, and I would've known, and no drugs, no way, no how—whoever this Sammy guy is, he didn't have nothing to do with Tarvis, I swear to god . . ."

"Okay," Streator said, "You would know, that's why I asked." Streator heard Duane's car ripping down the gravel drive from around back. *Shitbag car,* he was one to talk, his car sounded like ten sticks rattling in a can. "Well, I better go," Streator said, trying to muster his most empathetic smile. "You've been *very* helpful, you'll never know, thank you *very* much." He made his way to the door. "I'm much relieved, to tell you the truth. I think Sammy is going to be okay." He nodded and gave a thoughtful smile. "Yes. Okay." He opened the door and stood in the doorway. Megan held the door, practically hiding behind it. Like she could really hide that belly, Streator thought.

"By the way," Streator said, "I know this is odd—but did Tarvis ever mention anything about Frederick Gunther? Or Gunther relatives or anything?" If he was going to fish, he might as well really chum the waters.

"Gunther? No. Not that I remember. I think his uncle worked at Gunther Hall. Like maintenance or something. Why?"

Did he indeed. "Oh, nothing. Just something he said one time about Gunthers in the family. Must've been different Gunthers. Well, thanks again, and I'm sorry to bother . . ." He stepped on to the porch.

"My dad was killed at Gunther Mills," she volunteered, in that free-association way he was accustomed to with these students.

"Is that right? Like an accident?"

"Yeah. Some guys were cleaning a tank or something and the fumes got them, they weren't wearing the right mask, my mom said my dad went in to get them and he died too."

"Wow. That damn company, they treat their labor like just so much grist for the mill."

"Yeah," she said. "My dad was like a supervisor and everything. Mom said those were his guys, that's why he went in. He was like that."

So much for the labor vs. management angle. "I'm so sorry." Now he was really getting cold.

"I was five. I don't really remember it much. Mom married Duane's dad and we moved out here."

"Well, thanks again, I shouldn't keep you . . ."

"Mr. Streator," she stopped him again as he started for the steps, "the reason I know that Tarvis . . . his mom . . ."

"Yes. I know."

"We was . . . he wanted to get us—away . . . he worked so much, we was wanting to get out of here."

Dream on, sister, Streator thought—Jesus, did stupid little girls still buy those lines when it was painfully obvious that what Tarvis the Savior really wanted was bearing fruition under her baggy sweatshirt? But now she was crying. He thought about stepping back to comfort her, but he was just making his escape. "I know, I know. So, how much longer?" he said with as much concern as he could fake, giving a quick but knowing glance at her belly.

She looked very confused, then it dawned on her. "I'm not pregnant!" she sobbed.

"Sorry, sorry . . ."

"Jesus! Just cause I put on a little weight, god!" She turned and shut the door hard.

116

So except for the last bit—which was a little embarrassing, though he wasn't convinced he was wrong—that all went pretty well, Streator thought.

A light snow was falling, tiny icy crystals that tinked on his windshield. Once he left Megan's drive, the road east was very dark, just a black ribbon with no markings, now with a bit of shine from the snow. A crappy night, but he was glad he made the drive—he definitely made some progress. He was starting to feel like this was going to work. He dug into the bucket of cold hot wings as he drove one-handed. Megan was scared, hiding something, he could tell, and that brother was a poster child for methamphetamine abuse. Must've been cooking it somewhere out there, probably that barn, probably what Streator had smelled earlier. He realized now that it wasn't the safest idea to sit in a meth addict's house asking about gangs and drugs, but he'd been too focused on what Megan could reveal to be scared. The dots were starting to connect. Tarvis was likely running the crank back into town for Duane, likely met him through Megan, or vice versa. He was on that side lane because he was headed toward Duane's barn, not because he was lost or taking a shortcut. Megan was right about how easy it was to miss a turn at night—only it wasn't the turn onto Hackydale that Tarvis had missed but the sharp turn near the barn.

And on top of all that, ol' Uncle Archie worked at Gunther Hall, wasn't that interesting . . .

But Tarvis had mentioned his book idea to Megan; that was going to be hard to get around. He definitely needed to get into those notebooks. It occurred to him that when she described his plot, she didn't say, "Just like that Gunther guy, wasn't that weird what happened?" Could she not have heard? Did she not watch TV? He couldn't remember seeing one in the living room. No Internet providers out there?

He was licking hot sauce off his fingers when he realized he was on the wrong road—in the dark and snow, with his attention swirling everywhere, he had missed the turn onto Hackydale, just as Megan had said, and now he was coming up quickly to the right-angle corner where Tarvis had wrecked. He thought he saw something parked on the left side of the road, in the dirt drive heading north toward the barn, but he couldn't be sure in the snow fall. As he tried to make out what it was, he bit into another wing and came into the turn to the south faster than he realized and hit his brakes harder than he wanted—he could feel a little slide, his old Nova without antilocks, but still no problem. . . But just as he entered the corner, bright high headlights suddenly blasted him from the left and lurched out like they'd cut in front of him or ram him in the side. "Jesus!" Streator yelled and dropped the wing and jerked the wheel with his one hand harder than he intended to avoid the wreck, and in a blur of motion his car spun on the icy road, missed the curve, hit the ditch sideways and rolled over twice, landing on its wheels in the dark.

Streator sat in a daze. His headlights pointed out across black, bare fields, the light snow wispy through the beams. He was breathing hard, his heart racing, his hands shaking on the wheel. He felt battered and shaken and dizzy.

He was crunched down in his seat, the roof crumpled in somewhat from the roll. He slowly took stock. He seemed to have all of his parts. Legs and arms moved. His shoulder ached under the seat belt. His left leg seemed a bit stuck or something. There was blood everywhere, but nothing hurt much. Not a good sign.

Bright lights shone on him from the left. He squinted out the driver's side window. His neck ached when he turned. Headlights from the road, pointed right on to him. Must be the driver of the other car, he thought. Good. At least some help. He sighed and waited for the driver. In the light he looked for the source of the blood. He could find no gaping holes. He looked in his mirror. His face was red, his eyes burned. He licked his bloody lips. Mondo habanero. The carnage of his bucket of wings was everywhere inside his car.

He looked again toward the light but saw no movement from the car, no one getting out to come help him. He waved into the light. Nothing. Streator didn't understand. *Just come help me, you bastard—you caused this, now come help* . . . No movement from the car. *Come on* . . . He unbuckled his seatbelt and tried his door. He was surprised that it creaked open when he leaned his shoulder on it. He slowly swung his left leg out—it hurt now, seemed to be bleeding around his knee. He pulled himself out and waved again into the headlights. *Little help here, huh*? The headlights were high and narrowly spaced, and he could see nothing in the cabin. He heard the engine rev a bit, and the lights lurched down and up as it crawled across the ditch. It stopped, its lights square on Streator. He took one shaky step toward the light and the car lurched forward again.

All of this was too confusing for Streator. He was beginning to shake in the cold, perhaps from shock. He fished his cell phone out of his pocket and sat back down in his car. He dialed 911.

The headlights glared on him while he described to the dispatcher where he was, as near as he could remember road names and mileages. Then the headlights backed up, lurching across the ditch again—some sort of old four-wheeler, Streator thought— and turned around very quickly when it hit the road, tearing off loud and rattling west into the dark night.

16.

Nobody at the hospital seemed too worried that he was going to die. He did have some non-wing-related bleeding from a decently deep gash on his left leg, probably from the after-market speakers he had installed in the door himself that had never fit fully flush. He needed stitches, and his knee and ribs were pretty bruised, his shoulder, too, from the seatbelt as he rolled. He had knocked his head but didn't seem to have a concussion. They gave him some Vicodin and a muscle relaxer while the doctor stitched his leg. He drifted off into a woozy near-sleep while they worked.

Some time later, someone was shaking him gently and talking to him. When he found focus, he saw a pretty ER nurse with dark wavy hair. "Hey," she said, "hey in there, how we doing?"

"Okay," he said.

"Super," she said. "We'll get you going then. Unfortunately, your pants"—she held them up for him to see that both legs had been cut lengthwise cuff to waistband— "are just 'pant.' The EMTs see all that blood and don't mess around looking for a source." She scrutinized the jeans a moment. "Though that doesn't look like blood, really."

"No, not really," Streator mumbled. He couldn't begin to explain.

"Someone could bring you another pair."

Actually, no, Streator realized. There was no one in this town he could ask to go to his house and bring him some pants. How pathetic was that. "I'll just have to make do with these."

She laughed. "That's not going to work," she said. She left for a moment and came back with some thin folded cotton. "Here," she held up a pair of flowery hospital pajama bottoms, "these will get you home." Baggy one-size-fits-nobody with a tie. "And so cute to boot. Here, I'll help you."

He sighed and slid to the edge of the examination table. She squatted in front of him, rolled the left leg up and slid it over his bandages. "Ok, super," she said. "Still teaching at Kickapoo?" She smiled up at him.

Most excellent. Ex-students helping him pull on his pants. The way things were going, the next student he ran into would be his proctologist. He had thought she looked familiar. "Sorry," he found her nametag, "Mora. Didn't recognize you, out of context and everything. Here, I can get the rest." He took the pants from her and slid on the other leg.

"No problem," she said, standing. "You were pretty out of it. And it's been a while."

He stood and pulled the drawstring tight. The jammies were so big they bunched at the ankles and ballooned at the hips. "*Hammertime*," Streator said.

She looked him over and smiled again. "Like I said, very cute." He remembered that smile. Creative writing class, last fall, but she had dropped early. Same dark eyes, dusky skin, smooth and tight. Her baggy scrubs had thrown him.

Now she was all business. "Ok, then, I don't mean to rush you, but you're all set, and it's really hopping in here tonight, you know those icy roads are great for business." She gave him his meds and his directions for checking the bandages and for following up with his family doctor (*no family, no doctor* he didn't tell her), suggested crutches, which he declined, and told him to wait in the ER lobby because the sheriff's deputy needed to talk to him.

The deputy was a jovial big guy with a thin moustache and a bad haircut, his brown shirt spilling over his gun belt, not the young stud stormtrooper types in the city force. He was yukking it up with the nurses at their station when Streator finally hobbled out.

"Mr. Streator, how we doing?" the deputy said. "Jake Donaldson. Let me get a few things for my report, it'll just take a second."

They went into a small family consultation room for privacy. He of course wanted the full story, but something made Streator pull back. Some things he needed to get his head around. He said he was out at a friend's house, on his way home, the road was icing up, and he didn't see how sharp the corner was until it was too late, those country roads were so dark . . . He didn't mention how the lights startled him and the driver of the four-wheeler didn't help him. Maybe it was sitting there in those loaner droopy drawers that made him feel like a kid who had just peed his pants and didn't want to admit it, but his instinct was to lie. Besides, details were coalescing in his head, he was on to something, and he wasn't ready to spill.

"Well, I'm afraid I'm going to have to cite you for speed unsafe for the conditions," Donaldson said as he finished writing and drawing the report, "I know that seems like rubbing it in what with your car totaled and your leg and all, but that just makes it harder to let one slip by, you know what I'm saying."

"Sure. I guess."

"But really, you're pretty dang lucky. Good thing you were wearing a seatbelt. Last kid that wrecked on that corner got ejected and his own car rolled over him, killed him."

"I knew that kid. He was one of my students."

"I'll be darned. Ain't that a shame." He worked on his forms.

"His car rolled over him?" Streator said. "That seems pretty unlikely."

"No, you see that sometimes." He stopped his writing and demonstrated with big hand gestures: "On a first roll or so they get flung out ahead of where the car's rolling, like a catapult, and then the car catches up and rolls over them too. Like in one of them Roadrunner cartoons, where the coyote falls off the cliff and he hits the ground and then his own anvil or something hits him in the head too."

"How can you tell that's what happened?"

"Well, you find your body closer to the road than the car and you got your massive internal injuries, like you been run over." He went back to his paperwork.

Streator looked over his arm at the forms. "So, I guess you've got all your CSI, your 8 by 10 color glossies with circles and arrows and a paragraph on the back of each one . . ."

Deputy Donaldson blinked at him, frowning. "It was pretty damn cold out there tonight. I'll swing by tomorrow and take some measurements."

"No, I meant, back with the other kid, I assume when someone dies and all . . . Is there like an inquest?"

"Maybe. It's all pretty straightforward. You can tell a lot just by looking. His looked just like yours. Except there wasn't no corn all flattened down tonight. Big old skid marks coming around the corner and a car upside down out in a field. Take some measurements to get the speed maybe, but there's not a lot to figure. Look for cans and bottles and dope and stuff—speaking of which, we did give you the tests, right?"

"Yeah-yeah. Zero point zero."

"Super-duper. Sign here." He handed Streator his clipboard with the citation. "Yeah, they didn't find nothing in that kid's blood either, that's just a real bad corner, we're going to have to talk to the township road commission about that corner, get some better signage or something."

"They could start by putting the old sign back up."

Deputy Donaldson didn't seem to hear him. He tore off a yellow copy of the citation for Streator with a smile, told him where his car had been towed to, smiled again, and left with a hearty, "Hey man, be careful out there!"

Streator used the phone at the nurse's station to call a cab. As he finished, Mora came back by with charts.

"So he didn't throw you in the tank?" she smiled.

"No, no."

"Got your meds? Your directions? Know what to do with that bandage?"

"Sure, got it covered." He gathered up his pills and paperwork, stuffing them in his parka pocket.

"You still writing?" she asked, fiddling with her own paperwork. "Get that novel published?"

"Novel?"

"You told us you were working on a novel."

"Oh, yeah, no—no luck with that one. Still plugging away, though."

She smiled again but didn't say anything.

"How about you?" he said. "Still writing, I hope?"

She laughed. "No, not since your class."

"Yeah? Why not? You had some talent."

"Sure, yeah, thanks."

"Seriously."

"Well, I got my boy, this job is a killer for time . . . Guess it'll be a while before I'm the next Toni Morrison."

"You like Morrison?"

"We read *Beloved* in your class, remember?"

"Wait—what? My class? Creative writing?"

She laughed and whacked his arm. "I knew you didn't remember me when I came back last fall! I took Intro to Fiction from you, too, about eight years ago? That little room in the library? Thanks a lot!"

"Sorry—" and then he placed her years back: directly across from him, locked on so intently he felt a bit uncomfortable. A long, thick braid she often pulled in front and twirled absently while he talked. "Oh yeah, I remember, the seminar room in the back of the library. You laughed at my jokes. Your hair was longer—a braid." She used to wear tight jeans and tight tops, scooped a bit low, he remembered, especially for someone in her early twenties still living at home with her Asian family—Indian? Pakistani? But she never played the shy demure type. Too smart for that. So much confidence. She came by his office once or twice, it was all coming back. She wanted to be a novelist and he was encouraging, not falsely so for once, but her family was putting pressure on her to get some practical education. Or just get married. Family won, he could see. He remembered her in his office chair, very short denim shorts, long tan legs crossed tightly at the ankles. Notebook held to her chest. But not hiding or protecting, no. Like now. That wide white smile and sparkling black eyes, a face as direct and assured as a searchlight. He didn't know why he hadn't remembered her when she came back for creative writing. More and more he was wiping his memory disk clean every year. It sort of worried him.

"My last name was Kontos then, too, so I guess I'll give you a break."

"Well, anyway," he said, "I bet you get lots of good material here." The waiting room was nearly full of comatose patients staring at the TV in the corner.

"You'd think." She leaned in and spoke a bit lower. "But

really, it's pretty boring. Anymore just the same stupid stuff, same stupid people doing stupid stuff over and over and wanting us to clean it up for them."

Who would've thought that such a bright light would be such a cynic? Now that was interesting. "Well, I was just thinking, you know, you'd get the real scoop on things in a place like this —like I keep hearing some priest on your board gave some kid AIDS and the hospital is forking over hush money to the family?"

She rolled her eyes. "Please. Give me a break."

"What?"

She sighed. Almost coyly.

"You *do* know something," Streator said. He edged in closer and made a show of glancing around to reassure her that no one was near. "Come on, spill. You know, fiction writer, I live for the dirty details."

She shook her head and lowered her voice even more. "Not some priest. I don't know how that got started. That Gunther guy, the one who just died."

"Frederick Gunther?"

Mora shrugged.

"Are you kidding me? Frederick Gunther gave some kid AIDS? And they're paying off his family?"

"Hers. Some real young black girl."

"See, you do have good stuff in here."

"Naw. Everyone knows that one." Her nurse colleagues were coming and going from the station, some sort of commotion in one of the rooms down the hall drawing her attention. "Oops, gotta go, hey it was great seeing you again." She smiled once more and made to move away.

"Yeah, sure, thanks. Hey, Mora, look, I'm dying to know—I mean you've really got my curiosity piqued . . ."

She waved her ring finger at him. "Nope. Not married, no boyfriend, ask away. "

Now he was really embarrassed—"No, that's not what I was . . . I meant my writer's curiosity."

She looked hurt. "*Professor*."

"No, it's not that—"

She smiled again. "Jeez you're easy, I'm just messing with

you. You want some dirty details, but I don't know anymore, so
. . . I guess this is *farewell*. Seriously, I've really got to go." She
walked down the hall briskly.

"Sure, okay, maybe I could give you a buzz later though?"

Now she looked genuinely puzzled as she glanced back.
Damn, he thought, he finally found someone who really seemed
to know something and she thought he was hitting on her, even
standing there in those cute baggy pants, or she was hitting on
him, whatever, really crappy luck any way you sliced it.

It was late by the time he got home. He wanted to sit and
think and figure out where he was, but he ached all over and the
thoughts and images racing through his head could find no center,
just a swirl of incoherence. He went to bed in a drugged stupor
with his leg on a pillow.

He was exhausted but so dizzy when he shut his eyes, he
couldn't sleep. Once in college some friends talked him into
bungee jumping from a big crane contraption set up at a local
street fair. For the next couple days, every time he closed his
eyes he felt like he was falling and flying. Now he felt the same
vertigo—his room, his bed, his body spinning ass over teakettle
across a dark field again and again.

17.

He awoke in a haze when it was light and lay in his bed under his heavy covers, dozing off and on for most of the morning, getting up just for the bathroom and more drugs.

His late sleeping had always been a raw spot with Roni: "Maybe if you got your butt out of bed before noon, you'd get something done!" she'd inevitably bring out in one of their fights. That his mom had made the same complaints all through his teen and young adult years made it even worse. Roni and Mom were devout early risers; he was an unrepentant night owl. He never understood why preferring a different portion of the clock for waking hours was such a moral failing.

He finally pulled himself out of bed after ten and stumbled downstairs. His head felt light and disjointed, his senses dulled. "A wombly bubble," Roni used to call this feeling, when they overslept after afternoon sex. What he wouldn't give for that kind of wombly-bubble now. This one came from painkillers and fitful sleep punctuated with dreams of flying—and landing hard. He'd heard that if you hit the ground in your dreams, you would die. No such luck.

His stomach was queasy, but he thought he should get something in it besides buffalo wings. He had no milk for cereal, so he made himself some buttered toast and finished off the last of his coffee. Then he curled up on his couch with a comforter and tried to figure out where he was, what he had, and what he was going to do.

His mind still spun and his head hurt inside and out. He couldn't focus. Stressed, distressed, aching, empty. This was Tuesday. He was supposed to be in New York in three days. He was having a hard time working up the energy to care about any dead Gunther or dead student or dead novel. He was just so tired. He needed to call his insurance agent about his car, now in some junkyard somewhere. He should figure out that COBRA thing, see how he was going to pay for the hospital visit. He needed to get some food in his house. He should call Det. Cruiks and tell him everything, which was really nothing, and just forget it all.

He needed some air or he'd just sleep all day. He was feeling a little hungry again. Might as well start with lunch. Might as well be Subway.

Even in his heaviest parka, thick gloves, and a wool scarf, Streator froze his ass off riding his motorcycle across town. His leg was so stiff from the bandage he could hardly shift. His cheap old helmet did little to keep his ears warm and he had no face shield. At a stoplight he tried to tuck the scarf up under the helmet and over his face, but as soon as he rode away, the scarf blew back down.

By the time he made the truck stop at the interstate, he was so cold he hurried inside shivering and got a cup of coffee from the convenience store side of the building. There were six Subways closer to his house, but this was where Tarvis and Megan had worked.

He had also remembered that during the "Gangs In Our Town" workshop, Det. Ramage had said the truck stop was a focal point for drug trafficking. Seems that drug runners needed gas and a john like everyone else. The detectives apparently hung around the parking lot, looked for likely out-of-state vehicles and "suspicious individuals," which of course was not to be confused with "profiling," then sidled up to these individuals, made small talk, showed a badge, and asked them if it would be okay if they took a look in their car. "They always say yes," Ramage had said, shaking his head. "These are not the sharpest knives in the drawer. Apparently they think that if they agree, then we'll think they aren't carrying so we won't bother to search. We always search. Or they think they've got it hid so great we'll never find it. We always find it. We know every secret cavity, we can tell if any dashboard screw's been tampered with . . . And of course, we've got dogs. I could be standing there with my dog at my side and they still say yes. Like I said, not the sharpest individuals to come down the pike."

Streator sat a table near the Subway counter, thawing out. The place was busy with truckers and interstate families unloading from minivans. No one looked local, and certainly no one looked like drug traffickers. Or police officers. Streator wondered if drug running was a seasonal business. No one liked being out in the cold.

The line at the Subway thinned out. He finished his coffee and had stopped shivering enough to eat. He ordered a sandwich from the teenage girl working the counter. She was thin and very short—he could hardly see her over the counter—with a long black ponytail sticking out of the back of her Subway cap. She did not look familiar. Her name badge said "Tiffany."

"Busy today, huh?" he offered as she fixed his sandwich.

"Yeah. Not too bad. Cheese?"

"Sure, and lettuce, tomato, pickles. You worked here long?"

"About a year. No peppers, olives, anything?"

"No. You must've known Tarvis Conner, then."

She perked up a bit. "Yeah. That was so sad. Mustard, mayo?"

"Mustard. Yeah, he was a student of mine. Liked him a lot. His girlfriend Megan worked here, too, right?"

"Yeah. She was really broke up when he died, poor sweetie." She wrapped his sandwich and passed it down to another bored girl at the register.

"Meal? Drink, chips?" this bored girl said without looking at him.

"Yeah, sure. You knew poor Tarvis?"

"Nuh-uh. Just started a couple weeks ago."

Streator paid and took a seat near the register. After a few minutes, Tiffany came out to wipe down the tables around him. He was the only customer at that end of the store.

"Yeah, as a matter of fact," Streator said between bites as she cleaned the table next to him, "I just happened to see Megan, what, yesterday I guess."

"Really?" Now she really perked up. "How's she doing?"

"Ok, I guess."

"We were all totally worried about her." She abandoned her half-hearted cleaning and came to his table. "She quit here, we none of us seen her since, she don't answer her texts or calls. She really took the Tarvis thing hard. I think she blamed herself."

"Really? Why?"

"I don't know, I never got all the details, but the night he wrecked he was going out to see her, I heard she had some big blowup with that asshole druggie stepbrother of hers. Tarvis was all, 'I got me some business to take care of with that dude' or something and he went flying out of here. That's what I heard."

Now that was worth coming out into the cold. As he thought, Tarvis and Duane had some unhappy dealings. "Wow. That's really sad."

"Yeah." Tiffany nodded and looked far away. "If you see Megan, tell her to IM or something. I chatted with her like once on AOL a long bit ago and she said something about a new boyfriend or something, but I think her Internet or cell is dead or something, I don't get nothing but a busy signal when I call."

"Sure, I'll tell her." A customer came in, an older man in a business suit, and got a sandwich to go. Streator nibbled on his own sandwich, picked at some Sun Chips, his stomach queasy again, and finally gave up and threw the rest away. Although Tiffany obviously didn't know much, he thought he might as well ask as he left: "Say, you ever know a guy named Sammy who was a friend of Tarvis's?"

Tiffany had never heard of Sammy.

He decided to try again for Angela Conner's teacher in prison. Kickapoo Community College was not far from the truck stop. Faculty didn't come in the week after New Year's, but staff sure did. Streator smiled at their Division Secretary, Mrs. Lois Forney, the World's Nicest Human and the One Who Knows Everything About Everything. She seemed surprised to see him, his not working there anymore and all. He told her he hadn't quite finished clearing out his office, which was true. She was surprised he still had a key. She would need it back.

He puttered around in his office a few minutes and then came out with fat file of random papers. He told Mrs. Forney he needed to return some material to a Keller developmental instructor but had no contact information. "I've never met her, Loren passed along the name and essays, and I'm embarrassed to admit, I don't even remember who it was. You know how I am with details."

"Yes, I know," she said sweetly. She quickly was able to find for him the name, Natalie Anderson.

"Yes, that's it!" Streator said. "You are the best. Don't suppose you have a phone number handy?"

"Well, yes, but I am so sorry, you know, it's not listed for release to students or anybody, and since you don't work here anymore, I'm so sorry." No sense trying to argue; she would never breach a confidentiality rule. "I can get that to her for you." She reached for the file.

"Sure—well, you know, I better talk to her about it. She won't be able to make heads or tails of my notes. You know."

She knew. "Tell you what, I seen a lot of Correctional folks out here today, I do believe they have their meetings this week, they start their semester way earlier, Natalie just might be out here."

It was not a breach of confidentiality for Mrs. Forney to make a few calls and find out for Streator that the Correctional instructional staff was meeting with other support staff in the conference rooms at the back of the library beginning at 2:00 and to describe to him the appearance of Natalie Anderson.

Streator waited in his office, pretending to sort papers and clean. The hallway was quiet, but he did notice the light on under Phyllis Nash's office door. Not surprising that she'd be in working more than a week before classes started.

He hadn't uncovered anything about her student Sammy. He should go ask her. He didn't want to. In truth, she still intimidated him.

She opened the door with a smile when he knocked. "Henry! I didn't know you would be in today. Cleaning out your things?"

So cheery, so unexpected. Then again, everyone was always in a better mood between sessions.

"Yeah, packing up, hitting the road."

"Good for you. I didn't have a chance to congratulate you on your book. That's really terrific!"

"Thanks, yeah, it certainly was good news."

"I'll say. Well, when we hired you, we knew we couldn't keep you forever. But maybe a little longer than expected, no?" she said with a twinkle.

"I'll say. Listen, I don't want to interrupt, I just had something I wanted to ask, if you're not too busy."

"Please, glad to get away from this. Always something ugly left over, isn't there? I was just thinking about getting some coffee before the canteen closes. Want to join me?"

In ten years, he had never gone for coffee with Phyllis Nash. "Sure, I could actually really use some coffee."

As they made their way to the canteen, she noticed his limp and asked if everything was okay, genuinely concerned. He explained somewhat about his accident. "I'm fine, though," he said, "lots of good drugs."

"I thought you looked a little bedraggled," she said with a laugh. She asked about his book, the timetable for publication, what it was about. He answered vaguely. He had included a Phyllis-like character, a shrewish department chair. Perhaps he could revise that part, if it came to it. Or at least include a "You're not in it!" disclaimer, though surely no one would believe it.

"I'm just so glad for you," she said. "I was thinking the other day how unfair it was that someone like Derrick Doolin," she rolled her eyes, "gets all the acclaim and someone like you with real talent doesn't get a shot."

"Thanks. Turns out talent isn't the most important ingredient."

"I'll say. I haven't read his book, but I had Derrick in class. Talk about tone-deaf sentences." She lowered her voice and put a hand to her mouth, "And what a pain in the patootie. He really thought he was God's gift."

Wow, Phyllis Nash trashing a student! Would wonders never cease!

She insisted on buying him a congratulatory cup of coffee. "I bet you won't miss this coffee," she said. "I'd give anything for a Starbucks in this town. Donut?" She pointed to a plate of gooey glazed bars.

"You know, I'd love a donut, thanks."

"My weakness. If they ever get the culinary program up and running, maybe we'll get something decent around here for a change."

They took a table near the window in the empty café. The sky outside was clear and bright over the plowed fields past the parking lots. Streator asked her about Sammy from last semester, describing him, wondering if he had ever let on anything about gang or criminal activity. She had no Sammy in her classes but was sure from his description she was talking about a kid named Ty Bonafile.

Megan had mentioned a friend called "T-Bone." Who knows how many nicknames a posse might hand out. Had to be the same guy.

"I had Ty twice for 101," she began thoughtfully, licking her fingers. "The first time he didn't make it, I thought he was stoned all the time."

That would fit, Streator thought.

"The second time, though, last semester, I came to think there was something else going on. He just couldn't get things, it just wouldn't sink in. I think there may be some learning disability. I tried to get him to go get tested in Accommodations, but I don't think he ever did."

Ah, Phyllis . . . Streator never realized how sweetly naïve she was.

"He definitely has anger issues, that's for sure," she said. "And I know he comes from a pretty rough family—his brother is in jail, I think. So, I suppose a gang background wouldn't be out of the question."

"I suspected so," Streator said. "My friend thinks his little brother—" he could hardly keep his lies straight now—"is headed for trouble, and he hangs with Ty all the time."

"Well, that would really be a shame," Phyllis said. "I thought he'd turned a corner. We got him through 101 by the skin of his teeth last fall, finally convinced him he had to live in the Writing

Center to have a chance, got him hooked up with TRIO for some more support. He told me once he nearly dropped out of high school his senior year, but someone at Truman got a hold of him, his coach, I think, and he squeaked through. Apparently he was a big baseball player, he said he was going to get drafted to the pros, but maybe that was just his talk. Does that happen, high school players get drafted right to the pros? I don't follow sports."

Streator didn't follow sports, either, but his father sure did and was always filling him in on players from their old high school who were drafted. "Yeah, in baseball, lots of them go into the minor leagues right out of high school."

"Ah, then that may be why he's so angry. He had some horrific knee injury his junior year and that was the end of baseball. That's why he limps. I think he was one of those guys just passed along through school because he was good at sports, and now . . ."

"Yeah, and now." A sad story, sure, but this place was so full of train-wreck lives, he could never figure where to even begin, where to jump in. And when one wreck leads to a bigger wreck—what to do then? He took a big bite of his donut and thought about telling Phyllis all he suspected about Tyrone, and Tarvis, just to prove to her how futile it was to work so hard.

Ten minutes before two, Streator hovered over a library table pretending to read a newspaper near the aisle to the back conference room. The place was empty except for one clerk behind the counter. After a while, a few unfamiliar staff came through chatting in twos and threes. He made straight for the only short, dark-haired, thirtyish woman.

"Natalie, right? From Keller?"

"Yes." She looked vaguely familiar but did not look like she wanted to talk to him.

"I'm glad I caught you. Henry Streator, from English."

"Yes, I know."

"Sure, yeah, I thought we'd met. Hey, the thing is, I was finishing up that program review, looking through those essays, and I had a couple questions about some of the students, about some of their experiences in the essays . . ."

"The program review?" she interrupted, puzzled and angry both. "Seriously?"

"Yeah, just a few things I was curious about."

She shook her head and chuckled. "You are a piece of work," she said. "Or, should I say, in terms of shit, you are full of it."

She left for her meeting. The clerk behind the counter pretended she hadn't heard that.

Back home, he called Locke. "Slow down, slow down," Locke said when Streator rushed through a breathless explanation that still left out Tarvis's story. "English 091? At Keller? And, why, again? Have you talked to the police yet, Henry?"

Streator took a long breath and tried to collect himself. Given the state he was in when he left Locke's house two days before, he realized he must be coming across as seriously manic-depressive. "Someone who was out there, one of the prisoners, can help me get a handle on this whole Gunther thing. She was in our 091 last spring. She's released now and I don't know where she is, so I tried to ask this Natalie Anderson, her English teacher out there, but she was just—a major dick. And no, I haven't talked to the police, not yet, but I will, I have a friend who's a detective."

Locke hesitated. "Well, you didn't really think you'd get anything from Natalie Anderson, did you?"

"Yeah, I know, FERPA laws and all that, but seriously, she could help a guy out, huh?"

"Natalie Anderson?"

"Am I supposed to know her?"

"Ah. Remember that department meeting last fall when we looked at the Keller classes? You missed the introductions. She was there. You managed to insult her and didn't even know it?"

"Crap." He could sort of picture her in the corner. "But really, she won't even talk to me?"

"You really don't pay attention to anything, do you. Natalie Anderson has worked for us for three years. The first two she was Natalie Fray. She married last year."

It took a moment for the import of the name to penetrate

Streator's buzzing brain. "Malveeta's daughter."

"I'm afraid so."

"Could this town be any fucking smaller?"

"Apparently she coached Mom into the refund thing. I don't think she likes you."

18.

Surrender. That's all he wanted to do. Give up and crawl into bed. He was exhausted. His leg hurt. He took another Vicodin. He wandered his house listlessly, finally settling at his desk. He clicked on his computer out of habit. He tried to prop his leg up on another chair but couldn't reach the keyboard sitting that way.

An e-mail from Medina, asking him to call, getting peevish now. He made it very clear that he was losing trust in Streator, and if he didn't trust him then Kendall certainly wouldn't, and that would be bad for Brent Medina, and the first order of business was preserving the delicate web of relationships that his living depended upon and that he had nurtured so carefully for so many years. And that there was not necessarily any order of business with Henry Streator's name on it.

He poked at the papers on his desk absently. Under a pile of messy drafts and notes next to his computer, he found his MFA thesis, where he had left it last time he swiped a few bits from a story. It was an official black bound edition with gold lettering. *Deep Water Passages.* Didn't take him long to really hate the title. After he had paid for the two bound copies for the department and one for the grad school, he couldn't afford a copy for himself. This one was a gift from Roni the next Christmas. She had sneaked out with his loose manuscript and taken it to the bindery. It was the best present she had ever given him.

He pulled out the snapshot he had been using to mark a page. It was a photo of Streator, his thesis advisor, and Roni. She had buried it in the book when she gave it to him. He always kept it there.

Streator, like most men, had little use for memorializing the usual benchmarks of a relationship: first date, first kiss, first sex, first fight, first night apart after marriage, etc. But he did have a secret set of firsts he carried with him that marked the arc of his relationship with Roni in ways more significant to him:

First time answering the other's phone. First combined batch of laundry. First borrowing without asking. First door left open in the bathroom. First sleepover without sex, mutually approved. First photo together.

The latter was this one in his hand. It was taken at an awards reception when Streator won the department fiction prize. The photographer, one of their fellow students, had a grievous lack of social grace, as did so many of their grad school friends. She insisted Roni be included in at least one of the shots of Streator and all but pushed her into the frame. She had already decided that Streator and Roni were an indivisible unit. But at that moment Streator wasn't so sure he thought they were a couple; they hadn't been dating very long. So they stood awkwardly in the photo, Streator always uncomfortable in a coat and tie anyway and never one for posing. Roni pointed out to him later that he didn't even put his arm around her. He pointed out that it took two hands to hold his plaque in front of him for all the world to see. Actually, Streator was the only one looking uncomfortable. His advisor looked jolly but distinguished, a veteran of such poses. And Roni had taken Streator's arm with both of her hands and looked happy for all the world to see. Proud of him, happy with him, so much joy in her face just from locking onto him. But as goofy as he looked, and even though Roni in her heels was noticeably taller than he was, Streator had always liked this picture. This is when I thought, hey, this chick digs me, Streator told her much later. Who needs a wedding vow—we got a picture that seals the deal. Essence of two souls captured in a photo. Just ask the Amish. Or Hopi. Someone like that. She had laughed.

Now he hadn't seen her in five months, had only a couple of short phone calls, and couldn't remember the last e-mail. He hadn't told her anything about the book: he fantasized about mailing her a first edition, inscribed *"In yo face!"* Or something a lot wittier that would come to him later. Now, though—now she would have the last laugh. Though the bitch of it was, she wouldn't laugh at him. That was maybe even harder to take.

He put the photo back in the book and tossed it onto the desk. He realized he had always liked that photo so much because it helped to reassure him that they really were souls attached like

Donne's compass. He always needed a lot of reassurance.

She was the one who suggested they move in together, "to save rent." A year after he finished his MFA, he finally found a last minute one-year position at a small college in South Carolina. "I kept waiting for him to ask me to come," she liked to joke with new friends when they shared their life stories, "but if you wait for Streator for something like that you'll wait forever, so I finally just said, so is there room in this U Haul for my books or what?" She taught as an adjunct and studied for her qualifying exams, and when his South Carolina gig ended, the only job he could scrape up was at a community college in Illinois. She said she wouldn't go with him unless they married.

He remembered when they first moved there, how they had few friends and no money, so a good night out was dinner at a little Greek café on the edge of town next to a wood throbbing with cicadas. The family that owned the café came to know them and welcomed them with cheap spanakopita and moussaka, or a plate of chicken and salad and strong olives for a few dollars. Afterward he and Roni would take a slow drive around the lake in the late evening sun. He remembered the nights as soft and warm, with a hazy sunset over the water, fireflies blinking over the lawns. They'd try to convince themselves that this was all right, that they were happy, that they should feel something like contentment. But still he remembered feeling melancholy and alone, cut off and adrift, and their talk inevitably turned toward how they were going to get out of there.

Once in their second late spring, just after school was out and grades were in, they invited another young couple out to the Greek café with them. He was a quiet fellow just out of grad school at the state university, like Roni teaching adjunct that year at Kickapoo and nearby community colleges. Roni got to know him in the adjunct office, and they occasionally shared rides. His wife, also an English teacher, was the talkative one, so Roni took to her right away. With a two-year-old girl to care for, the wife taught just one section at Kickapoo—Streator saw them playing tag-team parenting as she came in for a night class, and the husband would get the girl a cheese toastie for supper at the canteen in the building. They brought the child with them to dinner, naturally, and the café owners fussed over her with crackers and treats. She was a blonde cutie, a bright girl, talking far beyond her years, using words like "actually" and "perhaps," holding up her chubby little pointer finger to punctuate her thoughts. The husband wanted to pick Streator's brain about job-search advice. Streator thought he was kidding at first, but then realized, *no, this guy really* does *want to know how to get a job like mine.*

After dinner they all walked out to the vacant lot at the end of the parking lot, where rabbits were running in and out of the grass and bushes through the low summer light. The girl said, "There sure are a lot of bunnies!" and ran after them, until Mom and Dad saw the broken bottles and tires in the lot and corralled her. Streator and Roni watched the three of them track bunnies, the little girl comfortably in Dad's arms. Later Dad swung her up onto his shoulders, and they reached for the new moon low in the dusk and put it in her pocket. Mom played at fishing it out again, and all three of them laughed.

Though this couple was actually a few years younger, Streator had always assumed that this was a vision of his own future, his and Roni's—not just the child, maybe not even the child at all, but this vision of happiness, of these two people with each other, how they were entirely absorbed into each other's lives, into one life really, their own one life.

By late June the young dad was offered a tenure-track job at a community college in Iowa and they were gone. A couple of years later the Greek family closed their café and moved to Florida. A print shop bought the building and paved the bunny lot for more parking.

It occurred to Streator that Tarvis and Megan must have bought into the same fairytale. *It will be all right, everything will be all right, as long as we have each other, because we have each other.*

Who could resist that siren? Tarvis was turning out to be more of the dreamy romantic than Streator gave him credit for. If he knew half as much about Tarvis Conner as Phyllis Nash knew about her students, he wouldn't be in such a muddle now.

Tarvis had come by his office, what? Three times maybe? What had they talked about? All Streator could remember was trying to urge him out the door. Always something about that damn car—Streator probably knew more of the bio of the LTD that killed Tarvis than he did of the dead kid himself. All he could remember about Tarvis were the movies he liked, plots related in excruciating detail. Streator could see now that Tarvis was feeling him out, trying to see if his idea of *story* matched Streator's, if there was some secret code he was missing. And there were the handwritten sheets of rap lyrics that Streator had barely glanced at—about what? Clichés of perseverance and making it, believing in yourself, keeping it real and right . . . all so fuzzy, then and now. In his first go-round in creative writing, Tarvis had mentioned or written about living in housing projects in East St. Louis or somewhere, about how dull this town was in comparison. Wasn't he the one with the story about his mom leaving the projects to come here to live with relatives when the drugs and gangs got to be too much? Gunshot through their toaster one night? Or was that some other kid?

He wished he could get into Tarvis's notebooks but couldn't think of anything halfway plausible to convince Megan to let him have them. He fished through a deep pile of papers and files and found Tarvis's floppy disk of school work. He had glanced at it months before but wondered now if there was something useful he had missed. He popped it into his computer and pulled up the files. But no, not much. Some more lyrics, but not raps as he had thought when he first looked—more like *oh bay-ay-bee you are my ev-a-ree-ee thang* sort of sappy croonings. Written for Megan, no doubt. Lots of *i'm so scared too but with you i feel strong* sort of stuff. Embarrassingly vulnerable, Streator thought. But even the street toughs figured out long ago that "vulnerable" was a good sell to the ladies. He was sure that the notebooks at Megan's house had piles of this stuff.

Tarvis's few English 101 essays on the disk didn't reveal much either. One made the case that not all rap music was lurid gangsta rants, apparently in response to an *Ebony* article given to the class about misogyny and materialism in hip-hop. Tarvis's essay recounted briefly the politics of early hip-hop artists like

Public Enemy, reaching for a point about "keeping it real" and fighting the man. He gave some half-baked examples of socially responsible and even Christian hip-hop. A second essay argued about the injustice of the city's loud music ordinance: that spring Tarvis had been ticketed in his LTD, resulting in an outrageous $500 fine and impoundment of his car on the spot. "If they take my car so I can't get to work or to school how I'm going to pay the fine? And how is it fair that a speeding ticket is only $125 when you could kill someone?" Good point, Streator thought, though perhaps more importantly, an impounded car would put a crimp in your drug-running. Surprising that they found no evidence of his dealing when they impounded; surely they would've searched the car, which seemed to be the whole point of the loud-music law. Tarvis didn't even mention that the ordinance was chiefly enforced in certain neighborhoods against certain drivers thumping certain kinds of music.

The last essay was a surprisingly conservative blame-the-victim rambling mess about how, sure, some cops were racist but if young black men didn't put themselves into bad situations they wouldn't get themselves beat up or harassed; he apparently saw no ideological discrepancy with the point of his previous essay. In the middle of the third essay he slipped in an example: "Like I know someone got AIDS and died from shooting up, and I'm sorry but if you get AIDS from drugs or whoring or gay sex why should you expect some rich guardian angle to come make it better, you made your mess now you got to face up and take care of it, its not the employers job or government job to babysit us and bail us out." Angela's essay from Keller had mentioned "guardian angels" helping out her cousin who had HIV. There seemed to be a difference of opinion in the Lloyd family about the proper role of earthly guardians in helping to solve one's problems. But at any rate, Tarvis knew someone with AIDS who was helped by a wealthy benefactor.

From there the essay degenerated into a rant about the lowering of morals in society today apparently brought on when They took prayer out of school and legalized abortion and wouldn't let law-abiding citizens carry weapons to protect themselves like what worked so well back in the old west when a man took care of

142

himself by his ownself and so didn't get hassled by the sheriff or something.

The essay didn't mention if Tarvis was packing a weapon to protect himself, but Streator had to wonder. Uncle Archie sure was loaded for bear. It wasn't hard to hear Tarvis's essay coming out of Archie's mouth. Certainly Tarvis was under the influence of the old man. So much for positive male role models in the lives of kids raised by single moms.

It was late afternoon, but Streator could barely keep his eyes open. He retreated to his couch and fell asleep under his comforter, dreaming of Tarvis in his classroom with a gun, first threatening Streator, then saving him from Chinese methhead vampires in the seats, no one taking notes.

19.

He was hungry when he awoke a couple of hours later in the afternoon dusk. He made himself a grilled cheese sandwich (he couldn't get himself to call it a *cheese toastie*, even if the locals did) on a hamburger bun and sat at his kitchen table. The American cheese and soft bread tasted as good as anything he'd had in days. He felt alive—the drugs were wearing off, which made various aches and pains worse but made his mind and soul more functional. He was desperate for a shower but didn't want to hassle with wrapping his bandaged leg in plastic.

His neighbor's car pulled into the drive they shared alongside his kitchen. The headlights played across the ceiling and walls. Streator remembered the headlights that ran him off the road and then stared him down in the field. High and narrow. He had seen lights like that before—old Landcruisers. When he had been out there in the daylight, he had seen some old beaten up Landcruiser or something like it off next to the meth-lab barn, down the dirt lane running north from Tarvis's corner. It had to have been that old Landcruiser out in the dark that night he wrecked.

And whose Landcruiser? Had to have been brother Duane's. The rattling tin can sound it made as it tore off, the same he'd heard in Megan's driveway, had him thinking even at the time, and now after turning it all over for a couple days, he was convinced: Duane had waited for him, then ran him off the road. Then waited but didn't help. In fact, not only didn't he help, there was something threatening about the way those lights inched forward as soon as Streator stepped from his wrecked car. What would Duane have done if Streator had approached closer? Run him down. Finished him off. He'd been listening in the kitchen. He knew Streator was getting too close to the truth.

Now Tarvis's wreck became clearer. How could an old-lady driver like Tarvis take that corner so fast? If he was run off the road, as Streator had been. Would be easier in the summer to lie in wait on the dirt drive, with the high corn blocking the view. Or maybe he just ran him down from behind. Either way, out into the field he went tumbling. Except that he always wore his seatbelt, and that car was a tank.

Surely Tarvis survived the wreck, just as Streator had. But his body was found closer to the road with massive internal injuries. He would've walked away from the crash. Toward the road, toward what he thought was his friend in a Landcruiser. And then run down before he knew it. What kind of crime scene investigation would ol' Deputy Donaldson and his buddies do for a wreck like that? For a victim like that? Would've all looked pretty obvious. Wouldn't get much in all that downed corn. Any extra tire marks would be attributed to the paramedics or ambulance—the first responder to Streator's wreck was a fire truck that drove right out to his car. The ambulance was right behind, and a tow truck later. An autopsy—if there was one—wouldn't likely tell the difference between an LTD rolling over him and an old Landcruiser running him down.

That paranoid schizo Duane could have had it in for Tarvis easily; drug deals go south all the time in big nasty ways. And Tarvis, like Streator, knew too much. Maybe he said too much. Tarvis's friend Sammy—T-Bone—was outside Streator's open office door when Tarvis was describing how Gunther was going to get it. Sammy was not at all happy with Tarvis. And a couple of days later, Tarvis was dead.

He found Tyrone Bonafile's home address in the Kickapoo records. A street in the Burke Hole area. A few blocks from Tarvis. In the local paper archives, the only mentions he could find for Tyrone were in some sports stories from a few years back. Phyllis was right, he had been a star baseball player at Truman High, even set some home run record. But there was a small news item about a Tremarias Bonafile who was arrested in a drug raid, also in the Burke Hole neighborhood. Weapons charge as well. Phyllis had mentioned a brother in trouble. It was all coming together.

He remembered that Det. Ramage had never returned his call. It was well past five o'clock, but he figured it wouldn't hurt to leave him another message. He found his card and called. He was surprised when Ramage answered the phone.

Ramage apologized for not getting back to him earlier—
"We're all a little swamped here, all hands on deck, you know,
when you get a high profile case in a small department."

"Sure, sure, I understand," Streator said, "I won't take your
time, just wondering if you can help me a bit, I remember how
helpful you were on Staff Development Day . . ." He gave him his
story of his little buddy he was worried about because he had been
running with Tarvis and this guy Ty Bonafile, T-Bone, sometimes
called Sammy, a story getting more convoluted with each telling.

"Tarvis Conner? No, I can tell you that name was not on our
list of known gang individuals. Ty Bonafile, that name sounds
familiar, didn't he play ball at Truman? We sent up a Tre Bonafile,
must have been three or four years ago, maybe they're related, but
to the best of my knowledge he was never referenced as T-Bone."

Not what Streator had expected or hoped for. "Hmm,
interesting, that's good news for my little buddy—but now, some
of these guys I know worked out at the truck stop, at the Subway,
and I remembered you said you made a lot of drug busts there."

"That's all out-of-state traffic out there, just passing through,
nothing local. Wait—Tarvis that little kid with the braids, kind of
hyper?"

"Yeah, I guess so."

"Yeah, I remember him. I bought a lot of sandwiches there.
He was a funny guy, always busting my chops about a ticket he
got for loud music. No, you got nothing to worry about if your guy
was hanging with him."

"You're sure?"

"You get a nose for these things, you can tell the kids getting
messed up. And really, after our big multi-agency task force a few
years ago, we broke down all the real organized gang activity."

"No Vice Lords?"

"A few. Not like five years ago. Now, we're seeing a little
spike in some local teen crews, 'squads,' they call themselves,
there's the Brick Squad out of Truman High, but they are definitely
low-level wannabes, a little mob action, no weapons we've seen
yet. Maybe your guy is getting hooked up with them."

"Selling drugs?"

"They may be moving a little weed in the high school

bathrooms, not much more."

"What about meth?"

"Meth? With the Brick Squad? That's way out of their league."

"No, I meant with the gangs in general, like the Vice Lords."

"Sure, I suppose, I'm not hearing anything specific about meth, but they'll move anything that sells, and meth sure sells. But like I said, Vice Lords and the others aren't well organized now around here. You gotta know what you're doing to make meth for very long and stay alive."

Again, not what Streator was hoping to hear. "Well, thanks very much, that's very reassuring."

"No problem. Unless, hey," he laughed, "if your guy was messing around on New Years, maybe he's starting up a V2K Squad!"

"Is that, what, a real thing?"

"No, not really," Ramage said with a chuckle. "Just this Internet thing going around, a joke really. Hey, I gotta go . . ."

Streator took one more stab: "Say, one last question: how about a guy named Bruckner, Duane Bruckner? Any history with him I should know about?"

"Bruckner?" Ramage's tone changed. He paused for a minute. "Your guy hanging with that loser?"

"No, I don't think so, but he may be a friend of a friend."

"I'd have to check, but if he's who I think he is and we're talking about the same individual, he is one scary-ass loser that I would not want anyone I know to associate with in his circle of influence."

Streator wasn't sure what to make of all this—it was all more complicated than he had figured. The possibility of gang activity didn't seem as great but was not out of the question and he couldn't help but think there were, literally, signs of such; the possibility of dangerous drug trafficking from Bruckner of Hackydale seemed very high. But the connection to Gunther? A rich old perv dying of AIDS?

Streator turned on the television for a distraction but ended up checking the six o'clock news to see if there was anything new about Gunther. The local station had little more than Streator had already heard from Det. Cruiks. The police were talking to Gunther's home healthcare attendant, whose name they wouldn't release and who apparently was a holiday fill-in. Graceland Nursing and Home Health Care had no comment.

Graceland. Tarvis's aunt worked for Graceland, in their nursing home, not home health. But that was still close. She would probably know this person. Another reason he should talk to her.

But Alberta wasn't seeing anyone. The woman at her door had made that clear.

All that fuss at Alberta's house.

Couldn't a Graceland CNA also do some home healthcare for the same company?

Reporters often know more than they can say in print, Streator thought. None of his students had ever become a journalist or ever made a profession out of writing, except Derrick fuckhead Doolin. But he did know the guy on his TV screen yukking it up with the weather woman: NewsWatch 15's Don Hamel, the local anchorman. He lived at the end of Streator's block and taught morning speech classes part-time at Kickapoo. Hamel was about Streator's age and also hadn't managed to make his way up to a bigger market. When Streator and Roni had just the one car, he used to bum rides from Hamel. He wasn't a bad fellow, despite his perfect brown hair and crisp shirts. Decent company for a ride: they would rip through ten topics of conversation in a fifteen minute drive to school.

He would have to wait until after the news, when Hamel came home for dinner, he remembered. In the summer he often saw him, still in his orangish make-up, playing with his kids on the sidewalk between the early and late news shows. Streator kept watch out his window until he saw Hamel's black Camry go by. He decided to take some air and hobbled down the street. He was finding that the chats rambled more freely in person than on the phone.

Hamel's wife answered the door holding a baby. She smiled when she saw him and touched his arm. "Henry! Good to see you! It's been forever!" She ushered him in out of the cold into their noisy living room, the TV blaring in the corner, two more kids running around her feet, the debris of a pink and blue Fisher Price tornado scattered around the room.

Streator felt unexpectedly embarrassed to see her. He had included versions of Hamel in his novel, and more prominently, his wife, Nora. She was in her late thirties, sparkly blue eyes, a pleasant round face and a quick laugh, brown curly hair with massive bangs. She always looked tired to Streator and a bit worn-out in her baggy sweatshirts, maybe a bit chunky from three kids in five years. In his novel he moved her next door to Rosetta, took off a few years and a few pounds, got rid of the kids, kept the nursing-sized breasts, and invented a torrid affair: she was so afraid of getting caught she wouldn't let Rosetta come over except at ten o'clock on weeknights, but then she would tear off her clothes as soon as she saw her husband's face on the news, and they would have a quick bang with hubby's voice low in the corner of the bedroom, his face peering out at them (which Rosetta thought was weird but to have this tigger bouncing on his lap with those boobs in his face he'd let her husband watch in person) and always only at her house in case he called from the news desk at commercials, which he did a few times and she had to explain her breathlessness as rushing up from the basement with the laundry; by the time she heard "And finally tonight . . ." and the cutesy story about a water-skiing squirrel, she was hurrying Rosetta to finish and rushed him out the door as Letterman's theme music started . . . A good scene, Medina had told him.

Hamel came in the living room eating a sandwich, his face still orange, his tie tucked into his dress shirt. When Streator was writing his novel, he had been so desperate for material and so frantic to finish, it hadn't really occurred to him that he would inevitably face off with all the lives he had strip-mined and ridiculed. Recalling that sex scene now, he could hardly look at Nora or Don and was sure he was turning red as he stammered through his story about his wrecked car, his banged-up leg, his need for a ride to the before-school meetings the next week, hoping that Hamel hadn't heard that Streator was no longer teaching.

"No problemo," Hamel said, and though the kids were now hanging on his leg and he was clearly pressed for time, Streator kept him chatting, finally leading around to the Gunther story and how badly the at-home nurse must feel and how lots of his students worked for Graceland. "So I'm sure I'll hear all about it from Alberta, she sure can't keep her mouth shut."

"Alberta?" Hamel said. "Alberta Jameson? She's one of your students?"

"Yeah, you know her?"

"Uh, I know *of* her," Hamel said with a little smile. "I don't think you'll be hearing much from her—Graceland's lawyers would have a shit fit."

"Oops—so you're saying it would be pretty awkward if I asked her about it?"

"You didn't hear it from me, but let's just say I don't think you'll get much of a chance to ask her much of anything, if you know what I'm saying."

"I hear ya. Mum's the word." He couldn't believe he'd said that. He hurried out into the cold. He was glad to get out of that living room and hoped that when he said goodbye to Nora without looking her in the eyes, he hadn't been staring at her chest.

So his hunch was correct, he thought as he walked back home. Alberta Jameson was the home health worker who was supposed to be watching Gunther on New Year's Eve. Not the regular worker, but a fill in. Wasn't that just too convenient. Come to think of it, Uncle Archie had made some cryptic comment about Alberta needing God on her side now; Streator thought at the time that Archie was just talking generally about their messed-up family. That would explain why no one would let him in at her house. She was the last person to see Frederick Gunther alive. Streator could just imagine the holy wrath of the Gunther family's lawyers coming down on her, let alone the police and the press.

Now he was getting somewhere. Now he was sure he was right on top of the whole truth. What must have happened? The good Christian woman, she gets herself a little tipsy and out goes the old guy . . . Or—or she wasn't drunk at all. She let this happen. Or she *made* this happen. Tarvis knew it was going to happen.

But that was a detail that had been bugging Streator for a long time: in August, Tarvis knew about a hit on Gunther that was planned for January. Why would they wait that long? There had to be something important, something symbolic, about New Years 2000, some message they were sending with that date.

Det. Ramage had joked about a "V2K" squad. Something about "V2K" was familiar to Streator. He had seen those letters before, could picture them typed out, Times New Roman, 12 point font, in a cluttered sentence . . . He found Tarvis's original plot outline on the filched disk. He had written "the alarm don't work because V2K took it out." Streator had assumed it was a typo, there were so many, but Y and V aren't very close together on the keyboard.

A long, slow search on the Internet put some half-light on what Ramage must have been talking about. Streator found a sort of end-of-millennium meets Keyser Soze conspiracy mentioned in bits and pieces in different whackjob right-wing message boards and websites but had trouble putting it together; it was always referenced as if the readers were well aware of its accuracy and needed no explanation. But apparently the black-helicopter crowd had it in their heads that on New Year's Day, when the Y2K bug crashed prison security systems, the doors would swing wide open, sending tens of thousands of pissed-off Negro criminals swarming the streets. V2K, a vast underground cabal of young black men, apparently the youth brigade of Vice Lords and other street gangs—clearly identified by the "Our Time" motto already tattooed on thousands of black youth in and out of prison, and throughout the NBA—would lead the rampage, taking advantage of the wide-spread chaos of crashed communication systems, collapsed financial markets, broken electronic locks and security systems. Their first target? Rich white folks, of course, but the message was clear—ALL white America better lock and load!

It was all too crazy. But maybe—maybe Tarvis and some of his friends had bought it, were starting their own little V2K revolution. Maybe the rumors were fueled by some hint of something real, or it was becoming a self-fulfilling prophecy amongst little wannabe gang-bangers. Earn your colors on New Year's 2000 by taking out rich whitey?

He had to make himself stop. Stop and think. Back up. He ached to go for a long walk, as he used to do when he was writing and had confused himself, walk for a few miles through dark neighborhoods and let the cold clear his head. But the short stroll to Hamel's house had left his leg achy. He put on his parka and sat on his front steps. It didn't take long for his boogers to freeze.

Back up. Everything he knew about Conner/Lloyds, and everything he knew about Gunther: he had to draw the connection.

Alberta Jameson and Angela Conner were sisters. In her essay, Angela said her cousin "got treatment" because of guardian angels. And Tarvis had mentioned guardian angels bailing out someone with AIDS contracted by drug use. So this cousin, that would be Alberta's cousin, too, and Travis's second cousin, and what to Archie? His granddaughter? Great niece? Everyone in town said the Gunthers were paying off somebody to keep shut about the old man giving somebody AIDS. Mora at the hospital said it was a young black girl. Just like back in the day when Gunther was the randy son of the plantation owner.

More. There had to be something tying the two families together more tightly. He went back inside to his computer and searched "Lloyd and Gunther." Up came a ton of hits, all unhelpful, as far as a quick scan could tell him.

He returned to the newspaper archives. After a long search, he found it. A thirty-year-old photo of the dedication of the viaduct under the railroad tracks that let Frederick Gunther into his factory office without being stopped by a train. Gunther in the back seat of his big black Lincoln, window opening, a big hearty wave for the ceremonial first drive through the viaduct. And who was that behind the wheel, also window open, also a big wave? ". . . *driven by long-time chauffeur Archie Lloyd."* Streator had to read it again for the significance to hit him. Archie Lloyd, at least at one time, was a daily companion of Frederick Gunther's. Now he was shaking with excitement. Now he was getting close. He could smell it.

He poked around on the Gunther Hall website but found nothing about Archie Lloyd. The site didn't really list staff, however, probably for security and confidentiality, and what was the chance of a company listing a janitor anyway? That must've been something of a step down for ol' Archie, Streator figured, from Frederick Gunther's personal driver to a hospital janitor. A falling out? Dereliction of duty? What kind of resentment must he be holding on to? And yet, whatever had happened, he was still in a Gunther circle.

He remembered that Gunther Hall did have another clientele: drug addicts. Rehab. Surely the girl with AIDS had spent time there.

The website also described a relatively new venture: Gunther NEST, which stood for Nurturing Environment for a Successful Transition. A half-way house, a state-approved transitional facility for parolees. He'd bet anything that's where Angela Connor was safely nestled.

The girl with AIDS, Archie Lloyd, Angela Conner, and the Gunthers: the locus was Gunther Hall. A place of secrets, where you took your problems. If this were a movie, he'd just grab his flashlight, head on over, break into an office, and the answers would come up in the first file drawer he opened. The reality was tens of thousands of personal files, thousands of personnel files, computers with passwords and firewalls and all that stuff.

So he'd just have to go in the front door in the light of day. See what someone would blab. So far that had been the best investigative technique he had come up with.

He was surprised to see it was after midnight. Searching with his slow computer and even slower connection had been so interminable, he hadn't realized how many hours he had been sitting there. He wished he were out at Kickapoo with his fast office computer and T1 connection. He realized that may have been the first time he had ever wished he had been at school instead of at home. He took more Vicodin and crawled off to bed.

20.

Wednesday morning he had trouble once again getting himself upright and more trouble busting his wombly-bubble. He was out of coffee, and cereal, and bread, and milk, and everything. He couldn't remember the last time he had been to Kroger. He couldn't figure out how he was going to get groceries home with just his motorcycle. A backpack?

He found one last tea bag in a box of Earl Grey that Roni had left behind. Streator had always thought that weakly flavored hot water was a poor excuse for a breakfast drink but made a cup anyway, to warm himself.

When he was more fully functioning, he took stock of what he needed to do. Some time that day he should poke around Gunther Hall, see what he could find. But it would help to know more about what or who he was looking for. He wished he knew more about the Conners, Lloyds, some cousin with AIDS. Alberta would know, but she wasn't going to talk to him. Angela was who he needed to talk to; he was counting on finding her in the Gunther NEST. Their website was vague on visiting hours and procedures— no Approved Visitor's List mentioned!—but it looked like he couldn't get in there until evening, unless he came up with some other story, like inquiring about services they offered.

He wrapped his leg in plastic and took a long hot shower. Leaning against the tiles, he meditated on his options. How to find information about a girl who died from AIDS in a town this small: hospital personnel would know. Some of the Kickapoo nursing faculty took shifts at the hospital, and they were as blabby as anyone, but still they were unlikely to spill a name or any details to him, not with a confidentiality issue as touchy as AIDS. Same with former students now working healthcare, like Mora in the ER. He thought of social workers he knew, clergy, cops—he couldn't think of how to pry information out of any of them.

He decided to kick it old school: ask a reference librarian.

On the way to the library downtown he stopped for lunch at McDonald's because it was closest and fastest and the coffee was hot enough for a lawsuit. He immediately regretted it. The indigestion hit him before he made it to the library. He couldn't imagine how he had lived on that food in college.

The reference librarian was an eager beaver but perplexed by Streator's task. He was a scrawny little guy with an unfortunately large nose he tried to hide with an unfortunately large black moustache. "You're trying to find the name of someone who died of AIDS in 1999, but you don't know exactly when?"

"Right. Though I guess it could've been before 1999."

"In this county?"

"Yes. Well, maybe. I hope so."

The librarian frowned and tapped on his computer. "The thing is," he said as he searched, "county death records are over at the court house, and they are so understaffed, they are not very . . . helpful . . . especially for just, you know, this kind of browsing . . . they are quick to remind anyone who comes in that they are not a library . . . nor are they librarians. And their records probably aren't indexed by cause of death anyway. So that leaves the *Dispatch-Telephone*'s obituaries . . . but they are not well indexed at all, in fact their whole online archive is, pardon my French, horseshit, the search function as clunky and unhelpful as they come."

"Tell me about it."

"But I think that's your best bet. Probably means plowing through them one at a time. You can use one of our computers, or we've got last year's full set on paper over in Periodicals."

He wasn't missing old-school research enough to flip through a few hundred yellowing, moldy newspapers. At least the library's computers and connection were faster than he had at home.

The librarian was wrong about the search functioning of the obituary records: it wasn't clunky, it was nonexistent. He could search by name—which he didn't have—or he could search by year, names listed alphabetically. He started with "Lloyd" and "Conner" and "Jameson" in 1999 and then 1998, hoping for good luck with the cousin's name, but no likely candidates came up. So he went back to "A" 1999 and started skimming.

Because he had in his head a young drug-addicted prostitute, at first he limited his attention to women under forty, but then realized he had no idea how old she had been. So he went back and only eliminated women over sixty. No obituary ever mentioned AIDS, as he expected; most mentioned no cause of death at all. He realized, too, he had no idea of how past-tense Angela and Tarvis were talking in their essays; could've been years. He went back three years. He could definitively eliminate many with family connections or life stories that obviously didn't fit but was still left with a long list of unconfirmed but possible.

He was hoping for an obituary matching the parameters with a list of survived-by or preceded-in-death-by family that would include a Lloyd-Conner-Jameson he recognized. He found none.

Except one. Except that it didn't. "Misha Dawkins, 23." Very little other information. Preceded in death by her mother, Harriet; survived by a son, Terrence. No life details. No other family listed. But services were at Broadway Temple of the Living God, the Conner's church; memorial donations were requested to The Glaser Foundation. A quick search showed that the full name was the Elizabeth Glaser Pediatric AIDS Foundation.

The problem was that Misha Dawkins died in November of 1999. Angela's and Tarvis's essays mentioning their cousin's death were written in spring of 1999, though come to think of it, Tarvis never actually said she had died.

Maybe there was some sort of mistake, his or theirs. Since it was the only name he had, he found a quiet corner of the lobby and called Broadway Temple of the Living God from his cell phone.

Sister Bernice, the church secretary, was very pleasant when Streator asked if she knew where Misha Dawkins had been buried, as he was a friend who had missed the funeral and in fact had just found out about her passing and wanted to leave her flowers.

"Bless your heart, child," Sister Bernice said, "I don't know that I know that, I'll look in the files, I recollect she might could've been cremated. Sister Alberta handled poor Misha's service, I can ask her . . ."

"Alberta? Jameson?"

"Yessir, bless her heart, poor sweetie lost her little angel and insisted taking it all on, we tried to tell her, Sister, you got to let God and us help you, sweetheart—you know Alberta?"

"Yes, ma'am. I didn't know she was family."

"Well, we all God's children, ain't that right, Misha one of Alberta's Gunther Hall kids, from when she worked there? Alberta tell you about it, better than I can. She'll be at Bible study tonight, why don't you come round, I'm sure she want to know someone so fond of little Misha."

"I just might do that," Streator said. A little prayer certainly wouldn't hurt him now.

The timeline was way messed up, but that had to be the right girl. Misha, Alberta, Archie—all at Gunther Hall. He was sure Angela was there right now. He had to find her. Gunther Hall must somehow connect them all to Gunther himself.

He noticed that the Local History Room was open, but only for a little while longer. He poked around the dusty books, wondering if there was a way to confirm the rumors that Lloyds were Gunther's throwaways.

The blue-haired volunteer staffing the room was little help, but she pointed him to the wall of city directories. These didn't seem to be government records but culled from those records by a private publishing company, one for each year, each listing heads of households, addresses, members and ages of each household, occupations. He found Albert Gunther, manufacturer, and his five children, including Frederick, on Vapor Springs Road, no number, until 1942; then the address was listed as 1847 Vapor Springs Cove Road, which must've been when the city finally annexed the area, assigned street numbers, and standardized wobbly road names. Frederick disappeared off the family listing in 1944, which must have been when he entered the Army. There were no Lloyds listed until 1943, and then there was a John Lloyd, millwright; wife, Bea; and three children, Esther, Samuel, and Rosalie. The following year the sixteen-year-old eldest had moved out but a baby Thomas had joined the family. Interestingly, the address was Vapor Springs Road, probably too far out still for a number, but still not likely to have any connection to Gunther. This was the only Lloyd listed through 1954, when the run of directories ended. Any Gunther kids named Lloyd would be too young then to be listed by heads of households, and the directory of course had no listings for Gunther Hall for Wayward Girls.

"Do you know anything about these directories?" Streator asked the volunteer when she came over to tell him it was time to close the room. "They don't seem to be official records—do you have any idea how accurate or complete they are?"

"Well, my daddy had a little grocery store on Walnut Street, this was back, oh, 1930s, and he always kept one behind the counter, they did a lot of home delivery, you see. So I guess they were kind of like a phone book for businesses and such before you had phone books. But no, I don't know how accurate or complete they'd be."

"I'm wondering particularly about African-American families."

"Well, you know, I pretty much doubt coloreds were in there much at all."

He decided that Angela Conner was his most likely way into Gunther Hall, if she were there. He was certain she was. Gunther Hall's visiting hours didn't begin until six o'clock. No mention of a pre-approval list. He tried to rest, watch TV, eat some canned soup. But he felt like he was waiting for his first date.

The temperature plummeted when the sun went down. Just before six, he bundled up as best he could and rode over to Gunther Hall. He paused at the bottom of the long driveway, so cold he hurt all over. The grounds weren't fenced, but he could see a lighted security shack up the drive near the parking lot. Streator hoped it would be unmanned, or at least that any checks would be pro forma. He rode up the hill slowly, trying to remember the story he had concocted.

As he approached the guard shed, he saw a sign that said, "All Visitors Please Check In With Security." There actually was a bar lowered across the drive. In Streator's head an image flashed of gunning his bike, crashing through the rail, or peeling off across the lawn around it like Steve McQueen, and then . . . well, then nothing. Making polite inquiries at the front desk.

A baby-faced kid in a blue parka and a blue Ellets Security

hat slowly slid open a window as Streator stopped at the gate. "Can I help you?" he said wearily. He didn't bother standing up or putting down the book he was reading or turning down the death metal on his radio.

"Yeah, sure," Streator said, "I just came to visit a friend."

"Sorry, visiting hours are Sundays one to five."

"Really? I thought the website said six to eight on weekdays."

"That's just for a couple of the juvenile programs."

"Ah, I thought she said it would be okay tonight, I think they gave her permission or something because I couldn't make it Sunday." He was feeling panicky, making too many mistakes, telling lies too easy to check.

The kid frowned, put down his book, and picked up a clipboard. He scanned it for a moment. He looked familiar. His hat was pulled low over his eyes and the bill was bent in a tight curve "Sorry. You're not on the Special Authorization list."

Enough with the fucking lists already! Streator bit his lip and composed himself. He noticed that the guard had checked the list without asking his name. He does know me, he realized. "Really? Not on the list? That's surprising." The kid looked at him blankly. A face was coming, a class . . . "So, I can't just, like, go up and check?"

The kid froze him with a stare for a moment and then picked up a phone. "Yeah, this is Mike, front gate," his voice impatient and self-important. "You have a Streator down for Spec Aut?" He listened for a moment, waiting, even picking up his book again. "Okay, thanks," he said finally. "Sorry," he said, still scowling. Must have really pissed him off, Streator thought.

The hat. The kid from 101 with the KKK essay he ripped up. "No, okay, I understand, Mike, must've been a mix-up somewhere, I could've sworn she said that in the NEST program, you could come later."

"Wait, NEST? That ain't even on this campus."

"The website said—isn't this Gunther Park Place?"

"Yeah, but NEST is out on Gunther Parkway. Near Kickapoo."

"Ah. Guess I read it wrong. My bad. I bet that happens a lot, what with those street names and all." He started to say, *Guess I better read the addresses when I'm not so strung out on drugs!* but was smart enough to keep his mouth shut.

Mike slid the window shut and picked up his book. Streator recognized the yellow cover. *The Scorpio Aspect* by Derrick Doolin.

Gunther NEST was a two-story duplex in an area of apartment buildings. No sign out front, but they sure wouldn't advertise to the neighbors who was living there.

A stern, thick woman answered the door. She kept the storm door closed between them and eyed him suspiciously. She had a pager on her belt and wore the short spiky hair in fashion amongst the radical feminist critics back in Streator's grad school a decade earlier.

Streator asked for Angela Conner. Several women watching TV in the living room behind her turned their heads. The woman at the door asked him what he wanted her for.

"I wanted to talk to her about her son, I was his teacher," Streator said.

A thin little woman jumped off the couch and came quickly to the door. "Skyler? What about Skyler?" She had blonde hair in cornrows, couldn't have been more than 25, and looked frantic.

"No, Tarvis," Streator said.

"Tarvis?" the young woman said, still worried.

"You know this guy, Angie?" the first woman said.

"No—not Skyler? Skyler's okay?"

"I'm looking for Angela Conner, mother of Tarvis Conner, I was his teacher at Kickapoo . . ."

"My boy's in the third grade, I don't know any Tarvis," the mother said.

"You got the wrong place, bud," the first woman said and shut the door.

That just didn't make any sense, Streator thought as he drove off. He obviously had the wrong half-way house, but the name . . . He would have to backtrack and figure out where he went wrong. Damn. He really wanted to talk to Angela Conner.

160

Streator waited for traffic to clear on Gunther Parkway to make a left, toward home—when the image of Mike's hat and jacket came to him and a slim possibility presented itself. Streator turned right, toward Kickapoo Community College.

He made it to the school stiff and shaking and let himself in to the darkened building. After hours on days when classes weren't in session, he was supposed to sign in by the main entrance, but he didn't bother. Yesterday, he had managed to slip past Mrs. Forney without giving back his office key. He sat shivering in his office with the door closed and the light on, switched on his computer, and pulled up the Gunther Hall website again. Yes, he had remembered correctly. And now, if he was lucky, he would just have to wait.

He poked around on other Gunther sites while he waited, rereading articles from the newspaper archives, looking for any other connection he might have missed. Flipping through the company history page again on the Gunther Mills website, he saw the family picture of the Gunthers by the old mill, the same photo from the local history book. In the background was the family home, a squat square one-and-a-half story farm house, big front porch, next to a wood line. Something struck him about that house. Looked like thousands of other houses around there from early in the 20th century. But how it sat on the lot, the two upstairs dormers, the big front porch . . . He printed off a copy. Then he took a pen and drew half walls and storm windows on the front porch. Spitting image of Archie Lloyd's house.

Millhouse Estates Road. Millhouse Estates across the street. The location the stories described would put it right there, before all the new postwar housing. The mill was long since torn down, but this was the Gunther's old place. How could he have missed it earlier? He hadn't jotted down any notes in the library, not thinking he was on to anything important, but he remembered Vapor Springs Road. At some point they must have changed the name when all the new development went in. He wished he could get back into the historical room at the library and study old street maps. Still, there was no doubt. Archie Lloyd lived in Frederick Gunther's former home.

Streator jumped when his lock rattled behind him and the

door swung open. He'd been waiting for this, but still it startled him. "Oh, hey, professor, how you doing," the security guard said, "just checking, saw the light."

It never failed: whenever he worked late, someone from security—usually this guy, Smitty— unlocked his door without knocking, scaring the crap out of Streator.

"Hey, Smitty, how's it going, just catching up on a few things." He wondered if Smitty knew that Streator was no longer an employee of Kickapoo Community College and should no longer have a key. He had never struck Streator as the fastest gun in the posse. Smitty was short, a little paunchy, with white hair and thick glasses. He wore a white uniform shirt and blue cap, the thick square-front kind favored by truckers and farmers, but instead of a seed or implement company logo, it said "Ellets Security" in a badge. Just like in his picture on the Gunther Hall website, where his grandfatherly smile at the guard gate was a comforting reassurance on the "Security and Privacy" page.

"Moving out?" Smitty asked. He was apparently quick enough to notice the empty shelves.

"Yep, you know. . ."

"Didn't know you still had a key," Smitty said.

So ol' Smitty and the entire security apparatus at Kickapoo was much more on the ball than Streator had ever given them credit for. "Yeah, I hadn't finished clearing my stuff out, I'm still officially on the clock for a few days I think."

"We got first of the year, but it's always a little loose for faculty, ain't it. Just be sure to turn the key in . . . and now don't be taking the computer or nothing!" He laughed.

"Computer, stapler, phone," Streator pointed out, "just like I found them."

"All righty then. Sorry to see you go—what're you going to be doing?"

"Oh, I got a few irons in the fire," Streator said. "Interviewed over at Gunther Hall for a counselor spot, still waiting to hear. Say, didn't I see you over there the other day?"

"Maybe. They rotate me over there a few nights a month. But unless you were interviewing New Year's Eve, you wouldn't have seen me anytime soon."

"New Year's Eve? That can't be much fun."

"Oh, I always volunteer, good double-time. Not like me and Irma's going out on the town. It's quiet there, hardly anyone in or out. Got me a radio and a heater . . . not like all the walking I do nights here, and driving around the parking lots."

"Say, you know a guy out there, Archie Lloyd?"

"Oh yeah, everyone knows Uncle Archie. Practically runs the place. Thinks so, anyway."

"That'd be Archie all right!" Streator said with a laugh.

"He a friend of yours?"

"No, a student, way back." He was getting to be an awful liar.

"Well, that musta been some fun," Smitty said, shaking his head ruefully.

"I'll say," Streator said, picking up the tone. "So he's his ownself out there too, I take it?"

"Well, let's just say there are the rules, you understand, and then there's the Uncle Archie rules."

"That can't be easy in your job then."

"No sir, not a bit, especially when you ain't one of his full-time compadres out there, you understand what I'm saying."

"Sure."

"Like just this last shift, on New Years, who's coming back in the gate at 12:40 in the a.m. with some pretty little colored gal, obviously a client, and he's giving me grief because she ain't on my list—I don't make the rules, if she ain't on my list . . ."

"Puts you in a bind, sure . . ."

"So he's hopping mad because I call into the desk to get the okay, and they give it of course, he's got buddies everywhere. Hey, I don't make the rules, I tell him, but he's giving me the what-for in ways I don't appreciate, not one bit, let me tell you."

"Been there," Streator said. "Try giving him a low grade."

"He's a piece of work, all righty," Smitty said. "And between you and me and the mice in the walls, they don't get a handle on that guy, they're looking at some major trouble." He gave Streator a knowing look, "I mean big time, I mean, I know those girls in there been around the block a few times but even still they ain't most of them 18."

"Yeah? I take it that wasn't the first time a girl was in his car?"

Streator guessed.

Smitty sniffed. "Now what do you think. Guy like that. You get out there—" Streator was momentarily confused, then remembered his job interview—"you best keep an eye on ol' Uncle Archie."

21.

So Uncle Archie was bringing pretty little colored gals in and out of Gunther Hall at all hours for who knows how many years, Streator thought on his icy ride home. Didn't take a lot of brains to figure out what that was all about.

He passed Family Video, and something clicked. He made a U-turn.

He hobbled straight across the store to the Adult Room in the back, not caring which of his former students saw him going in there. On a Wednesday night, he had the place to himself anyway. He was momentarily dazzled by the bright colors of the movie cases, the pinks and reds and flesh spilling out everywhere. He hadn't been in one of these rooms since college, when they were tucked away behind covered windows on the seedy side of town, where quiet grungy men and rowdy college students were the only patrons. It took a minute to get his bearings, but amidst the orgy of parts exploding around him, he detected a system of little handwritten cards on each shelf: "Amateur," "Hardcore," "Lesbian," "S & M," "Barely Legal Teens" —he wondered if it was giggly little Amanda's cutesy handwriting he was reading— and there, "Ethnic."

Most in that section featured big black men or little Asian girls, but he found the title of one he had noticed in Archie's pile: *Bang That Funky Poontang, White Boy.* He saw the titles Amanda had read to him when he returned Tarvis's rentals: the *Hot Brown Sugar* series and more *Ivory Does Ebony.*

He climbed back on his motorcycle and rode toward home. Curious flavors of porn for Archie or Tarvis. They must have been for someone else. Some white man with a thing for black women.

Gunther was at Archie's house. No, Gunther was at his *own* house. Probably how Archie got that really expensive home theater system. Certainly how he got the house. Taking care of Gunther's little hideaway, and not just for porn, Streator figured.

Misha Dawkins, the girl who got AIDS from Fred Gunther? She was "one of Alberta's Gunther Hall girls." It was all coming together—Gunther's old driver Archie, probably continuing with one of his duties as a driver, procures Gunther's favorites and brings them not to Gunther's current home, under the watchful eye of Miss Marta, not to some seedy motel or anywhere else he might be recognized, but to Uncle Archie's, the ol' homestead in the sticks. Off his nut, my ass, Streator thought.

Tarvis knew all about it. He was in charge of the porn. Apparently the old farts hadn't figured out the Internet yet. Or maybe they were just old fashioned.

But why the ice skating, Streator thought as he pulled up to a stoplight, almost missing it in his distraction. Out on the lake— why that? And there at the stoplight, staring at the streets around him, a map of the city came to his head, the one from the phone book, stretched over two pages—Streator had little use over the years to look at page two, the south side of the lake, but he had glanced at it before he went over to Archie's. When he had turned off Millhouse Estates Road to Archie's lane, wouldn't he be pointed toward the lake, at least the long cove off the main body, Vapor Springs Cove? Those woods around Archie's house must have been on the bluff over the cove. And here he strained to see the map in his head—on the other side running along the shore, that was Vapor Springs *Cove* Road, he thought, a newer road built after the lake and the cove were created. To be sure, he should pull off and look at a map. Or he could just go out there and see.

He made a quick left and headed south, across town, over the dam, down into the tracts on the south side, over to Millhouse Estates Road, out to Archie's lane. He parked his bike at the end of the lane but left his helmet on because it was the only thing keeping his head and ears thawed, and he was shivering hard already. He pulled out of his pocket the crumpled copy of the old house picture he had printed off. Even in the dark, he could tell it was the same place.

He made his way over the snowy open ground toward the trees, keeping a wide berth from Archie's house to avoid the dogs. His leg was stiff and painful as he limped into the trees and brush and picked his way carefully in the dark. The ground started to slope in front of him, as he knew it would, and he had to go slowly in the snow and dead leaves. He couldn't quite see what he knew would be there, the brush was so thick, so he moved closer to the house where it had been cleared more and edged down the slope carefully.

Through a break in the trees, he saw it, just as he thought: the end of the cove, Vapor Springs Cove, shining frozen white in the moonlight. But more importantly, less than a half mile away on the far shore, brilliantly lit by outdoor lights and two-story windows in the arched living room, shone Frederick Gunther's sprawling estate.

When he was standing on the shore with Det. Cruiks looking out to where Gunther drowned, they had been looking straight across to Uncle Archie's house, the old Gunther home. Probably wouldn't even notice it up on the bluff, back in the trees, if you didn't know it was there. An easy straight shot across the ice, especially if you were an expert skater, even if you were old. And there—yes, long wooden steps from the shore up to Archie's house. Streator made his way over to them, directly behind Archie's house. He could practically see into Gunther's living room from here. Probably been coming over since he was first married, his own little hideaway with Archie, who had easy access to desperate young black girls and whatever else a rich guy needed. A fun time for all.

A panicky thought came to Streator: maybe the horny old goat was just coming on over as usual on New Year's; after all, Archie had a girl waiting for him. Maybe he just fell through the ice. But no—Tarvis. Tarvis knew it was going to happen. He knew how it would look: legs up in a V. No one would fall through the ice head first. He said it would be a sign. And he knew when: New Year's, turn of the century. "Our Time." It was all planned.

He made his way down the long wooden stairs, leaning on a rickety free-standing rail to take the pressure off his stiff leg. Then the rotten rail gave way with a snap and Streator yelped "whoa shit!" before he realized it. He reached for another section as he lost his balance and twenty feet of rail and two posts came snapping and crashing down as he fell into a tangle of dead branches.

He sat in the snowy mess for a second taking a breath. That

was a lot of racket on a snow-quiet night. But Archie's house would be shut up tight. He was probably deaf to boot.

But the dogs sure weren't deaf. He heard them barking wildly inside the house. He saw the back porch lights come on. He heard the back screen door open and the wild barking come flying out. He heard Archie's raspy voice yelling, "Go get 'em, girls, who the hell sneaking around my place, I swear to God . . ."

Streator scrambled to his feet and limped down the stairs as fast as he could, no direction in mind, just away from the advancing dogs. He could hear them snarling as they ran, he could hear Archie cursing, he turned and saw the dogs at full tilt—and then the ground under his feet was transformed, some new kind of world where friction was optional. He realized he had backed out on to the ice of the lake, and he slipped and caught himself with his hands. The dogs kept flying down the hill and Streator found himself unwillingly backing up, shuffling to keep his balance, until he was ten feet or more from the shore, but not far enough for the dogs who came flying out after him with a snarl—and flying right past, their legs in a tangle as they frantically scratched for a grip and slid across the ice. Archie was yelling and Streator was yelling at the dogs and trying to yell at Archie—and then he heard a bang and something kicked up ice not far from his feet—god damn it, the old fucker was shooting at him! He jumped with the crack and nearly lost his balance forward and yelled some more as the dogs tried to circle back, running in place trying to get a grip. Then Streator's shuffling heel caught a clump of hard icy snow and he thought *how the hell could anyone skate on a lake like this that hasn't been cleared of snow* just as he lost his balance and fell hard backwards.

He couldn't get his arms back to catch himself and with his stiff leg he could do nothing but land full force on his back, and his head snapped back and cracked hard. All was hazy from that point on, but the next thing he felt was the shock of very cold water pouring over his face and into his open mouth and then it was darkness and icy cold and dizziness and choking all at once. He had a vague realization that he had cracked the ice when he fell and slid backwards, head first into the hole. His legs kicked for something solid but with his toes up, his heels just banged the ice and broke it more, and he sunk head first backwards, his legs thrashing the air wildly and widely, his arms thrashing over his head but now weighed down by his suddenly soaked parka. But then he did touch something—mud and plant debris, nothing solid to push off of. His head hit the bottom, the foam of the cheap helmet soaked full so he felt like he had a bowling ball on his head. His legs and feet seemed free, kicking in the air widely; he must've only been down three or four feet but he couldn't find anything to kick on to, he couldn't push off the soft bottom, his head felt stuck, his lungs were bursting, and in the icy dark cold of his panic he thought, *my god, a man could die like this* . . .

Then the clear starry night exploded into his face and he gasped for air. Then he was looking into the angry faces of Archie and his barking dogs. Archie had grabbed him by the legs and pulled him up on to his back on solid ice.

Archie sat him on his couch with an old comforter around him. He got him a cup of coffee. Streator's teeth were chattering and his head was foggy.

"You okay?" Archie said, more annoyed than concerned.

"Yeah, I think so."

"Better get your head looked at."

"Yeah, maybe. I'm feeling okay. My helmet."

Archie showed it to him. The back was cracked. "Where'd you get this piece of shit, Toys R Us?"

"I'm okay," Streator said again.

Archie tossed the helmet on to the couch and pulled his gun out of the back waistband of his pants. "Then tell me what the hell you doing snooping round my place for?" Now he was worked up to an angry lather and poked the very large gun at Streator. "You real lucky you ain't dead, professor man, I ain't fucking around, someone comes snooping around my place . . ."

"A little jumpy, aren't you there, Archie?" Streator said, his head throbbing so hard he couldn't even feel frightened.

"Man lives out here by himself he gonna be ready to take care himself."

"Yeah, yeah," Streator said, shutting his eyes, drifting away from Archie, the pain almost like a beer buzz gone very bad, "though I guess I would be too if I had gangbangers using my place to put a hit on someone, they got you pretty spooked, I would be too, they must know, you know," he was rambling but couldn't stop, like his tongue was having an out of body experience.

"What the hell are you talking about? How hard you bash your head?"

"And hell, who knows what they think in the first place about that little side action you were running for Gunther, maybe they didn't approve, maybe they want a little slice, probably one of their own whores you were working on the side . . ."

He could smell cigarettes and beer and when he opened his eyes all he could see was Archie's face: bulging eyeballs, yellowing teeth, a scraggly beard. Then all he noticed was a very large gun barrel way too close to Streator's head. "You coming into my house calling me a pimp? That what I'm hearing?"

"Come on, Archie," Streator had no time or patience for excuses or theatrics, he had a head to get clear and had no idea how he was going to do it, "pretty sweet set up for a janitor," he waved at the room around him.

"Janitor? *Janitor?*"

"I know you were taking girls out of Gunther Hall, all these years I bet, old man Gunther's going out for a midnight skate—sure, yeah, skating his horny ass over the pond to his old homestead, just like in the old days for Gunther, wasn't it."

Archie stood up straight and dropped his gun to his side. His face was as much confused as angry. "So you think, what—you saying I was pimping that girl I brought out on New Year's to Fred Gunther?"

"I'm just saying, I hear a lot of young girls come out of Gunther Hall with you, I'm guessing those addicts get pretty desperate, willing to do about anything—" he had no idea what was coming out of his mouth, he could hardly hear himself with the throbbing— "though you didn't really need to pimp anyone New Year's anyway, did you, I mean, did Gunther even make it up to the house that night? And you're pretty wound up with that gun, aren't you? What, you spooked those Vice Lords or V2K or whoever took out Gunther and took out Tarvis, hell, what's going to keep them from taking you out too . . ."

"What in the *hell* are you talking about?" Archie stood in the middle of the room, all astonishment.

"Come on, Tarvis told me . . . some of it anyway, the rest wasn't that hard to figure out, if I can do it the police will pretty quick."

"Tarvis told you *what*?" Archie said, beyond exasperation.

"He told me exactly how Gunther was going to get it, four months before it happened. Look, I know Tarvis was running meth in from the county to Burke Hole, I know the Vice Lords control all that, so I know Tarvis was running with some real bad boys." Here he could feel himself slipping away again, his tongue just a release valve for his teeming brain, as if he were back in his downstairs room at his computer, or up writing on his walls, Archie a distant vision. "And I know that Gunther gave that girl AIDS, that must've really pissed you all off—or maybe her V2K posse back in the hood found their target—so they set up New Years Eve, I'm thinking maybe you didn't even know, or maybe you did and didn't give a shit . . ."

"Who in the hell you talking about? What girl with AIDS?"

"Angela wrote about her, Misha, she was a cousin, so she'd be a Lloyd too . . ."

"Angela wrote about Misha? Where?"

"In her essay at Keller, I've seen it."

"What essay? Why they have her write a goddamn essay?"

"Kickapoo classes up there."

"Why the hell she be taking classes up there? What the fuck you talking about?"

"They all do, looks good on their record, gets them out earlier. . ."

"Gets them out?"

"You'd be amazed what students will tell an English teacher— hell, that was Tarvis's problem, he knew, he heard what was going to happen New Year's Eve either from you or his Vice Lord boys, he was too dumb to keep his mouth shut, he was going to write about it in his class assignment, maybe he thought they were just talking and would never really do it. But that Sammy guy—T-Bone or whatever—he overheard him talking to me, and I know he's deep in the Vice Lords or V2K or whatever, and now they're really pissed. So Tarvis has himself a pretty convenient accident—you probably didn't even know that did you, same way I had an accident, his meth friends run him off the road and then run him over in that field, I know how they did it, they almost got me too, I'm surprised mine didn't come earlier, they knew I knew . . ."

"What the hell?"

"Then come New Years, Alberta—she was in on this too, wasn't she, she's a Lloyd, she's ticked about that AIDS girl, is that her niece? I can't keep it straight. She knows Gunther infected her, doesn't give a shit he's making some payoff, who knows what that's about, why does Gunther care about some ghetto crack whore—but she's a Lloyd, so maybe she's blood to him. So you bring that girl up here from Gunther Hall, Alberta's the fill in nurse, 'lets' him or helps him relive his old tomcatting ways, sends him across the ice, on back home, just like the old days, and then someone at this end—you? A few V2K? You get him steered up the creek with a few well placed shots, I know what that's like, don't I, up where the ice is thin and the mud stays soft from the springs, yeah I know what that's like, and son of a bitch if we don't got one dead billionaire and some sweet sweet ghetto justice for The Man. Can't tell it's not an accident, even the V2K aren't dumb enough to take credit for a hit like that, as much as they'd like to brag, but they got to leave a little calling card so at least their homies know—those legs up in that V . . ."

Here his rambling started sliding in his head with memory so he didn't know if he was talking or thinking, he had written about all of this, it was already in his head, not exactly the same—didn't appear to be any South American drug cartel involved, but Jesus he was close—drugs, prostitution, street gangs, pornography, old factory boss tomcatting all over town, obviously big money buying silence or at least a wink wink nudge nudge from police and city officials—Streator had imagined it all already—which meant he was the fucking Zebra storyteller! And he had bagged himself one hell of a Siamese cat!

"Hold on, hold on, hold on," he heard Archie saying—Streator wondered if he had said that last bit aloud or just thought it, "am I hearing you right? You come here with that movie bullshit about Tarvis and come snooping around tonight cause you think me and Tarvis and Alberta and some 'gang-bangers' put a hit on Fred Gunther?"

Streator pulled himself a little straighter in his chair and tried to pull himself back to someplace where a man named Archie was standing in the middle of a room with a gun asking him questions. "Tarvis wrote about it for class. I saw the thing. Rest of it falls into place once you look at it the right way."

Archie stared straight at him, dumbfounded. Well, hell, that's what the truth will do to you, won't it. Strike you dumb. Streator shut his eyes again, looking for a happy place. "So, Charlie Chan," he heard Archie say, his tone changed now, not surprisingly, "you got it all figured out, all us Lloyds, the whole shitting shooting match. Guess I should've left you feet up like old Gunther, huh? Guess I'm just going to have to 'off' you with some 'ghet-to justice,' too, don't you think?"

Here was a new possibility Streator hadn't even counted upon. "Except that I've told, like, twenty different people about all this, I'm writing this book about it, so if I'm dead they'll know . . ."

"Won't help your dead ass much though, will it? Either way, I'm on death row, right?"

Good point, Streator allowed. He really should've thought this whole thing through. "Look . . ."

"No, you look, motherfucker. This all coming clear to me. I'm really getting it now. I understand. I understand."

He saw Archie gather himself together. Streator had the feeling that something was coming, and it was going to hurt.

22.

Streator tried to drive himself home from Archie's on his motorcycle, but the farther he went through the city streets, the more his headache roared, the more blurred his vision became. His clothes were still damp, especially his soggy parka, making the cold of the ride hurt like a burn. He started shaking nearly uncontrollably. On Shorewood Avenue he was having so much trouble determining which were lane markers, which were side reflectors, and which were oncoming headlights, he slowed to a crawl and was nearly run over from behind. Finally he turned off on a side street and wound his way over to St. Anne's Hospital.

He told the ER nurse he had fallen off his bike and hit his head on the pavement hard enough to crack his helmet. They wondered why his clothes were damp. He mumbled something about falling into the snow. They thought he might be hypothermic. And they were pretty sure he had a concussion.

They traded him his damp clothes for a hospital gown, which led to another set of tiresome questions about the bandages on his leg, a pulling of his records from what, just night before last are you kidding me? And a numbing cycle of jokes about how we aren't having the best week are we, maybe we better stay home and off the roads . . . They put him in a bed under warmed blankets and gave him some painkillers. Some of the stitches in his leg were pulled out and they had all gotten wet, in direct violation of the orders they had sent him home with. They wheeled him down the hall for a CT scan. When they brought him back to a curtained area in the ER to wait for the results, he dozed off.

He woke to find Mora standing over him again, shaking him gently, smiling. "We've got to stop meeting like this," she said. "People will talk."

He was a little lightheaded but felt considerably better. He was embarrassed to see her but not disappointed.

She said the scan results didn't show much but his symptoms

indicated he had a slight concussion, his shitty helmet saving him from anything major to worry about, but they'd like to keep him overnight for observation.

"No," he said. "I'll be okay. I'll just go home and sleep." He no longer had insurance and had forgotten to do the paperwork for that COBRA thing but didn't want to explain why. Yesterday's ER would be hard enough to pay for, and then today—a CT scan? He didn't even have a car to get a title loan—would a payday loan place know that his last pay stub was really his last pay stub? No way he was staying with this meter running.

"Well, see, that's the problem," she said, "the sleeping—we really don't want you to sleep and not wake up, someone needs to wake you every two hours to make sure you're okay. Someone at home gonna help you when you get there? No, or you would've called them to come get you. Where's your wife?"

"Minnesota."

"Minnesota? Who in their right mind goes to Minnesota in January? What's she doing there?"

He looked at the clock on the wall. "Right now, probably sleeping with some long-haired grad student, maybe the chair of her department, she's ambitious, you know, maybe the dean or. . ."

"Okay, okay, I get it," she interrupted. "Sorry, I should've known, you're not wearing a ring but you got that nice white stripe on your finger. I wouldn't have asked, but you shouldn't be alone—there's snow and ice on the sidewalks and driveways, you could faint or fall, I bet you got an upstairs bedroom, don't you, that's just nuts, and you really need to be woken up, that's why we should admit you."

"I'll set an alarm," he said.

She argued, explained, scolded, did her nursely duty, fetched the doctor again, but Streator wouldn't give in. Eventually the overworked doctor threw up his hands and had Mora get the paper work for Released Against Medical Advice. He signed it all, and she helped him with his pants again. "I spread these out under a lamp," she said. "They're pretty dry now." She started to argue with him again—was it sweet that she was so worried? Or just professional? Streator couldn't tell. But then she just sighed and walked out of the examining room.

He took his new discharge instructions and new pills and made his way to the exit.

Mora spied him and intercepted him at the door. "When's your ride coming?" she said.

"Got it covered," Streator said.

"Don't even think about riding that stupid bike home," she said.

"It's not that far."

"I will call the cops, don't make me call the cops . . ."

"All right, all right, I'll get a cab."

"Thank you," she said.

He took a seat near the exit and she called for the cab. "They said ten minutes," she said. "Which in Kickapoo Kab code means half hour minimum." She stood next to him with her arms crossed.

"Last time it meant 45 minutes," he said.

She sighed and sat down beside him. He slouched in the chair, his bad leg straight out, his head back.

"Are you okay?"

"Yep."

"Dizzy though, aren't you."

"Not much."

She looked at her watch.

"You're not going to wait here, are you?" he said. "Aren't there, like, dead people you should be shocking back to life or something?"

"Not now."

"Just letting them find the blue light on their own?"

"For one thing, I'm off my shift—" he just noticed she was wearing her coat over her scrubs and carrying a purse—"and for another, I'm not leaving until I see you in that cab, so don't even think about it . . ."

"Don't worry, I'm not presently capable of thinking at all."

"Yeah, that's the problem, you're not thinking, you should be up in a room."

He closed his eyes and slouched deeper. He could feel her chair rocking his attached chair. She was restless, fidgeting. He opened his eyes and saw her look at her watch again.

Across the room up on the wall a TV flickered, sound off,

closed captioning on. Some late-night sports show. He couldn't read the captions from that distance. Maybe a year in review thing. Some guy who hit home runs. Something about him looked familiar. Big head, little ears sticking out, short hair, and kind of a thin crooked smile. In the dugout he mugged for the camera with a series of quick two-fingered signs from his lips to chest.

"You follow baseball?" he asked Mora.

"Go Cubbies. You?"

"Not a lick. You know that guy?"

"Sammy Sosa? Sam-may?"

Sam-may. "He's real famous, I take it."

"Oh yeah. Kind of a joke, too, though. Bazeball been berry berry good to me."

A joke. So someone calling you Sam-may all the time because you bore a passing resemblance might tend to piss you off. "And all this business—" Streator did a half-hearted chest and lip tap.

"That's his thing. Something about blowing kisses to his mother."

"So, not like a gangsta sign or anything?"

She looked at him funny and laughed. "Don't you have any guy friends?"

He shut his eyes again. Sure he had guy friends. Just give him a minute and he could come up with a list of a half dozen or so. At least two or three. Mostly in other states.

"Ok, look," Mora said after a couple of quiet minutes. "That cab could take all night, so I'm going to give you a ride home, make sure you at least get that far without killing yourself, and don't even think about arguing with me, I've had enough of your smartass back talk, I got a four-year-old boy who thinks he's all that, too, but he learned real quick . . ."

He didn't even think about arguing. As he waited for her to bring her car around from the parking lot, his head swam with Gunthers and Lloyds and accidents and illnesses and houses and beds, wandering here and there, passing but not connecting, or connecting but not how he thought. Not how he wanted. Odd, but he'd had this sensation before. When he was writing. When he read something of his own that on further review made no sense. When he knew he needed to rethink the whole scene. Or the whole story. Or throw it all away.

He stumbled into his house with her hand on his back and went straight for the downstairs lav under the stairs, where he peed a river, one hand on the wall to steady himself. In the kitchen he found his prescription bottle from before and took a couple of Vicodin.

When he came out, he found her in the back room where he had been writing. He had left the door open and the light on. She was standing in the middle of the room turning slowly, looking at his mad scribbles all over the drywall. She turned toward him with a look of mock concern and waved a questioning finger at the walls.

"My novel."

She nodded and went to examine a section more closely. "Gonna be hard to get these walls on a store shelf. Might want to consider something smaller."

He sat at his desk chair to keep from falling. Tapped an untidy pile of papers.

"Is it finished?"

He laughed. "Yeah, it's finished all right. Done, finished, deceased, bereft of life. An ex-novel."

She didn't seem to understand. "I don't suppose it's any good or anything."

"Used to be brilliant."

"Not any more?"

"Nope."

"What's it about?"

"It's about a rich old goat who didn't have the common decency to let a starving artist make a buck or two off his death."

She looked at him quizzically. "Is that why you were asking me about Gunther?"

"Pre-cisely, you've hit the nail on the head."

"Can I read it?"

"You could. But then I'd have to kill you."

She shrugged. She absently picked through the books on his shelf. He really wanted to go to bed. It was after two o'clock in the morning. Did she think he was in any state for visitors?

She picked up his thesis from the desk, read the title and author, and smiled at him.

"You don't even want to look at that—" he reached for it.

She turned away and flipped through the first few pages. She found the snapshot and took a look. God she was nosy.

"Wow," she said, turning the picture toward him. "You look really proud of all that hair. Who's this with you?"

"My thesis advisor."

"The one who looks like Judi Dench or the one who looks like Halle Berry? When she was fifteen?"

He took the picture from her and put it face down on his desk. "My wife. Ex-wife. Wasn't my wife at the time. And she was—" he had to calculate a bit—"twenty-three." Were they really that young? That explained so much . . .

"Ah," she said, knowingly. "Well. Here's the good news. You think it's hard being married in this town? Wait til you see what it's like being single and over thirty."

Something else on his desk pile caught his eye. The photocopy of Angie's essay. He looked at the name. He showed it to Mora. "What do you think this name ends with?" he asked. "An 'or' or 'er'?"

She studied it. "Hard to say. Her o's and e's look a lot alike, they're so loopy. And the copy is dim. But I'd say 'or.'" She gave it back to him.

Streator looked at it again. She was right. "Angie Connor." Which is not the same name at all as "Angela Conner."

He pushed himself up out of his chair. "Listen, that Vicodin is really beginning to kick in—I think I better get to bed."

"Vicodin? You took a Vicodin?" She looked puzzled.

"Yeah. I got them Monday. They always make me sleepy."

"Aargh!" Mora grabbed her head. "*Monday*, you didn't have a concussion! *Today*, we're trying to keep you from sleeping too long, remember?" She found his coat and took out his new prescription bags from the pocket. "Extra Strength Tylenol for today, remember? Not the never-wake-up berries?"

"Hmpf. Well, isn't that interesting." Now he realized what his students felt like when they screwed up the easy directions for an assignment. He decided not to tell her he had actually taken two.

Mora sighed heavily and took his arm. "Come on, Professor Dumbshit."

He let her help him upstairs, one arm over her shoulder, her arm around his waist. The more they climbed the dizzier he became.

She led him to his bed and pulled back the mess of covers and sat him down. He kicked off his shoes and nearly fell over pulling off his socks—she righted him and helped swing his sore leg up and his swimming head down. She arranged extra pillows for his leg and head both. She unbuckled his belt. He could smell her hair.

"Excuse me, miss, FERPA or HIPAA or Furry Hippos or something says I should keep these records private, or these privates recorded or something . . ."

"Shut up, I've already been in your pants."

She slid them off his stitched up leg, took a quick professional look at the bandage, and pulled the covers over. "Where's this alarm clock you were talking about?"

"My watch, or my cell phone, in my pants."

"Christ. Like that's going to work, even without the Vicodin." She switched off the light.

He struggled to sit up and pull off his sweater and shirt—a hot sleeper, he could never leave a shirt on. She sat on the edge of his bed and helped him pull the sweater and t-shirt over his head. As his face emerged from his shirt, her face was so close to his he could hear her breathing; even in the dark he could see her long lashes as she took in his face, reading him, he could tell, nervous now to look him in his eyes. She was shivering slightly. Probably because it was so cold in that room. He could smell her hair again, something vaguely spring-like about it, and her hands or clothes, just a touch of something hospital clean, like the bed he'd been in, and he remembered a girl at summer camp in the Berkshires when he was a sixteen-year-old counselor, another counselor he'd been flirting with this close as they scrubbed camping cookware in the old kitchen, her hair her skin this smell, but it took him the rest of the summer to kiss her—he had a story in his thesis about that girl and that summer. Now Mora looked at him and he wouldn't wait this time, he kissed her. She pulled back a bit and gave him a quizzical look like she couldn't quite read the message, so he kissed her again longer so she would understand it was no accident though he had no idea what the message actually was. She sighed and looked at him again, now with a smile. And she kissed him. She lay his head gently on his pillow and kissed him again. He put his hands on her thin shoulders, shaking a bit under her scrubs, and kissed her back as hard as he dared. He heard her shoes hit the floor. She slid slowly on to the bed next to him and made her way under the covers, still kissing him.

Streator, never a player, always careful not to expose himself to anyone he couldn't trust, had taken only a handful of lovers in his days. Sex was always part of a relationship package, tied so intricately with everything else it was hard to separate. He'd never had a one night stand before, no casual "well that was fun, I'll call you again if I can remember your name" sort of thing, and he was sure that's what this would be with Mora—he wasn't even sure how attracted he was to her.

He barely had the energy to slide his hands over her back and through her hair, but she seemed to be in no hurry, sliding slowly herself, an arm, a hand, a leg, as if she were trying to find him, and why not, two strangers, it takes years to find someone in bed. It occurred to him that what he had there was a short story when all he'd read before were novels—there was no long arc of first meetings, planned and chanced second meetings, phone calls, should-or-shouldn't I call her, first dates and kiss goodnights, how long should I wait before I try to get her in bed, don't want her to think that's all I'm after, the days between spent rereading the previous parts, all anxious and plotting, fantasizing, wondering. . . Here he had classical unity of time and place, beginning *in media res*, no chapter breaks, what Poe said was the ideal, one uninterrupted experience with nothing of the workaday world intervening to break the spell, and when it reached its climax, the story quickly finished with little fuss, the characters and lives frozen there eternally, no more chapters or sequels, everyone evaporating into shadows . . .

That Poe had a point, Streator allowed, this was a rush,

washed up on the shore of her strange land before he even knew he was shipwrecked, *what country, friends, is this*—but now he was mixing metaphors, and Jesus was his mind wandering, even with this woman next to him, her scrubs and underwear peeled off one piece at a time, no help from him, he was useless, the damn drugs, the fatigue, his head so dizzy he could hardly see the shapes over him dark as an eclipse, skin and eyes and thick brows and hair and breasts, he should never take Vicodin, it made him so sleepy . . . His leg propped on the pillow was aching now, that may have been his boxers coming down, really he couldn't tell what all was throbbing below his waist, she was asking in a breathy lover's voice if he had something, something she needed, it was some kind of code he was supposed to understand but she might have just as well asked for the moon, he had no idea what she was after, she was looking for something in his beside table but she won't find it, she was slipping off, she was slipping away, she wouldn't find what she's looking for . . .

23.

When he awoke several hours later facing the wrong wall, in bed with the wrong woman, not dead but not feeling fully alive, he had no intention of giving up anything of himself.

But she asked the question he couldn't resist.

What's the story.

The story. Yes, he'd tell the story. This is what he'd do for Tarvis. God knows he'd never done anything else for him. Uncle Archie was right. Streator knew nothing about someone like Tarvis. Streator had leaped to every negative conclusion, swallowed every assumption whole, couldn't see an inch past the surface of Tarvis and his family. Streator owed him big time. All he had to give was a story. Maybe the police would listen, maybe not; maybe Kendall Books would listen, maybe not. But at any rate, he'd figure out a way to tell it, all of it, some way or another. Starting now. Mora said she wanted to listen.

So he told her. Everything. Starting with a knock on his office door and recounting every inch of the last few months. It was the drugs, the warmth of her skin, the way she asked, the look in her eyes like she was interested: she was an audience, and he was a storyteller. He didn't care that prudence said he should keep his mouth shut until he had figured out how to parlay all of his new story into something for Kendall and Medina. Hell with prudence. He wanted to tell the story. Felt good to tell it. Stories unheard had no existence—*I am told, therefore I am.* This was his place in the world, this is what he did well.

He spun the tale slowly in the dark, a spellbinding account unfolding for her ears only, over months of writing and days of misreading, of running around in the dark and cold until he fell through the ice and into Archie's living room . . .

Archie had paced the room like he was going to explode. Then he set his gun down on the shelf by the door. Then he came back to Streator and stood over him again. His arms and hands were twitching. He leaned over and put one large hand on Streator's throat. His grip felt like an iron collar. One tick tighter and Streator wouldn't be able to breathe. "That girl ain't no drug addict," he said slowly, like he could barely talk, "and she ain't no whore. She's sixteen. My grandbaby. She got clinical depression. I take her out on holidays. Home to her mother, her father, her two brothers, and her cat, like that's any of your fucking business." He squeezed tighter, his breath coming faster and faster, his other hand in a massive fist cocked and loaded just in Streator's peripheral vision. Go ahead, Streator thought as everything from his chest up felt like it was going to explode, just kill me, it couldn't possibly be worse.

Then Archie let go with a disgusted grunt and sat back in an old rocking chair across from Streator, staring at him, daring him to move or speak.

"You look real good, and you listen real good," Archie said slowly. "I ain't never killed a man in my life but I might make an exception for you, motherfucking egghead college professor come in my house and insult me and my family with your Charlie Chan bullshit. Malveeta Fray telling me at church all about you, I thought it was just her usual bug up her butt, but she absolutely goddamn right about your racist ass."

Jesus, that woman would be the death of him yet . . . but hold on—"Malveeta Fray goes to your church?" Sunday mornings were still the most segregated time of the week in America, and Streator had her pegged for Missouri Synod Lutheran.

"Course not," Archie said, "she just pick up her grandson sometimes, his mamma want him to get in touch with his *roots,* don't you know."

Yes, a "mixed grandbaby," she had mentioned. "But Malveeta, she always . . . I mean, I'd say something like nigga and nigger were both offensive . . ."

"Offensive? You wanna know offensive, here you are you don't know dick about me and my family or black people in this town, and you go, yeah, no black *janitor* could afford hisself a big TV and a nice house and nice car without he was selling drugs and pimping his kids . . . Unless he wasn't no fucking janitor but the Director of Building Operations for a 52 bed facility going on 15 years!"

Well, that was interesting, Streator thought. But didn't change much.

"Can't believe your sorry ass. Sure, we got us some kids messed up with drugs in our family, or got themselves pregnant in high school, one or two ended up in Gunther Hall. But I tell you what, there's a hell a lot more rich white kids in that place more fucked up than any Lloyd ever been."

"Maybe so," Streator just couldn't keep his mouth shut, "but Tarvis's mom, she got herself pretty fucked up, I mean, drug addict thrown in prison . . ."

"Angela? You think . . .?" Archie looked so dumbfounded he couldn't speak. He shook his head over and over. "Where you get this shit?" he said finally.

"Alberta told me she was up at Keller."

"Angela a *guard* at Keller," Archie said, angry and confused both.

"A what?"

"A fucking *correctional officer*! Maybe five years now."

No. Couldn't be. She was in jail. "Tarvis—lived with Alberta . . ."

"Angela got tired of that drive, especially for the night shifts, so when Tarvis graduated, she moved up there, he went and lived with Alberta so he could get to school easy."

No no no. Streator's head spun wildly. That made no sense at all.

And then it did. All that confusion at the Gunther NEST. There were two Angela Conners. One in the big house. One guarding the big house. That's why the guard at Keller looked funny and made sure he was looking for Angie Connor, inmate, and not Angela Conner, correctional officer.

And that's who answered the door at Alberta's house. Her sister, Angela Conner, correctional officer. Circling ranks for the sister in trouble. In uniform pants he should've recognized from Keller. Tarvis's mom. She looked familiar because she looked like Tarvis. If he had gone to the funeral he would've met her.

Streator's head really hurt. He couldn't put the pieces back together again. Something was still wrong. None of these revelations changed what Gunther did—and the lake . . .

"Gunther," he heard himself saying, "he gave that girl AIDS, Misha, that Lloyd cousin."

Archie laughed. "Fred Gunther and Misha? You go to college to get that dumb? Jesus, you make me sick. In the first place, Fred Gunther didn't have no AIDS. He was senile, Alzheimer's, on all kinds of new experimental shit only rich white folks can afford, but he didn't have no AIDS and if he did he wouldn't be able to give it to no one, I can tell you that. And Misha, god damn . . ."

This was too much for Streator—he had to get out of there. "Whatever—I'm going, I've got to—I'm sorry. Where are my clothes?" He started to rise, slowly, then sank back down.

Archie scooped a pile from the radiator and shoved them in Streator's arms. He wouldn't stop staring at Streator. Streator sorted through his clothes. They were still wet. "The thing is, okay, I guess I didn't know some stuff, but Tarvis, it all started with Tarvis, and I still think he was messed up with some shit, the night he wrecked, this girl said he was going out to get something settled with that Duane guy, Megan didn't even know that, at least she didn't say . . ."

"You talked to Megan?" Archie's whole demeanor changed—suddenly surprised, concerned.

"Yesterday. I was at her house."

"How she doing?"

How was Megan? Streator had no idea what he even meant. "I think she's pregnant," was the only thing that came to him. "She says she's not."

Archie rubbed his balding head quickly, nervously. "God *damn*— you think she's pregnant with Tarvis baby?"

"That's my guess. You haven't seen her?"

"Nobody seen her since Tarvis funeral. Where she at?"

"She lives way out in Hackydale with that methhead stepbrother of hers."

"Whoa—he ain't in jail? Tarvis told me about him. He's serious trouble." Streator could see that Archie was doing some serious calculating of his own.

"Tell me about it. I think he might've run Tarvis off the road or something. I think he tried to kill me."

"That's what you were talking about?"

"Least I thought so. But I—I don't know shit anymore. He scared the hell out of me. Looks like he was scaring the hell out of Megan, too." Streator found his boxers and started working them on under the comforter.

"So what you do about it?"

"About what?"

"Megan, dumbshit—what did you do?"

"Do what?"

"You telling me you left a helpless little pregnant girl out there in the boonies with some crazy methhead already tried to kill you and Tarvis? What kind of man do that?"

" I didn't know then—I thought . . ."

"Where she live?" Archie was in motion, getting his coat, his keys, his knit hat.

"Hackydale Blacktop, somewhere—why?"

"Why you think, dumbshit? I'm gonna go get her!"

Streator couldn't begin to explain how to get to Megan's house. And Archie hadn't the slightest interest in taking a moment to consult MapQuest. The only navigational aid he wanted was sitting on his couch.

Archie pulled his pickup around to the front while Streator put on the rest of his clothes. Archie came back in for his gun, his dogs, and Streator. There was no arguing with him. He had no intention of waiting until a more decent hour. Streator dragged the comforter with him out to the truck. The dogs rode in the back. Streator envied them.

"We should call the sheriff," he said as they ripped down Archie's gravel lane.

"What for? They ain't doing squat, not tonight, unless there's some sort of action in progress. I ain't waiting."

Streator pictured their pickup tearing up the Bruckner drive, Archie and the dogs leaping out, brother Duane and a posse of drug dealers busting out windows to open fire— "I'm calling them anyway." He pulled his phone out of his pocket but it was dead from his dunking in the lake.

They rode in silence through the South Lake neighborhoods and onto Sickle Street Road. The heater on the old truck was taking its time warming up. Streator pulled the comforter around himself and tried to steady his aching head.

Finally Archie said, "So where you get that shit about Misha?"

"Hospital. Church. Everybody seems to know something but me."

"Wrong. Nobody knows nothing."

"Who was she then?"

"None of your goddamn business, that's who!" Archie looked like he might reach over and punch Streator. "She got nothing to do with Fred Gunther, and she sure as shit ain't no Lloyd. That's all you or anybody else need to know."

That just didn't make sense: if there never were any girls, New Year's or other nights, waiting across the lake for Gunther. . . "So you're telling me Frederick Gunther, he just happened to be out ice skating toward your place . . ."

"Toward *his* place, fool. He thought he was going home. He grew up in that house and ice skating on that lake. The first old mill was down there at the bottom of the hill, underwater now. Second one right up there on the flat just across the road, where Millhouse Estates is now. His daddy sold that house to my granddaddy in 1942, when he built that big place across the cove."

"Yeah, I know," Streator said, thinking as fast as his aching head would allow, "but you never brought him back over there for nothing?"

"Fred Gunther ain't been in that house since 1943. My granddaddy wouldn't have him in there. My daddy wouldn't have him in there. And I sure as shit wouldn't have Fred Gunther in my house."

"You worked for him. I saw the pictures."

Archie laughed again derisively. "Just because I take a man's money don't mean I let him in my house."

Archie yanked the wheel hard, slamming Streator against the door, and they careened into the parking lot of a gas station on the edge of town. Archie left the motor running and went inside.

188

Streator shut his eyes and drifted for a bit until Archie came back with two cups of coffee and a pack of cigarettes.

He gave one cup to Streator and took off fast again, somehow drinking his coffee, lighting a cigarette, and manhandling the pick-up out into the dark of Hackydale Blacktop.

The coffee was old and bitter but so hot Streator kept sipping it down to try to stop his shivering from the inside. Archie filled the cab with smoke, turning Streator's stomach even more. He kept glaring over at Streator, holding his stare long, like he was trying to make up his mind about something. Streator desperately wanted him to keep his eyes on the road and at least one hand on the wheel.

Finally he said, "You one of those listening to all that mess about Fred Gunther and Lloyd girls, ain't you, I can tell. You like stories? All right, you sit there and I tell you a little story."

Please don't, Streator thought.

"Yeah, Fred Gunther got a Lloyd girl pregnant. 1943. Her daddy worked for his daddy. Old Al Gunther. That girl—her name was Esther—she ran off and tried to have that baby all on her own, she didn't want nobody to know. She bled bad and died two days after she gave birth. She was sixteen. Old Al Gunther so ashamed he sent Fred off to the Army. His momma so sick she started taking in pregnant girls, got that Gunther Hall going."

"And gave that baby the Lloyd name, for Frederick Lloyd."

Now Archie was furious. "That baby already had the Lloyd name, didn't need no one to give it to her! Asshole."

He rolled down his window and chucked out the coffee cup, lit another cigarette, muttering to himself. Streator wasn't sure he wanted to hear any more.

Archie started again in a slow growl. "My granddaddy John Lloyd worked for Al Gunther for near fifty years, from before either one was even married, from the day they built that little water-wheel on the creek fall."

He pulled long and hard on his cigarette like he was drawing his last breath. Smoke streamed out of his nose like a dragon. "Old Al Gunther trusted my granddaddy like he trusted no one ever. And that was back when black men was regular getting themselves swung from trees and burnt alive in this state, when every little town had a sign said, 'Nigger don't let the sun go down on you here.' Gunther didn't give no Lloyd a name. Gunther give his own kid a Lloyd name."

Damn, Streator thought, he wished he'd looked at those library records a little more, those old city directories and things . . .

"Tell me one white man in this town do that today," Archie said.

By the time they had bumped down the rough roads and slid around the icy corners out to the Bruckners' lane, Streator's head was so dizzy and painful, his stomach so queasy, all he wanted was for the truck to stop, no matter who might shoot at them. Archie parked by the porch, commanded his dogs to stay in the back, and left without a word to Streator. He huddled in the comforter against the door with his eyes shut, gripping the door handle so he wouldn't fly off the spinning world.

In a minute or an hour, the door opened and he almost fell out. "Let her in," Archie said. Megan was with him, head down, sniffling a bit, holding a small duffel. Streator stepped out and let her have the middle.

Archie cranked the heat to stifling. Streator's nausea rose again. He had a hard time following their fragmented conversation and was in no position to interrupt with questions, but he picked up that brother Duane and friends were not at home, hence the quick and clean getaway. With his eyes closed and head against the door, Streator was mostly aware of voices coming to him out of the dark: Megan's like broken glass; Archie's surprisingly soothing, tender, as one who had practice talking to those who were fragile, even if they were just guests in a facility he tended. Archie remembered her dad from Gunther Mills. He drew out of the crying girl that once the Bruckner parents left for Florida the winter before, selling off the fields and leaving Megan and her older stepbrother the house, Duane spiraled deeper into addiction and dealing, terrorizing Megan more and more to keep her quiet and in control, cutting her off from friends and the outside, so that by last fall, after Tarvis's death, Megan hardly left the house at all. Duane had of course hated Tarvis, and Megan didn't seem shocked with the idea that he might have had something to do with Tarvis's accident. And there was some guy named Bill, apparently Duane's friend or partner, who became more or less installed as Megan's new "boyfriend," at which point Megan started crying so hard she couldn't talk. It came to Streator that what he thought were rashes on her legs and arms were probably bruises. Or burns.

"I think I'm going to be sick," Streator said.

"Not in here you ain't," Archie said.

He pulled over and made Streator get in the back. He didn't protest. He needed air, he needed to stretch out, he needed to make the horror show unfolding in the cab to go away somehow. He moved a tube of sand up near the cab for a pillow. He curled up under his comforter in the bed of the pickup. Archie's dogs curled up next to him.

Streator was shaking violently from the cold by the time Archie stopped at his house. He climbed slowly out of the back. He thought Archie was dropping him off for his motorcycle, but then he realized they had only stopped to return the dogs. When Archie came back and saw Streator standing there, he looked surprised, as if he had just noticed him. He took the comforter and put it in the cab with Megan. "By the way," he said after he had shut her door, "she ain't pregnant."

"How do you know?"

He'd scowled at Streator like that was the stupidest question he had ever heard. Then he'd left with Megan for the Gunther Hall Domestic Violence Shelter.

Streator told Mora everything, ending with her handing him his pants a second time. He hadn't yet figured out how she would figure into the plot—she wasn't even a character a few hours ago—or he would've told her that, too.

When he finished, she was asleep.

And he was wide awake. He realized he had talked himself completely out of the possibility of any sex that morning, nothing remotely amorous in the mood of this cold house, not quite to classroom atmosphere, but something abstracted, distanced, full of noisy lives and conundrum not their own . . . not that he was confident he was up for anything anyway.

It wasn't full light, but it wasn't night.

She was curled tight under the covers up next to him. Apparently she wasn't ready to go home. He slowly slid out of bed. She clutched the covers around herself more tightly as he slipped away.

"Where you going?" she mumbled.

"Make some coffee."

"Tea?" she said sleepily. She'd be back asleep before the kettle boiled.

"Sure."

Then he remembered how bare his cupboards were—he had neither coffee nor tea. He slipped on his clothes and awkwardly but quietly made his way downstairs. He pulled on his boots and heavy coat and looked for his keys. Then he remembered: car in the wrecking yard, bike at the hospital. But he really needed to get out. He could borrow her car. He should ask her. But he didn't want her to say, no don't be silly, you can't drive, don't go out in the cold, just come back to bed . . . He really needed to get out and get some air. He found her purse and dug out her keys. It would just take a few minutes, he'd be right back, she'd never know. So off he went in the early morning dark for a can of coffee and a box of tea. Maybe a jug of milk.

He drove the few blocks to the Huck's convenience store because it was closer than the Kroger and already his head was beginning to pound again and his vision blur. He staggered into the store. He started to look for the coffee and tea but a wave of nausea came over him and he made straight for the restroom, certain he would puke all over the floor like all the other late-night drunks.

He couldn't bend over the toilet with his stiff leg and couldn't face the stinking bowl anyway, so he leaned on the sink and held himself, sweating, his arms quivering, his head swimming, waiting for the end, for the relief, for something to come out or come up or just finish him off, damn it, just finish him off and be done with it . . .

What had he done, he thought, what the hell had he done to himself. Could there be anything more pathetic than hoping to die by puking your guts out in a Huck's at six a.m.? Jesus had he fucked himself up, he couldn't even begin to count the ways. He was supposed to fly to New York—when? Tomorrow? How many days had passed? He had nothing. Nothing. Some sad-ass story about some sad-ass kid who may or may not have been killed and some predictably dull billionaire who couldn't even manage to be a proper murder victim. And back at his house was some strange woman wrapped up naked in his bed, and worse, he had spilled his guts to her, like that was going to help, now someone else knew the whole pathetic story of his whole pathetic life so he couldn't even fake something or make something up or spin things his way in public without her knowing it was all a lie. Only one thing he could do: he'd have to kill her to shut her up. And at that he had to laugh—how pathetic would that be to kill the only woman who was willing to go to bed with him in . . . well, it seemed like years.

The nausea passed. His head cleared a bit. He washed his face with cold water and wiped it with a paper towel.

Next to the towel dispenser was a condom machine. Down at the bottom of the white cabinet, in small neat letters from a black Sharpie, someone had written, *"everything will be alright."*

Now he really had to laugh. He looked at it again, like he expected the message might vanish. But there it was in black and white. Might have been the funniest thing he had ever seen.

What the hell. He fished a handful of change out of his pocket and bought a SensuRibbed. And in a fit of reckless optimism, he bought another.

24.

Mora was still in bed, dozing lightly, when the phone rang downstairs. By the time she realized that Streator wasn't going to pick it up, the ringing had stopped. Not that she would answer the phone in his house anyway. But apparently he didn't have an answering machine, or it was turned off.

When she eventually got up and dressed enough to be decent, Streator was nowhere to be found. A note on the table said, "Gone for coffee." She curled up on his couch under her coat and waited for him to return.

A weird night, all in all. That languorous sort of almost-sex with a man so doped up he hardly knew who she was, his head propped on two pillows and his leg on two more. What was she thinking. It wasn't that she'd had a schoolgirl crush on this guy, not anymore. And though he was certainly pitiful, it wasn't even a pity lay, which she didn't do. And she didn't do pickups. In fact, the two times in her life she had let a guy take her home from a bar or party, she had hated it—the lousy drunken sex, the awkwardness afterward—she vowed never to do it again. When her shift ended at midnight, she stayed to see him through. When she offered to take him home and helped him inside, she had no intention of staying the night, though she definitely had been flirting, almost out of habit. True, she was lonely, bored, her apartment empty, the only male who had been in her bed in nearly a year—her four-year-old son—off for several days with his father, the prospect of another cold bed painful to bear, one of the reasons she pulled extra night shifts whenever he was gone.

No, she hadn't been looking for a hookup, not really, certainly not in the ER. But at the hospital, she saw a man on the verge of something. Maybe cracking up. Maybe breaking through. There weren't many like that in this town, so few making anything happen. She had gone back to school that fall for this reason, to make something happen, to push the edges, pull back the covers.

But she had been disappointed. It was all mundane. Perfunctory. Her dreams of fires lit in a creative writing classroom had been naïve. Years earlier in Streator's lit class, she recognized that he saw everything in the world through a different slant of light. She came back to find that prism. But she could see right off it wasn't going to happen. She was disappointed that he didn't remember her, but worse, she could tell that he had no intention of giving anything of himself to a class. That had been the most disappointing of all. When she decided to drop, he hardly noticed.

So she worked the ER. At least there, something happened. But she soon realized that things that happened by accident were just events. And most were meaningless, random and inexplicable. She was no longer interested in the random, the inexplicable. Why is your young daughter dead and this drunk who hit her still breathing? Why should you fall from a roof when you're working a job off the books? How could you possibly have a stroke at age forty-three? Trying to make sense of this was like trying to make sense of the movement of smoke swirls rising from a lazy fire. And besides, it was all someone else's story coming through those doors. She was just a witness to the messy aftereffects.

But something was happening *with* Streator, not just *to* him. Something was going to happen, she could tell at the hospital. Something big. She wanted to see what it could be. She wanted to see. Maybe even standing in the shadows of something going on was like being a part of it.

As soon as she saw his back room she knew she was right, something was happening, though he might crack up before he broke through. That's when she decided she would need to do something to pull him together. To bring him to a focus, keep him in one piece, whole. By the time she dragged his Vicodin-drugged butt upstairs, she knew she would have to stay at least for a few hours. When he kissed her—almost reflexively, she could tell, without clear intention—she came into his bed, the best nursing she could think to administer. Maybe a dumb idea, she allowed, but it made a kind of sense at the time. When she couldn't find a condom anywhere in his house and came back to bed to find him asleep, she really didn't mind. She set the alarm on her own cell phone, crawled back in next to him, pulled the heavy covers over both of them, and slept better than she had in many a month. Maybe it was the sheer exhaustion of her life, long night shifts at an ER, single mother on her own. Maybe the fact that this man apparently wanted nothing from her but still let her in his bed—for whatever reason she just let go and fell dead asleep.

When her beeping phone awakened her two hours later and she awakened him to check on his condition, he told her his long strange tale of Tarvis and Gunther and car crashes and falling through the ice. She knew his rambling was partly the drugs—talking to the Vike, they called it at work—but there was something beyond that. As she lay in the dark the whole thing unfolded in his lulling voice like a film; when he finished and she was half asleep, she wasn't completely sure that she hadn't dreamed the story.

But now he was gone, and she felt more than a little foolish. She wanted a warm shower but decided not to, poked around his house for a bite of breakfast, found nothing edible, poked around his office, looked at his wife's picture again and wondered if that was his type—what had he joked? the dark exotic?—but truthfully he hadn't seemed that interested in her until she was pulling his clothes off, so who could tell what really attracted him. A funny thought occurred to her: somewhere in her scrap box of mementos was a photo from the Kickapoo student newspaper from years earlier of her, Streator, and some visiting writer, a friend of Streator's. It was taken after a reading the first time she was in Streator's class when the student photographer wanted to get a candid shot of the poet, the professor, and an admiring student. So Mora, never shy, stepped in so they could pose an obviously staged recreation of the visiting writer signing a copy of his book while Mora and Streator looked over his shoulder from behind, like the shots of the president signing a bill with senators jostling for position in frame behind him. She was sure he wouldn't remember, but she had saved the photo. She never threw anything away.

She looked at the debris of his novel, the bits and pieces of story on the wall, thought of what wasn't up there, Tarvis's story, and was convinced again that it was marvelous, all of it . . . she wished she had sometime been awash in something that rich, wished she had thrown herself in to the writing of anything with such wild abandon.

But he had abandoned her. In his own house, no less. "Gone for coffee." As if that would take more than an hour. Message received: he was waiting for her to leave. He didn't want to face her. He didn't want her help, had no part for her. She would just go. She resisted leaving him any kind of note—angry, hurt, funny, conciliatory, informational, invitational, anything. Hell with him. An odd night indeed.

When she went outside in the cold gray morning, she saw that her car was gone. Her keys weren't in her purse. That son of a bitch took her car. If he wanted her to go, how the hell did he expect her to get home? A sliver of worry crept into her head. She should've answered the phone; it might have been Streator trying to reach her. Maybe the car had broken down; it wasn't very reliable in cold weather. Maybe he'd had an accident. He shouldn't have been driving with that head and those drugs.

His phone rang again. This time she answered it.

The officer filled her in as he drove her to St. Anne's. Streator had been shot in the parking lot of a Huck's convenience store early that morning. Witnesses had said there had been some twitchy guy hanging out in the lot harassing people, probably a drug addict, probably tried to hit Streator up for money, probably Streator refused. Apparently Streator tried to hit the guy in the head with a milk jug.

The officer was overly chatty, trying to relieve the tension. "Funny thing is," he said, "my wife goes jogging every morning before work, like six a.m. when it's still dark, and she wanted me to get her some pepper spray, but I told her, I said, look, hon, the bad guys ain't out then, they're all finally asleep or passed out somewheres." He looked over at Mora. "Guess I was wrong."

"Just tell your wife not to jog through a Huck's parking lot," Mora said.

Her colleagues in ER filled her in: Small caliber gunshot wound to the chest, lost a lot of blood. He'd already been in surgery, and now he was in Intensive Care, critical.

She rushed up to IC. Her friend Allison was at his side. She gave Mora the rundown. Vital signs weren't great. Chest tubes, endotracheal tubes, drifting along under sedation.

"Is he going to make it?" How often had someone asked Mora herself that very question?

Allison shrugged. "You know. Maybe. Probably not."

The other staff weren't clear why she had such a hard time processing this news. Not like they didn't hear these stories in here every day. They supposed he had been some kind of special teacher to her.

She made herself a cup of tea and curled up in a chair in a corner of the staff lounge, crying softly off and on, trying to wrap her head around this, trying to pull herself together.

The story of the shooting was on the noon news in the lounge. Maybe twenty-five seconds.

But his story wasn't on the news. Never would be. Police would never find it. Not Streator's story.

She sat by his bed for most of the afternoon and into the evening. That night after the evening news played the story again, several people came by to see Streator. A few professors she recognized from Kickapoo, one with some woman who was the spitting image of Carly Simon. Nobody stayed long or said much. A couple of the women held his hand for a minute. She overheard talk about contacting his family and bad weather for travel.

Her car had been towed from the Huck's to an impound lot. Even after several calls and telephone tag through the police station, no one could give her a clear answer about when she could get the car back, whether it was considered evidence from the crime scene, or even where her keys were. She called her mother and asked if she could borrow her car for a few days. Mom came to the hospital right away, of course, full of concern and confusion. The price for borrowing the car was an awkward conversation about exactly how Mora's car had ended up involved in a crime

and why this Streator fellow—her professor? a patient? both?—
had her car so early in the morning, questions punctuated by
Mom's disapproving sighs and slow head shakes. The rest of the
bill, another lecture about Mora's "lifestyle," would be collected
later.

She drove back to Streator's house. She had been in such a
hurry to leave with the officer, she felt she needed to check to see
if she had locked the doors, turned off the lights, left anything
behind. Perhaps she could find phone numbers of people to call.

That's what she told herself, anyway, as she drove over. But
when she entered his dark, cold house, a house that looked and
smelled of lonely bachelor men, she realized that something else
had pulled her there. She found herself once again in the back
room. The only working light, a small lamp on his desk, cast
shadows across the writing on the walls. She ran her fingertips
lightly over the scrawls, trying to decipher the mad scribbles like
runes on a tomb. She leafed through the mess of loose manuscript
pages and notes on his desk. She felt an odd protective instinct
for all of this. She felt an urge to hide it all away before family
and others descended on the house and all of it became theirs. Not
Streator's. And not hers. Yes, the instinct was not just protective
but proprietary. Though he had sent the finished novel out into
the world, this messy creation was different, the private Streator.
Something only she had seen. She wanted to keep it that way.

But the more she thought, the more she poked through his
books and notes, the more she came to understand that this was
the wrong story to protect. That's was what he had been trying to
get her to see. The novel on the walls, the novel in the hands of
the editor, was nothing except in how it led him to the real story—
Tarvis's story.

She realized she was the only one who had heard it, all of it.
She could tell by the way he had told it, there in the dark, that it
was the first time out of his mouth. She sat at his desk and turned
on his computer. In his directory were hundreds of Word files,
coded with file names that meant nothing to her. She opened a few
of the more recent files. Not what she was looking for. It would
take hours to scour through these. Didn't matter. She was sure
he hadn't put any of it to type, that when he was telling her what

had happened over the last few months and last few days, it was the first time he had put any of it in words, as he breathed those words into the cold air between their faces. That was more intense and intimate than any sex they could have had, that was their real coupling, that was where he had been an extraordinary lover, with this complete unraveling of himself as they lay intertwined, stripped naked, strangers. His finest hour as a writer, she was sure.

And now it was her story, she was coming to see. He had passed it to her. He hadn't meant it to be hers, she knew—he was *telling* the story, which is not the same as *giving* it. But in a few hours, Streator might very well be dead. And no one else could put it together, except her. The guy in the Huck's lot, for instance— probably that girl Megan's brother, the meth addict. Duane, was it? She would find out.

She felt alive. Now something had happened to her. If he did die—if he did die, the entire marvelous screwy story was all hers.

"Hello, excuse me?" said a voice from the doorway—she jumped up with a gasp, bumping the desk, knocking papers to the floor, sending the rolling desk chair skittering into the wall with a clatter.

"Sorry," said the tall man in the doorway, silhouetted against the light from the living room. He fumbled for the light switch on the wall and clicked it several times but nothing happened.

"Who are you?" Mora asked, backing up, her heart pounding.

"I was going to ask you the same." He stepped forward into the pool of light from the desk lamp. He wore a long, dark wool overcoat and a fuzzy cap with flaps over his ears. He looked familiar. And deeply suspicious. He held a cell phone in one gloved hand. "Loren Locke. I work with Henry. I'm his dean." She had seen him at the hospital.

"Ah, you startled me. I didn't hear you come in."

"Apparently. And you are . . . ?"

"Mora," she said. "I'm . . ." What could she say? She was what—a lover, a girlfriend? Definitely not. A friend? Not even that. The deflating realization came to her that she had no title in Streator's life. "I'm from the hospital. I was his student."

Locke raised a skeptical eyebrow. "A student? Henry's student? In his house?"

"I thought maybe I could help out, find some phone numbers for his family or something."

"I've already called his family. His mother and father and sister are coming as quickly as they can get here. The weather's even worse in Massachusetts, though."

"Massachusetts?"

"Yes. That's where he's from, you know," Locke said.

"Right."

Locke stepped around the desk to see the computer monitor, glancing at her sharply.

"I couldn't find an address book in his desk," Mora said, "so I thought, maybe on his computer."

"Hmmm," Locke said. He powered down the computer. "Well, I was looking for Veronica's number in Minnesota. I hadn't any luck finding it online. She just moved, so maybe it's not listed yet. Or maybe she's keeping in unlisted. So students can't get it." He turned to face her.

"Veronica?"

"His ex-wife."

"Ah. Huh. So, you think he'd really want his ex-wife here, now?"

Locke studied her quizzically. "You really don't know Henry at all, do you?"

When she returned to the hospital in the morning, Streator was much improved. She was relieved. This was good news. Though deep back in her head she pushed back some primitive reaction— what was it? Disappointment, she almost admitted to herself. But relief, too, definitely relief.

By midmorning they took him off the sedation and removed the ET tube. He responded well, breathing on his own. Slowly he regained something like consciousness. He didn't seem to focus on her at first as he drifted in and out.

But eventually there was a flicker of recognition in his eyes as she talked to him. "You know we don't give frequent flyer discounts here, right?" she said. "No punch cards, anything like that?" He nodded slightly.

By mid afternoon he seemed more fully alive. He wiggled his fingers. She wiggled hers back. He seemed like he was trying to smile.

When she said, "You'll be okay. Everything will be okay," it almost looked like he was trying to laugh.

Eventually he licked his lips and spoke slowly. "All in all," he said, his voice slurred from the drugs and raspy from the intubation, "rather be in Philadelphia."

"Oh god, don't go all Ronald Reagan on me, I really couldn't handle that," she said. "Don't try to talk, you've been mostly dead all day."

"No, no," he struggled to speak. He pointed to himself weakly. "Lived in Philly. Really . . . really . . . rather be there."

He looked at her a minute.

"Sorry," he said.

"Yeah, you should be. You owe me big time, professor."

He nodded. "Pants," he said, "please?"

"What, again?"

He sort of shrugged.

"Sorry, cowboy, can't help you this time. Police took all your clothes for evidence."

He frowned slightly. "Cell phone?"

She called security and had them bring up his personal effects from the hospital safe. A guard brought in a small bag with the contents of his pockets. He motioned for her to bring the bag to him. She held it open for him. With one hand he dug around slowly. He pulled out a wrapped condom and tossed it at her weakly. Then he dug out another and tossed it too. She had to laugh.

He pulled out his cell phone and handed it to her. He said, "Call my agent. Cancel the meeting. *Major* rewrite."

She flipped open his phone and tried powering it on. "Dead." She held it up for him to see.

He sighed. He shut his eyes and rested for a moment, and then he mumbled, "Got to be a way to make money off of this."

His parents and sister arrived the next night. Mom and Dad Streator, both in their sixties, reacted in ways familiar to Mora:

they looked ready to collapse from fear and held on to each other's hands and then to Streator's as if they were afraid to let go, as if someone would float away like a red balloon if they let go. Sister Streator asked all the questions, grilling the doctors and nurses and aides, bossing and fussing in equal parts, a school teacher used to having a room run as she saw fit. Streator didn't introduce them to Mora and didn't speak to her much when they were around. She was just another one of the nurses in and out of the room.

Then the ex-wife arrived the following day, driving down through storms from Minnesota. The mood in the room grew tense. The family clearly did not want her there. But when she was in the room, she was the only person Streator saw.

Mora could see why. She was an electric presence, the kind of person who lit up any room she entered. She was quick and smart, at ease even with Streator's resentful family, funny and familiar with Streator himself. And so beautiful—bright eyes, perfect clear skin on high cheekbones, a brilliant smile—the kind of looks that made mere mortals uncomfortable. Mora was sure that no one ever stopped with just "pretty" or "attractive" with Roni but went straight to "beautiful." Mora herself had never made it past "cute."

25.

Once it became clear that Streator wasn't going to die, Roni drove back to Minnesota, where it wasn't as cold as a hospital room with Streator's mother and sister freezing her with icy stares and curt replies. Streator tried to tell himself that it was for the best. An unreasonable, unhealthy joy had seized him when he opened his eyes and saw her face over him so scared and concerned and beautiful. Better that she left.

In a week Streator was home in his own bed with his mother fussing over him like he was twelve and had broken his arm skateboarding. Upon touchdown in Illinois, his mother, Sandra, and sister, Francine, launched easily into a full-frenzy caretaking mode, cleaning his house top to bottom, washing every sheet, blanket, and pillow they could find, laying in groceries and filling his freezer with cooked dishes. His father, on the other hand, was lost; having him there was nearly as heartbreaking as having Roni around. Francis Streator had no idea what to do or what to say to his son. Usually unflappable and easygoing to the point of detachment, he was so scared in the hospital that he scared Streator. It was touching but disturbing. When the danger had passed and Streator was home, his father was still out of his element and off his game, trying to keep Streator company in his bedroom by reading him the paper and chatting about hockey games Francine's boys played, the weather, improvements Streator could make to his cold house.

No one could figure out what to make of Mora. She had been a near-constant presence in the hospital, but as family came in, she drifted into the background. Nobody knew quite who she was or how they were supposed to act with her. And then she was in his house so often. Was she a friendly home healthcare nurse? A "special friend" they had never heard about? A doting former student? Streator was in no mood to explain.

When they were alone, Mora kept bringing up the shooting, "the case," she said. "Did you explain to the detective about that stepbrother Duane?" she asked his first day at home as she checked his dressing.

"No. Why? It wasn't him. I would've recognized him."

"Still, he has friends, he might have sent someone or something."

Streator explained that back at the hospital, Detective Cruiks had shown him some photos of shooting suspects, and the long-haired, wide-eyed man Streator picked out was the one already in custody, a drug addict well known to the police and easily recognized on the store's security cameras.

"Really." She seemed disappointed. "They have a name?"

"I don't know, like Wilbur or Willy something I think."

"Willy? Not Billy? Bill?"

"Think he said Willy. Why?"

"Didn't you say that guy abusing Megan was named Bill?"

"Maybe, I guess."

Now she was excited. "They should check that out. He had a lot of reason to shut you up."

He could hear in her voice his own voice from the week before the shooting, and it pained his head.

"Please."

"I'm just saying, it wouldn't hurt to check it out."

It's hurting a lot already, he wanted to say. But he didn't know her well enough to know how to talk to her. He recalled how his college roommate by a cruel twist of timing became sucked into a family trauma not his own: when the girl he had been dating for a couple of weeks lost her sister in a car accident, suddenly he was her rock, her anchor, the one she leaned on from hospital to funeral to therapy sessions, though he hardly knew her and didn't even like her that much. When he waited for what he figured was a thoughtful interim and broke up with her, she hated him forever.

Streator didn't know how to tell Mora to feel no obligation. He was embarrassed that he had so little to say to her. When she was leaving on his third day home, after an afternoon filled with long awkward silences, she turned to him at the door and said, "You really didn't remember me, did you? From that Fiction class, back in '92?"

"Sorry," Streator said. "So many students."

She smiled weakly and left. She didn't come back.

When Francine decided she really had to get back to her classroom, her boys' hockey, and her husband, Dad decided that he should accompany her before Milton Bradley missed him, even though he readily admitted he was just punching the clock until his retirement in just a few more months.

That left him home with his mother. Retired from her special-ed teaching several years earlier, she was in no hurry to leave. The house smelled of her cooking. Usually something burnt. Roni had always said that his mom cooked by smoke detector. She was cheerful past his tolerance but thankfully left him alone. She felt no need for any heart to hearts, no dissection of this whole puzzling business; she was just relieved beyond words that her boy hadn't died.

Only a few others visited. One morning Det. Cruiks came to the house to fill him in on the timetable for the criminal proceedings. "Hey, maybe next time just let him have your wallet or what have you?" he laughed. "Easier to replace your credit cards than all that blood!"

Streator took the opportunity to tell him what he knew about Duane Bruckner and the likelihood of a meth lab out off Hackydale Road, not because he thought Bruckner had anything to do with the shooting, but because there was a meth lab out off Hackydale Road. Cruiks seemed intrigued and promised to have the sheriff's department look into it. Deputy Donaldson would be all over it, Streator was sure.

"And say," Streator tried to sound off-hand, "I've been pretty out of it. Whatever came of the thing with Gunther?"

"What do you mean?"

"The investigation turn up any signs of anything . . . amiss?"

Cruiks looked a bit puzzled. "No, no. There'll be a coroner's inquest, but there's nothing to suggest anything but an accident."

Nothing at all, Streator had to agree. In the quiet hours alone in his room, he had much time to meditate on the whole puzzling business his mother knew nothing about. The death on the lake wasn't even important. Uncle Archie must have been right,

Streator realized. They'd probably find out that Alberta had been drinking, leaving an old senile man to wander out, back to his glory days ice skating, going home, maybe going to see Esther Lloyd, maybe that's how he used to meet up with her way back when they were both nearly twenty years younger than Streator and Roni were now. That would be a memory burning through the fog all right, an urge to action you wouldn't resist. Wouldn't be hard for a gimpy old man with bad knees to fall head first through the soft ice into the mud of Vapor Springs Cove, Streator knew first hand—Gunther was probably all but dead when his head hit the ice, the autopsy would surely show. And really, Alberta probably hadn't let it happen, not likely to be drunk. How easy would it be to just doze off. She was probably just tired. Who wasn't. No conspiracy, except of fate. Shit happens. A novel that fits on a bumper sticker.

And it was Tarvis who saw it coming. He did—or was starting to do—just what Streator had preached, just what he himself failed at practicing: Tarvis took pieces of his experience, of stories from Uncle Archie, of crazy Internet rumors, added in a healthy dose of plausible what-ifs, made the imaginative leaps that Streator couldn't. Tarvis Conner, of all people, had made himself into a Zebra Storyteller. The world was indeed a wondrously weird place.

Too bad the story he was writing for himself didn't come true. Tarvis had seen what the drugs had done to his neighborhood, but he was no gangsta, nor was his buddy Ty-called-T-bone-called-Sammy—not likely that big-time drug runners would enroll in English classes at the local community college. He saw what was going on with Megan and her stepbrother. He wanted to get her out of there. He wanted to be a hero of his own story. Who doesn't? Tarvis was going to take Megan away, maybe get the cops in, at least the paranoid brother assumed so. Duane might have run him off the road and run him down—he'd need to talk to someone about that. What came to Streator there in the dark of his room was that all along, and once again, he'd been on the wrong track and missed the best story right in front of him: the barely noticed death of a good kid trying to do right.

One afternoon in the hospital the week before, Streator awoke to find two stern faces staring down at him, one familiar, one not so much.

"So you went and got yourself shot anyway!" Archie said. "And I didn't even get to do it."

"Nope." Streator was oddly glad to see him.

"Cause I wouldn't have missed, you know that."

"Yep."

"I just had to come and take a look." He bent over and examined the bandage. "Whoo-ee, that's a good looking hole. By the way," he motioned to the woman next to him, "this is Angela. Tarvis mom."

"Yeah."

Angela nodded. "How you doing."

"You one lucky sumbitch, I give you that," Archie said. "Guess your guardian angel looking after you!"

"Yeah, well, maybe next time she can give me a little shove a second or two earlier."

Archie laughed and made for the door. "Hey, you want to put a hit on the guy done this to you, you know who to call!" He cracked himself up as he left.

Angela stood by the bed and regarded Streator thoughtfully for a long moment. She really did look a lot like Tarvis.

"Uncle Archie told me what all you done," she said.

"Sorry, really . . ."

"No, no. I'm glad someone was at least paying attention. Seems like Tarvis, he just . . . disappeared." She choked a bit.

"I can't even imagine what that's like."

"Well, your family almost found out, didn't they!" She smiled. "We heard you was in here, we were down the hall with Alberta, she had a little heart thing."

"Oh, no."

"She's okay, probably from the stress, they said. She's had so much to handle in the last year, first Tarvis, then Misha, and now all this mess at the Gunthers they trying to blame on her."

The woman lost her son and was worrying about her sister. Tarvis was one lucky kid, Streator thought.

She pulled up a chair and talked for a good long while. How

she had moved him up from St. Louis to get away from the violence—yes, Streator had remembered the bullet-in-the-toaster story correctly—how he loved to sing, how he cracked up his family with his impressions of Archie, how she wished she hadn't ever moved up to Keller and left him behind because obviously God made life too short for needless separation.

And she told him about Misha, who for a time was like an older sister to Tarvis: a girl from their church whose mother died young, the Lloyd clan took her in, but she fell into drugs and landed in Gunther Hall, where Alberta tended her. The Jamesons took her in again when she was released, but she relapsed and eventually contracted HIV, perhaps from dirty needles, perhaps from unprotected sex. When HIV became full-blown AIDS, she was pregnant. Archie wanted the family to wash their hands of her, but Alberta would have nothing of it; she wanted Archie to ask the Gunthers for help, but he refused. Alberta and Archie went round and round and eventually all but stopped speaking, but Alberta finagled her way into home health care for Fred Gunther and bent his wife's ear. Miss Marta convinced the Gunther Hall Foundation to pay for the best AIDS hospital in Chicago for Misha, someplace they could deliver the baby without him contracting AIDS as well. Since she wasn't on the Board anymore and the foundation was run by St. Anne's hospital, Father Tolbert had to sign off on the confidential request—which was why half the town thought the hospital was paying off someone's family because of a priest and the other half assumed it was Gunther himself, Streator realized. The baby lived; Misha died last November.

"Uncle Archie—he would never admit he was wrong, but he took it all pretty hard when it came down to it. We all did."

"The baby?"

"Alberta's trying to adopt him."

"Ah. She would, sure." Taking care, doing what needs done. This family knew no other way. "Say, I've been wondering— Archie told me about Esther, the Lloyd girl who died? Gunther got her pregnant? Whatever happened to that baby?"

Angela frowned. "Archie told you all that b.s.? I thought he saved it for family."

"Wait—it's not true?"

"All I know is every Thanksgiving Archie gets going on with all this back-in-the-day stuff and the rest of the old folks tell him he's full of crap and sooner or later someone stomps off mad."

"What do you think?"

She shrugged. "It's a good story."

Brent Medina sent a get-well card with a note suggesting he could give a call "sometime this spring, if he was up to it." Didn't take a deconstructionist critic to figure out what that meant: *Iced on ice,* likely for good. Streator wondered why he didn't feel more disappointment. Then he realized it was because he knew that silly novel would never pay the debts he owed. To make those right would take the kind of writing he had never allowed himself to try, the kind that sprang from genuine empathy. He'd need to begin as soon as he could hold a fat pencil on a wall.

Loren Locke climbed the stairs at the end of the week. "Good lord it's cold up here," he said. He kept his parka zipped.

"Don't tell the realtors," Streator said.

Locke took a chair next to the bed and asked him about his condition: improving daily; his pain: talking to the Vike; his recovery timetable: weeks if not months.

"But . . . income. Insurance."

Streator shrugged. "Nothing to be done. Mooch off the kindness of strangers. Family." He nearly choked on his words. His father, in his own stumbling way, had let him know that he would have nothing to worry about. Streator also knew his hospital bills and rehab could destroy both of his parents' retirement.

"Let me give you an alternative," Locke said. He seemed a bit nervous. He took a breath. "Work for us."

Streator was confused. "Doing what?"

"Well, teaching, nitwit."

Now Streator was very confused. "How?"

"I've been talking to the right people. We can make it happen. Your resignation—it can go away."

"I was about to be fired."

Locke looked at him with something like pity, like how could a smart person know so little. "Circumstances change."

Streator shut his eyes and breathed slowly, trying to take it in. His mind had been drug-fuzzy for so many days, he had trouble finding the place where people made sense.

"Semester starts—what, couple of days? There's no way. I bet Phyllis snagged my creative writing class already, she's got the syllabus all done and every assignment ready."

"Term started two days ago, and we got Derrick Doolin to take your creative writing," Locke said. "Since he's going to be in town anyway."

Streator stared him down.

"Kidding."

"You're killing me."

"Yes, you're right," Locke said, pulling some papers from his parka pocket. "You're going to be laid up here a while, so this semester won't work. That's why you'd have to take the semester off." He handed the papers to Streator.

Streator struggled to read the papers. It was an Application for Professional Leave, all filled out, with a long description of Streator's proposed activities and a detailed rationale for Spring Semester 2000.

Streator couldn't focus on the document, couldn't get words to form. "Who—you wrote this? A sabbatical?"

"Professional leave—we don't do sabbaticals, remember. You'd have to do all this program review, outcomes assessment," he waved at the papers, "which looks to me like, what, a week's work in early August. In the meantime, on salary, no break in insurance." He gave him his best ironic smile. "Plenty of time to finish that book."

Streator couldn't get this to make sense, not the papers in his hand, not what Locke was telling him. "They decided these—like last February."

Locke sighed again. "Circumstances, Henry. They change." He looked a bit embarrassed.

Streator flipped through the pages back and forth. The last page had already been signed by Locke, the Academic VP, the President of the College, and the Chairman of the Board of

Trustees, all backdated. The only blank line was for Streator's signature.

"People are not all unkind," Locke said quietly without looking at him. "Not most. Not here, anyway."

Perhaps so, Streator thought, but as he looked at those names, he knew Locke was overly generous and too modest. It was painfully obvious that it must have cost Loren Locke a great deal personally and professionally to obtain those signatures. One more debt Streator would never be able to repay.

"Well. Thanks. I know I don't deserve this."

"True enough," Locke said with a smile. "There is, of course, the one condition."

Yes. Of course. He remembered. "Four years?"

"Four more years. The union contract is very specific, and everyone who signed your proposal made it clear that this point was non-negotiable, not now, not later. You can't leave, and you can't get yourself fired. Or you have to pay back the semester, salary and benefits. The last faculty who took a leave and didn't come back, the college sued. And won. As a matter of fact, that was the fellow you replaced."

Streator remembered hearing that story shortly after he was hired. At the time, he couldn't imagine what would drive someone to quit so foolishly. He studied the papers. "Four years indenture." He was having trouble thinking four days ahead. Four years sounded like a life sentence. "That's a lot of shitty papers."

"Yes, it certainly is. Of course, with a big fat advance, you could buy us out."

Streator put down the papers and regarded Locke. Streator had done nothing but purposefully make people miserable, and yet here Locke sat, helping him out of the misery of his own making. It made no sense, not without a complete recalibration of Streator's Unified Theory of Everything. This was going to be a bigger pain in his head than any knock on the ice could deliver.

And yet, four years. Four more long, cold years.

"What do you think?" Locke asked after a moment.

"I'm trying to figure out whether you're Mephistopheles, or—you know, one of those good angels, can't think of a name."

"Me, too," Locke said, standing. "Let me know what you

decide. We'll need to know in a day or so."

"You know," Streator said, holding up the papers as Locke made for the door, "I think I'm going to have a good cry."

Locke laughed. "From gratitude, or despair?"

Streator nodded. "Yeah."

"Ah, well. Could be worse. That's the only thing I've ever figured out." He left.

Yes. Locke was right. Alone in his cold bed, the windows dark already in the winter's evening, Streator turned it over. *Could Be Worse.* The title for his next book.

Robert Grindy was raised in the Mother Lode country of Northern California before graduating from California State University, Chico. Graduate studies at Indiana University, where he earned an MFA in fiction, brought him to the Midwest in the 1980s. He worked as a magazine editor and taught at several colleges in Indiana before moving to Decatur, Illinois, where he has taught writing and literature at Richland Community College since 1990 and raised two children with his wife, Rosemarie. His short stories, essays, articles, and poems have appeared in Fish Prize anthologies from Ireland, *Fiction Southeast, In the Middle of the Middlewest: Literary Nonfiction from the Heartland, Copper Nickel, Blueline, Illinois Times, The Saturday Evening Post*, and other publications.